D1235522

NOV - - 2019

THE SOUGHT SIX:
THE STERLING CONE

Emmie
PRESS

ST. THOMAS PUBLIC LIBRARY

ST. THOMAS PUBLIC LIBRARY

First published in 2019 by Emmie Press, an imprint of
Notebook Publishing,
c/o: 20–22 Wenlock Road, London, N1 7GU.

www.notebookpublishing.co

ISBN: 9781913206017

Copyright © C. A. Klug 2019.

The moral right of Catherine Klug to be identified as the
author of this work has been asserted by her in accordance
with the Copyright, Design and Patents Act, 1998.

All characters and events described in this publication,
with the exception of those known within the public
domain, are fictitious. Therefore, any resemblance to real
persons, living or dead, is to be considered purely
coincidental.

All rights reserved. No part of this publication may be
reproduced, stored in or introduced into a retrieval
system, or transmitted, in any form or by any means
(electronic, mechanical, photocopying, recording or
otherwise), without the prior written permission of the
publisher, aforementioned. Any person who is believed to
have carried out any unauthorised act in relation to this
publication may consequently be liable to criminal
prosecution and civil claims for damages.

A CIP catalogue record for this book is available
from the British Library.

Typeset by Notebook Publishing.

For my parents, who never let me believe I couldn't follow my dreams.

For Karen Frew-Paul and Debbie Schwantz, who allowed 11-year-old me to bring class to a halt so I could read the very first drafts of this story.

And last but certainly not least, for SC, MH, KN, SR and AW, who have all inspired me beyond measure.

CHAPTER 1:
AN ORDINARY MORNING

Jenna

"JENNA? JENNA?"

Jenna's eyes snapped open. She darted her gaze around the bedroom she shared with her twin sister Hallie, who was standing at her bedside and staring at her with an annoyed look on her face.

"You promised you'd listen to my science presentation," said Hallie, "but you're falling asleep."

"Excuse me, Hal, it's 7:20 in the morning," said Jenna, yawning. "Our alarm doesn't even go off for another ten minutes. At least *that* has a snooze button."

"Jenna Lee Dalmore, I am not in the mood for jokes."

"Quit middle-naming me," said Jenna. She yawned again. "I'm awake. I'm listening."

Hallie huffed and turned her attention back to the note cards in her hand. She tucked her sandy-blonde hair behind her ears; something she always did when she was nervous. She had done it a dozen times so far this morning—Jenna had counted.

Perhaps she wouldn't have been so nervous if she had had a more interesting topic to present to their class today, but there's only so much anyone can say about invertebrate sea creatures. Normally, Hallie wouldn't have gone within ten feet of a subject like that, but she was partnered with their friend Lindsay Peters, who had been at a late volleyball practice and who hadn't arrived to class in time for them to pick one of the more popular topics.

It probably wasn't all that bad that she had a difficult topic, which Jenna only thought but never said aloud, because Hallie had always been better in science. Jenna and Hallie Dalmore may have been identical twins, but their differences stood out like a sore thumb at times. Hallie was better in science, but Jenna was better in history. Jenna was more outgoing than Hallie. Jenna was left-handed, Hallie was right-handed. And yet, no matter how different they were or even how different they sometimes tried to be, the first things anybody always noticed about them were their identical hazel eyes and their identical sandy-blonde hair.

Hallie exhaled deeply when she was finally finished speaking and looked intently at Jenna, silently seeking her opinion.

"I think you're ready," said Jenna, rubbing her eyes.

"Really?" said Hallie, fidgeting with her note cards. "You really think so?"

"Yes. I never knew there were so many types of coral!" Their alarm clock buzzed its morning noise and Jenna checked the glowing green numbers—7:30 AM, meaning she had been awake and listening to Hallie practice for more than an hour. Right on cue, her stomach began to growl. "Let's go get some breakfast, okay?"

"Are you sure I'm speaking clearly enough? I didn't do Lindsay's part much justice, but she's better at public speaking anyway, so—"

"You're gonna get an A, Hal. Relax, okay?"

"I hope so. We sure worked on it long enough," Hallie mumbled, carefully placing her note cards back into her knapsack. "Of course, we all know *your* presentation is going to be top of the class."

"And how could we possibly know that? Because I'm partnered with Thomas?" asked Jenna, reading her mind. "Come on, Hal, that's not fair. At least I do my half of the work. At least I don't take advantage of him just because he's a genius."

"He's not a *genius*, Jenna."

"Okay, so he's never been tested," Jenna argued, trying and failing to straighten her covers by simply flinging them up to her pillow, "but he is. He could skip, like, two grades, easy."

Hallie rolled her eyes, but she couldn't hide the grin on her face. She knew Jenna was right, but there was no way she was going to admit it. "You said something about breakfast?" she said over her shoulder. "Come on, I can smell pancakes and bacon."

"Yeah, me too," Jenna said thoughtfully. Usually, breakfast on a school morning was cereal or toast. "Mom's probably been up for a while. Maybe she heard you pronouncing the different kinds of lobster."

"Well, excuse me for trying to be prepared."

The different smells were even stronger once they arrived in the kitchen. The table was already covered in plates of chocolate chip pancakes, blueberry pancakes, and fat, wavy pieces of bacon. There were bowls of grapes and strawberries. Jenna could smell and hear more bacon sizzling in the frying pan, and she could also smell the coffee brewing, but that was just for Lou.

Louisa Dalmore—'Mom' to Jenna and Hallie, and 'Lou' to everyone else—was standing over the stove, paying a watchful eye, making sure nothing was burning. She was all dressed for work at the Museum of Ancient History (where she was an examiner of old weapons), and her long, golden blonde hair looked just as warm and shiny as the sunlight streaming in through the kitchen window.

"Morning!" said Jenna. She wasted no time putting a chocolate chip pancake on her plate. "This all looks great, Mom. What's the occasion?"

Lou turned and smiled at them, her big blue eyes sparkling like the blueberries in the pancake batter. "Does a mother need an occasion to spoil her girls?" she asked, winking at them. "I was wondering when you two were going to come down. Do you have those science presentations memorized yet?"

"Told you she heard you," Jenna whispered to Hallie through a mouthful of bacon.

Hallie looked rather guilty as she glanced up at Lou. "I didn't mean to wake you," she began, but Lou shook her head.

"It's okay, sweetheart. Actually, from what I heard, it sounds like a really good presentation. But I didn't hear yours, Jenna."

"That's because I didn't practice mine," said Jenna, "at least not this morning. But Thomas and I are ready. We practiced yesterday during afternoon recess."

"You missed recess?" said Lou, shocked. "Who are you, and what have you done with my daughter?"

Jenna shrugged. "Well, Thomas couldn't practice after school because of his enrichment classes. They were learning trigonometry yesterday. Apparently."

"Trigo-what?" Hallie asked, pancakes filling her mouth.

Jenna nodded. "Exactly."

Lou chuckled at their conversation as she shifted down the counter where she was preparing their lunches. She began cutting up two different kinds of melon because Jenna only liked honeydew and Hallie only liked cantaloupe.

"Mom?" asked Jenna.

"Yes, baby?"

"Can we go shopping for Jules' birthday present after school? She mentioned yesterday that she wants a new floating toy for her pool, and there's some at the mall that are shaped like doughnuts."

Hallie let her fork fall onto her plate. "No fair, *I* wanted to get that for her!"

"Too late—I call dibs!"

"Mom!"

"Alright, alright, take it easy, both of you," said Lou, holding her hands up like a referee. She looked quizzically at Jenna. "Jenna, it's only the beginning of June."

"I know that. I don't want the store to sell out of the floating toys."

"Jules' birthday isn't until the first of July. I think there's still time. Anyway, I thought she wasn't having her party until July seventh this year…? Didn't one of you tell me she was going to spend the long weekend at her cottage?"

"Yeah, but her parents changed their minds," said Jenna. "Jules wanted to have her birthday party on the first of July. Her actual birthday. She wanted to do the pool party, barbeque, doughnut cake, and Canada Day fireworks, just like every year."

"Oh, well, that'll be nice for her," said Lou, "to have her birthday with her best friends. Will it be just the six of you, as always?"

"Yep," said Jenna. "Jules, me, Hal, Lindsay, Alan and Thomas. The Fantastic Six."

Hallie shook her head. "You're thinking of 'The Fantastic Four'."

"Okay, then, The Magnificent Six."

Again, Hallie shook her head. "And now you're thinking of 'The Magnificent Seven'."

Jenna groaned. "Then what is it for six?"

"There isn't one."

"There must be."

Lou cleared her throat. "That's enough, ladies. Yes, we can go shopping after school today,"—again, she held up her hands to silence them if they tried to mention the pool toy—"and we will find something nice for each of you to give her. Deal?"

"Deal," they said together.

"I hope her Uncle Levi will be there," Hallie added, grinning for ear to ear. "He's so cool."

"He comes every year," said Jenna. "He never misses Jules' birthday."

"Ah yes, Jules' uncle, the famous Uncle Levi," said Lou, nodding. "He's a fun guy to have around, isn't he?"

"He's awesome," Jenna agreed, "and funny, and so cool."

"Remember the water balloon fight Levi started last year?" said Hallie, a laugh escaping her as she thought about it. She reached across the table to grab a few strawberries from the bowl—her favourite. "I can still remember the look on your face after Alan threw a balloon at your head."

"Ha, ha," Jenna sneered. "That wasn't as funny as her sixth birthday party when Levi taught us how to suck helium out of the balloons. Remember Alan trying to helium-burp the alphabet?"

"He did what?" asked Lou, leaning over the table, but she didn't look entirely surprised. "What are we going to do with that boy? He's a sweetie, but such a goofball."

"That's putting it lightly," Jenna chuckled. She nudged Hallie's arm. "What excuse do you think he'll have today when he hasn't done the English homework?"

Hallie shrugged. "Who knows. But it'll make everybody laugh, no doubt."

"Speaking of school," said Lou, checking her watch, "you two had better go get ready or you'll be late."

They finished the last of their breakfast—which meant using spoons to make sure no maple syrup went to waste—and hurried upstairs. After a heated debate over who would get to wear their favourite purple T-shirt today (which Hallie won), they headed back downstairs and met Lou at the bottom, taking their lunches from her and giving her a kiss goodbye.

"Have a good day!" she called after them, watching them until they were out of sight.

What she didn't realize, and what Jenna and Hallie didn't realize, either, was that somebody else would continue to watch them once they turned the corner. And that they'd also be watched down the next street. And down the next street. And the next.

A strange woman with chestnut hair and striking green eyes would follow them all the way to school and watch their every step, but nobody would see her.

CHAPTER 2:
LIGHTS OUT

Jenna

MRS. SCHWANTZ'S GRADE SIX classroom at Landwood Public School was ripe with nervous energy that morning. Mrs. Schwantz had opened the classroom door early so that anybody wanting to practice their science presentations could do so, and while many people were already there when Jenna and Hallie arrived, only four people caught their eyes: a skinny red-haired boy, Thomas Brane; a tall blonde girl with freckles, Lindsay Peters; a bright-eyed boy with black hair and a devilish grin, Alan Zhang; and a small girl with brown hair and rosy cheeks, Jules Mansfield.

Jenna and Hallie walked to their desks and received smiles or nods of hello from Lindsay, Alan and Jules. Thomas, however, was focusing intently on his science notes. They took their seats, and Jenna tapped Thomas' shoulder with her pencil. He practically jumped out of his skin, but he smiled once he saw who had disturbed him.

"Oh, good morning!" he said, shaking his shaggy red hair from his eyes. "All ready to teach the class a thing or two about static electricity, partner?"

"As ready as I'll ever be!" said Jenna, opening her knapsack and getting her other homework out and ready for Mrs. Schwantz to collect. "You know, Thomas, it was a good call to practice our presentation yesterday at lunch. I spent most of last night finishing the English homework. Who knew one page of writing could take so long?"

Alan, who had been casually using his fingers as drumsticks on the edge of his desk, stopped and looked at Jenna, confused. "What homework?" he asked.

"The story report," Jenna said wryly. Just as she suspected, he hadn't done it. "We were supposed to read one of those fairy tales from the textbook and write a page about it for homework."

"That's due today? Aw, man!" Alan slid his hands down his face so hard they could see the underside of his eyelids.

Jules, who was squeamish at the best of times, covered her eyes. "Ew, Alan! That's gross!" she squealed. She peeked between her fingers to see if the coast was clear, which it wasn't. She turned around. "Someone tell me when he stops being gross."

"What am I going to do?" said Alan. He stopped being gross, as Jules had put it, and ran his fingers through his short black hair instead. "The last time I forgot to hand in my homework, Mrs. Schwantz told me she'd give me a week-long detention the next time. This is the next time!"

"Well, let's think about this realistically," said Thomas, whose desk was directly in front of his. He turned around and folded his hands on Alan's desk. "Perhaps, if you don't mind receiving a sub-par mark, you could scribble something up right now."

"What? No, I don't want to get a bad mark," said Alan. He sighed heavily. "But I guess I've got no choice, eh?"

"Well," Thomas began, "I suppose you can use my backup report."

Lindsay, who had been sitting with Hallie and reading over their notes on invertebrate sea creatures, suddenly turned her head so quickly in Thomas' direction that her blonde ponytail almost whacked Jenna in the face—well, more like the top of Jenna's head, because Lindsay was about a head taller than Jenna was, even sitting down.

She looked baffled, but not at all surprised. This was Thomas, after all. But still, she turned to him and said, "And on behalf of everyone here, I just want to say... your *what*?"

"My backup report," Thomas repeated. "I wrote two reports in case I lost one or in case I changed my mind about which one I wanted to hand in."

"Thomas, man, I can't take that," said Alan. It looked like he wanted to, though.

Thomas shrugged. "The way I see it, you've earned it. You've been helping me with my slap shot for weeks, and it finally paid off at our most recent game."

"But the puck hit the boards..."

"Yes," said Thomas, raising his index finger, "but it lifted off the ice, didn't it?"

Jenna never understood what enjoyment Thomas got out of hockey, since he was constantly tripping over his own skates or failing to shoot the puck when it came to him. He and Alan liked being on the team together, though, and since Alan was arguably the best player in the league, he was always happy to share his skills and help Thomas improve.

Thomas opened his briefcase, which he carried instead of a knapsack, and pulled out a clean sheet of paper covered with writing.

"Well, alright, if you're sure?" Alan said slowly, taking the paper.

"I'm quite sure," said Thomas, nodding his head so definitely that his rectangular glasses fell forward on his nose.

Alan grabbed a pencil and an eraser from his desk. "I'd better change some of the words or Mrs. Schwantz will know I didn't write it."

After the final bell rang and the playing of "O Canada" was through, Mrs. Schwantz began making her way around the classroom to collect the English homework. Jules' usual rosy cheeks became white as a sheet as she checked every compartment of her knapsack three times.

"Oh no," she said. She covered her mouth with one hand and kept rummaging, faster and faster, with the other hand.

"What's up?" said Jenna.

"I can't find my report!" she hissed.

"What do you mean you can't find it?" asked Hallie. "You never forget your homework!"

"Well, I must have today! I was thinking so much about the science presentations this morning that I forgot my English homework! It's probably sitting on the kitchen table—a lot of good it'll do me there!" She was practically in tears. "What am I going to do?"

"Miss Mansfield," said Mrs. Schwantz suddenly. She tilted her head down so she could look at Jules above her glasses. "Where is your report?"

"It's here, Mrs. Schwantz," said Alan, handing her Thomas' backup report. "She, um, she let me read it."

"Thank you, Mr. Zhang," said Mrs. Schwantz, taking the paper. Jenna noticed that Alan had written Jules' name across the top. "And where is yours?"

"Well, um, I don't exactly have it," said Alan. "Funny story, um, there was a wild tiger loose on my street last night. Yeah, probably from the zoo or something. But the police and the animal wrangler guys asked me to help catch him, and after that I was so wiped that I fell asleep on my porch swing, and then the mayor came over—"

By now, most of the class was laughing at his cheek, especially the girls. Mrs. Schwantz, however, wasn't so amused. Her look of disappointment could have burned right through him.

"A zero then, Mr. Zhang?"

Jules' eyes widened. "No, Mrs. Schwantz, he didn't—"

"Yeah, a zero," Alan interrupted, looking at Mrs. Schwantz and nodding his head. As she continued her way around the class, collecting other reports, Jules mouthed a silent 'thank you' to Alan, who shrugged as if it was no big deal. And it really wasn't a big deal to him. Jenna knew he would have done that for any one of them.

Soon enough, it was time to start the science presentations. Hallie and Lindsay were up first, and before they even started speaking, Hallie tucked and re-tucked her hair behind her ears three times. Jenna tried to catch her eye to tell her not to be so nervous, but Hallie was doing her very best not to look anybody directly in the eye.

Mrs. Schwantz took a seat behind her desk and opened her folder where she would record their marks. "You have five minutes, ladies. Please begin."

What happened next happened so fast that it took Jenna a few moments to comprehend that it had even happened at all. Before Hallie and Lindsay could utter one word about invertebrate sea creatures, there was a loud *CRACK*, like a bolt of lightning, and then everything went dark. The lights in the classroom and the hallway went out. There wasn't even any sunlight coming in from the windows anymore. In the blink of an eye, or with the crack of a lightning bolt, it looked like nighttime both inside and outside.

Some kids screamed at the sudden darkness. Others merely gasped. Jules did both.

"What happened?" she hissed. Jenna could feel her begin to tremble from head to toe. "I don't like the dark!"

"Alright now, everybody, remain calm," Mrs. Schwantz said as she stood up from her desk. Jenna could see her shadowy silhouette holding her arms up and waving them. She made her way to the window, like she thought there were curtains to be opened. When she realized they were already open and it was just incredibly dark outside, she, too, let out a gasp of horror.

"Is there an eclipse happening right now or something?" said Jenna, trying to see out of the window. The sky was practically black.

"To the best of my recollection, we aren't supposed to have a solar eclipse for another fourteen months," said Thomas' voice. "And besides, the likelihood of it casting this much darkness on the world is, well, slim at best."

"Then what the heck is happening?" Jenna responded.

"Haven't the foggiest! It is rather fascinating, though, you've got to admit."

Jenna rolled her eyes, which were starting to adjust to the darkness. She could just about make out the shapes of Hallie and Lindsay, still standing at the front of the room with their note cards. Throughout the school, she could hear cries of confusion from other classrooms travelling up and down the halls. They were getting louder by the minute.

Just when she was about to turn and console Jules, whom she could feel shaking like a leaf next to her, someone darted in front of her; she felt the wind as they ran and could smell a kind of fragrance she'd never smelled before. It was almost woodsy. *Strange*, she thought, since nobody in her class wore perfume. Then she felt someone—probably that same someone—step on her foot.

"Ouch! Who's there?" she snapped, reaching in front of her. She grabbed someone's shirt. "Who *is* this?"

"That's me," said Alan, trying to shake out of her grasp.

She pulled him close to her and smelled his shirt. *He* didn't smell woodsy. He just smelled like Alan.

Alan jolted away from her. "What the heck are you doing?"

"Someone just ran right past me and stepped on my foot!" said Jenna. "Someone who smelled like a forest."

"A forest? What are you talking about? Does the dark make you crazy?"

CRACK!

And just like that, the lights came back on. Even the sun seemed to come out from behind the blackness outside.

Jenna scanned the classroom. Twenty-six students and one teacher. There was nobody there who shouldn't have been there.

Mrs. Schwantz was standing at the front of the room with Hallie and Lindsay, relieved to see the sunlight coming in through the window once again. "Settle down, everybody, settle down," she was saying, even though she looked like she had just seen a ghost herself.

Alan nudged Jenna in the arm. "Did you just... kiss me?"

"What? No! Gross! I was smelling your shirt, you idiot!" Jenna exclaimed. "I told you—someone stepped on me and they smelled like a forest."

"Well, it wasn't me."

"Miss Dalmore and Mr. Zhang," said Mrs. Schwantz, noticing them talking, "I was just telling the rest of the class that I'd like to continue with our presentations, but perhaps you'd like to tell us what you find so interesting."

"It's nothing, Mrs. Schwantz," said Jenna.

"Well, young lady, it must be *something*."

"It's just, somebody ran past me when the lights were out, and whoever it was stepped on my foot. I was asking Alan if it was him."

"Which it wasn't," Alan added.

Mrs. Schwantz moved her gaze to the rest of the class. "Did anybody step on Jenna's foot when the lights were out?"

Everyone in the class shook their heads. Some of them felt the need to point out that they'd never even left their seats.

Mrs. Schwantz looked satisfied and turned her attention back to Jenna. "There, you see? Perhaps you imagined it."

Jenna sighed. "Yeah, maybe."

But she hadn't imagined it; she knew that much. Her foot was still throbbing, and she could still smell that woodsy scent if she sniffed in just the right spot by her desk. If it truly had been nobody in class, and it hadn't been Mrs. Schwantz, then who had it been?

CHAPTER 3:
ANNABEL SCOTT

Hallie

HALLIE AND JENNA LIVED on Metcalfe Street, number 47, in Peterborough, Ontario. Alan, Jules, Thomas and Lindsay lived on Metcalfe Street as well, and so the six of them always walked home from school together. Walking to and from school was good exercise, as Lou often told them. Unlike her sister, Hallie never argued with her on that point because she knew she wasn't going to win.

Lou knew a thing or two about exercise. Despite being a forty-year-old mom of twins, she didn't look it; nobody ever guessed she had been pregnant before, much less with twins, even though it was the first thing she mentioned whenever telling someone about herself.

Hallie was relieved to be leaving school today, and not just because of the strange—and still unexplainable—incident with the lights during her science presentation. Talk about humiliating! On top of it all, Landwood hadn't been able to get the air conditioning working again once the lights came back on. Even the thirty-degree heat outside felt much cooler than the stuffy air inside the school.

"If you ask me, the whole thing is super weird," said Jenna, kicking a stone ahead of her like a soccer ball.

Alan jogged ahead and gave the stone a second kick. "The lights?" he probed.

"That and the fact that someone stepped on me. Someone who smelled like a forest."

Hallie groaned. "Give it a rest. You haven't stopped talking about that all day."

"Have so!"

"Have not!"

"Come on, you guys, knock it off," said Lindsay, stepping between them. "Jenna, think about it. The lights weren't out that long. How could some guy have gotten into our classroom, run around and stepped on you, and then gotten out without anybody noticing?"

"I don't think it was a guy," said Jenna. "The woodsy scent was like perfume, not cologne."

"Regardless," Thomas spoke up, "I do believe Lindsay and your sister are right, Jenna. Security at our school is better than that. I think the real conundrum is neither the indoor lights nor the alleged visitor, but rather the fact that the sun simply went away outside! As proficient as I am in science, if I do say so myself, I cannot think of any possible explanation for such a phenomenon."

"I'm telling you guys: someone was in our classroom," said Jenna after a moment of puzzlement, trying to work out Thomas' words. "And that someone, whoever it was, stepped on my foot."

"And they smelled like a forest... Yeah, we know," said Hallie, rolling her eyes.

"Why doesn't anyone believe me?"

"Because you have the imagination of a five-year-old."

"You know, you sound like Mom. You're three minutes older than me, not three years."

Hallie rolled her eyes again as they approached the driveway of number 47. They waved goodbye to their friends and jogged to their front door. The second Hallie turned the key in the lock and pushed the door open, they were hit with a wave of air conditioning.

"Nothing like coming home to a cool house on a thirty-degree day," Jenna sighed as she dropped her knapsack on the floor.

"Jenna, for heaven's sake, pick that up. You aren't an animal." Hallie walked into the kitchen where she thought Lou would be. "Mom, we're home—"

She stopped dead. Somebody was in the kitchen, but it wasn't Lou.

"You're not Mom," said Jenna, stating the blatantly obvious.

This woman had wavy brown hair that fell to her collarbone and striking green eyes. Even from the doorway, Hallie could see just how green they were. She wore a grey pantsuit, much like the outfit Lou had worn to work that day, and no jewelry aside from two silver rings, one on each pinkie finger, with emeralds as green as her eyes.

"No," she said, "I'm not Mom." Her voice was silky—devious, almost. It made the hairs on the back of Hallie's neck stand up. And, yet, her manners were kind. She smiled at them. "Would you like a cup of tea?"

Neither of them said anything. For a moment, Hallie was tempted to make a run for the phone and call the police, but then the woman spoke again.

"Your mom should be home any minute now," she said, turning her back to them. She was waiting for the kettle to boil. "I just spoke with her about five minutes before you came home."

"You know our mom?" Jenna asked.

"Very well. We used to work together." She nodded her head to the kitchen table. "Sit down, please."

Hallie wasn't sure how she felt about a stranger inviting her to sit down in her own house, but, nonetheless, she sat, followed by Jenna.

Just as the kettle began to screech and steam, Hallie found her voice. "Who... who are you?"

"Annabel," said the woman, lifting the kettle and pouring it into three cups. "Annabel Scott. Assistant Department Head of Maple Cliff in Pawcombe."

Hallie stumbled over all of that. "Assistant what?"

"Assistant Department Head. It's like, there's the boss," she said, holding her hand up at about head-height, and then holding her other hand slightly lower, "and then there's me."

"Who's the boss?" Jenna asked.

"Jenna, focus." Hallie looked earnestly at Annabel. "What was the other stuff you said? Maple popcorn?"

Annabel laughed, but Hallie failed to see how any of this was funny.

"Maple Cliff, Pawcombe," Annabel corrected. "Maple Cliff is where I work. It's the place in charge of keeping the people of Pawcombe safe."

"The police?"

"You could say it's kind of like that, sure."

"But what's Pawcombe?"

"*What's Pawcombe?*" Annabel was shocked at the question for a moment, but then seemed to remember something as she sat down with the teacups. "That's right, of course, Lou was sworn to secrecy."

"Secrecy?" said Hallie. "What are you talking about? Our mom doesn't have secrets. She goes to work, takes care of us, and does Pilates twice a week. No secrets."

"Au contraire," said Annabel, sipping her tea. "Everybody has secrets. Even moms."

Hallie sighed. "Then what hasn't she told us?"

Annabel became serious. "First, let's make one thing clear. Your mom only ever wanted to keep you safe. She's not at fault, so don't be angry with her." Her affection for Lou might have been comforting had her tone of voice not been so heavy. She stared between them. "Okay?"

Hallie and Jenna looked at each other, confused, but eventually they nodded their heads to Annabel. She also nodded and cleared her throat.

"To begin with, there's another world out there beyond this one, and it's called Pawcombe," said Annabel. "It's a beautiful place. Full of forests and lakes, and some of the nicest people you'll ever meet. And Maple Cliff... Well, it's a sight to behold. The people who work there keep Pawcombe safe. You two were born there."

Hallie felt as though those last few words had slapped her across the face.

"What?" she and Jenna asked in unison.

"Haven't you ever wondered why there are hardly any photos of the first four months of your lives?" Annabel asked, very casually turning her teacup in her palms. Her pinkie rings sparkled under the kitchen lights.

Hallie paused. One glance at Jenna's puzzled expression told her Annabel's question had stumped her, too. Truthfully, she had wondered. All of their baby photos were dated August at the earliest, despite the fact they had been born in April. For a little while when they were growing up, she and Jenna thought they might be adopted, but they looked far too much like Lou to take that idea seriously.

Hallie swallowed and returned her gaze to Annabel, who was taking another sip of her tea. "How do you know that?"

A tiny smile spread across Annabel's mouth. "I remember when you guys moved here. It was twelve years ago. Twelve years ago this August, actually. It was just after Alan was born."

"Alan?" asked Jenna, leaning forward in her chair. "Our friend Alan? As in, Alan Zhang? *That* Alan?"

Annabel's smile grew wider. "Yes, *that* Alan. Anyway, all the parents had to move away from Pawcombe, and they were sworn to secrecy about anything to do with it. It was for your safety, of course."

Hallie shook her head. "What do you mean, all the parents?"

"The Zhangs, the Branes, the Mansfields, the Peters' and, of course, Lou."

"You mean... Alan, Thomas, Jules and Lindsay... they were all born in this place, too? In—what was it?— Pawcombe?"

Annabel nodded.

"Why did we have to move, then? And why couldn't Mom tell us about it?" said Jenna, squinting in an effort to figure it out herself. "And what does any of this have to do with our safety?"

"Very good questions, but I'm afraid the answers are quite heavy." Annabel lifted her eyebrows, as if the weight of what she had to tell them was sitting right there. "Do you promise to keep an open mind while I explain everything to you?"

Hallie and Jenna nodded.

"Drink your tea," said Annabel, before beginning. "It'll relax you."

Hallie didn't like the sound of that.

CHAPTER 4:
THE FIRST SECRET

Hallie

ANNABEL HAD ALMOST FINISHED her cup of tea before she spoke again. She was so comfortable in their kitchen that any casual observer might have assumed she lived at 47 Metcalfe Street herself, and that perhaps she was Hallie and Jenna's aunt or something. But, of course, she didn't and she wasn't.

"Okay, what's going on?" said Jenna with a huff. "What's all of this about Pawcombe and all of these secrets? What's actually going on?"

Annabel's eyebrows crinkled. "I suppose the only place to begin is at the beginning." She twisted the ring on one of her pinkie fingers. "August 11th, it was the night Alan was born. At that point in the year, the rest of you had already been born. Alan was the sixth."

Hallie and Jenna looked at each other. "So?" they said in unison.

"So, when six of Pawcombe's children are born on very specific days of the same year, they become connected with one another."

Jenna shook her head. "Specific days? What do you mean, *specific days*?"

Hallie nudged her sister in the ribs for interrupting, but Annabel didn't seem to mind.

"The specific days are the 6th, the 18th, the 1st, the 14th, and the 11th," said Annabel. "The months don't matter, but there must be all five of those dates."

"Hey, our birthday is on the 18th," said Jenna. "April 18th."

Annabel nodded. "Exactly."

Hallie's stomach began doing somersaults when she realized Thomas' birthday was January 6th, Jules' birthday was July 1st, Lindsay's birthday was March 14th, and Alan's birthday was August 11th. Adding their own birthday of April 18th, those were all the numbers. All the right dates. It didn't even matter that there were six of them and only five dates because, of course, Hallie and Jenna shared a birthday.

She swallowed hard. "But what's the big deal with our birthdays? How do they connect us?"

"They make you into a team." Annabel pursed her lips. "It's the most sought-after team at Maple Cliff, and certainly in all of Pawcombe. You're called the Sought Six."

Hallie wanted to ask things like *how* and *why*, but she didn't. She had a feeling the answers would only confuse her more, anyway. "What does a Sought Six do?" she asked instead.

"You asked that at just the right time. See, your birthdays don't only connect you with each other; they also connect you to somebody else. Another man in

Pawcombe. Actually, the *worst* man in Pawcombe. He's rather extraordinary. His name is Zyngor. Frank Zyngor."

Hallie wasn't sure why, but that name sent a shiver up her spine.

"Tell me," said Annabel after a moment, "what is the sixth letter of the alphabet?"

Hallie took a moment to count in her head while Jenna used her fingers to count.

"F," they said in unison.

"And the eighteenth?"

Counting took a little longer this time. "R," they responded.

"And the first?"

"A."

Then Hallie understood. Their birthdays—all the numbers—spelled the name Frank. Frank, as in Frank Zyngor. *That* was what connected them to this man who was apparently the worst man in Pawcombe.

"But... you still haven't answered my question," Hallie said slowly. "What is a Sought Six supposed to do?"

"Well, I've half-answered it," said Annabel, thinking. "The birthdate connection to Zyngor is the answer, basically. A connection like that is extremely significant. It makes the Sought Six the only people in the world with the power to get rid of him once and for all."

"Whoa, whoa, back up!" said Jenna, waving her arms. "You're telling us that a bunch of kids is supposed to—what?—defeat this guy? *Kill* this guy? And *we're* that bunch of kids?"

"Yes."

"Are you insane?!"

"Jenna!" Hallie snapped. "You're being rude!"

"Can you blame me?!"

"Don't shoot the messenger, girls. I didn't make the rules." Annabel's voice dropped a little. "I know it sounds crazy, but I'm telling you the truth. I don't expect you to understand how serious it is because you haven't seen what he can do yet. Trust me: he's ruthless. He must be stopped—and you're the only ones who can do it."

"Why, though?" asked Jenna, settling down a little. "I mean, what's his deal?"

"He wants control over Pawcombe. He has followers, most of which are only loyal because they're afraid of him. They're all helping him gain control over our world, and they'll kill anybody who gets in his way."

"But you just said it was a Sought Six's job to kill him," said Hallie. She could feel a headache coming on. "And if we're the Sought Six, that means we're going to be getting in his way. He's going to try to kill us, too, isn't he?"

Jenna's head snapped quickly in Hallie's direction, as if she hadn't thought of this yet.

"He's already tried to," said Annabel. She was smiling, but it was a sad smile. "I'm guessing power outages at your school don't happen often, right?"

"You know about that?"

"Who do you think fixed it?"

"Wait a second," said Jenna, leaping up from her chair and burying her nose in Annabel's shoulder to sniff her jacket.

"Jenna, for heaven's sake!" Hallie exclaimed.

"It was *you*!" gasped Jenna, bolting back a step and pointing at her. "You're the one who smells like a forest! You're the one who stepped on my foot!"

Hallie directed her gaze to Annabel. "Wait, what?"

"Yeah, sorry about that," said Annabel to Jenna. "I had to check on you—*all* of you. I had to make sure Zyngor's man hadn't gotten to you."

"His *man*?" said Jenna.

Annabel nodded. "A follower he sent to fetch you. He's dead now. That's why the lights went out. Whenever someone from Pawcombe dies in this world, there's a cross-connection and it disrupts any nearby electricity. Even the sun goes away for a while, if it's daytime."

"Well, that explains a lot," Hallie muttered. "So, you're saying you killed this follower guy?"

"I was protecting you," said Annabel.

"How did you... I mean, what did you...?"

"That's not important."

Hallie disagreed.

Annabel earnestly leaned forward on the table. "Don't you see? You guys are the secret. For nearly twelve years, the Sought Six has been our secret." Annabel absentmindedly twisted one of her pinkie rings. "But the attempted attack at your school today means Zyngor has found you. You aren't a secret anymore—and you aren't *safe* anymore. That's why I'm here now. I've come to take you back to Pawcombe."

Hallie swallowed. "What? Take us back?"

"I want Mom," said Jenna, slumping in her chair. "I'm not going anywhere until I talk to Mom." She sounded like she was on the verge of tears. Truthfully, Hallie felt like she could cry herself.

Right on cue, they heard a key in the front door lock.

"Well, here's your chance," said Annabel, peeking into her empty teacup. She stood up and walked back over to the kitchen counter. "Anyone else need a refill?"

Hallie and Jenna shook their heads; neither of them had even touched their cups yet. The front door opened and closed, and Lou's frantic footsteps came racing down the hallway. Her speed alone made Hallie nervous.

CHAPTER 5:
THE SECOND SECRET

Jenna

A WAVE OF RELIEF FLOODED Lou's face when she saw Jenna and Hallie sitting at the table. It was as if she hadn't expected them to be there.

"Oh, thank goodness," she said, sprinting forward the extra two steps to wrap them in a hug. "Are you okay? Are you hurt?" She looked both of them over, her eyes darting around like little blue marbles.

"We're not hurt," Hallie answered.

"Why would you even think that?" Jenna asked, staring at Lou. She wanted to hear everything from her mouth—actually, she wanted to hear Lou deny everything, but she doubted that was going to happen. "What aren't you telling us?"

"Oh, girls, so much," said Lou, letting out a heavy sigh. "So much, and I'm so, so sorry. I don't even know where to begin. I just—" She stopped talking suddenly as she caught sight of Annabel in the kitchen, standing against the counter. She was watching them, patiently waiting for this exact moment. When Lou's eyes met her own, a coy smile spread across her face.

"Hello, Lou."

"Oh my God," Lou breathed. She stood up straight but her knees began to shake. "Oh my God... You... You're here!"

"In the flesh."

Lou walked into the kitchen, slowly at first, but her speed increased with each step. She clapped her hand to her mouth, then her stomach, and then her mouth again. Her eyes filled with tears as she flung her arms around Annabel's shoulders and squeezed her tightly. A few sobs escaped her mouth, but they weren't sad sobs; they sounded like relief. They sounded joyous. One of the first things Annabel had said to them was clearly correct: she and Lou knew each other very well.

"Shh, it's okay," Annabel murmured as Lou cried into her shoulder.

"I missed you," came Lou's muffled voice.

"I missed you, too."

Jenna shot a dumbfounded look at Hallie, and then at the reunion in the kitchen. "Um, hello?" she said, waving her arms.

Lou and Annabel broke apart, looking slightly embarrassed.

"Sorry," said Annabel. "You mom and I haven't seen each other in a very long time."

"Twelve years," Lou agreed, "and you still look the same, An."

Annabel chuckled. "I don't know about that."

"You do," said Lou, "and thank God."

"Twelve years?" Jenna repeated. "You haven't seen each other since we were babies?"

Annabel led Lou back to the table. "I told you. She was sworn to secrecy. She had to cut contact with everyone when she moved away, even her best friend." Annabel pointed her thumb at her own chest. "She couldn't even mention Pawcombe without putting you guys in danger."

"So, you've already told them about Pawcombe," Lou said nervously as she sat down in a chair opposite her daughters. "What else have you told them?"

"Oh, nothing much," Jenna said wryly, sitting back in her chair. "Only that we were born in another world called Pawcombe, and so were our friends, and our birthdays make us into something called a Sought Six, which means we're the only ones who can kill a bad guy who also wants to kill us."

Annabel tilted her head. "Yeah, that about covers it."

Lou leaned forward, reaching across the table to take their hands in hers. "Talk to me. Are you okay?"

"How can we be?" Hallie muttered.

Jenna almost snapped at her to not answer for both of them but, in this particular scenario, she shared her sister's feelings.

"Oh, and we know you kept it a secret because you were trying to protect us, and we're not mad at you." Hallie glanced briefly at Annabel.

Lou looked relieved. "It's okay if you're a little mad."

"*I'm* a little mad," Jenna said quickly.

"I'm sorry, baby," said Lou, her eyes once again glossing over with unspent tears. "This is a pretty crazy thing to take in, eh? I know. But I'm going to be right there with you, every step of the way. Annabel, too."

Jenna felt ever so slightly better and Hallie's shoulders relaxed.

"You... you are?" She looked at Annabel. "You didn't mention that part."

"Of course," said Lou. "After all, we've been through this before. We know the kind of stuff you'll have to—" She stopped speaking then as Annabel put her hand on her shoulder.

"Lou."

Jenna's heart began to race. "What do you mean? You've been through what before?"

Lou suddenly went very pale as she turned to face Annabel in her chair. "You haven't gotten that far yet, have you?"

Annabel slowly shook her head.

"How far?" Hallie practically gasped. "What else could there possibly be to mention?" She looked from one face to the next, and then turned back to Lou. "Mom?"

"Alright, alright." She took a deep breath. "You guys aren't the first Sought Six team Pawcombe has ever had," she said slowly. "There was another, years ago. Annabel and I were both part of that team. That's how we know each other. We worked together."

Jenna's eyes grew as wide as golf balls. "You *what*? But you... you... you work at the museum, Mom."

"Yes, here in Peterborough I do. I had to get a job when we moved here, and the museum was the obvious choice because I already knew all about swords and daggers, thanks to my life in Pawcombe."

Annabel cleared her throat and tried to muffle her voice, but it didn't work: "I hadn't mentioned weapons either, Lou."

Jenna wanted to ask, but she didn't bother.

"Anyway," Lou said quickly, "before we moved here, I worked at Maple Cliff with Annabel and... well, with another familiar face as well. Remember Jules' uncle? Levi?"

Hallie grabbed the edge of the table as if to steady herself. "Stop it. *What*?"

"He was also part of our Sought Six team, all those years ago," Lou continued. "That's sort of why all the parents decided to raise you guys in the same city. We wanted to stay close to each other."

"And Levi never thought to mention anything either?" Hallie went on. "We've seen him at Jules' parties every single year, for heaven's sake."

"Secrecy," Annabel repeated into her teacup. "He couldn't tell. He comes out here for his niece's birthdays, but he has to swear he won't mention Pawcombe. He can't even visit Lou," Annabel said, shooting a mischievous look at Lou, "as much as he might like to."

"As much as he might like to?" Jenna felt less than amused. "What, is Jules' uncle your boyfriend or something, Mom? Is that another secret?"

"Of course not, don't be silly."

"Hang on," said Hallie, sitting up straighter, "if you guys are also a, um, a Sought Six, why do *we* have to be one, too? I mean, if you guys are already doing the job, there mustn't be much for us to do."

Jenna felt a flicker of hope in her chest, but Lou shook her head.

"We aren't a team anymore, sweetheart. We can't be."

Hallie dropped her shoulders. "Why not?"

"Zyngor killed two of us." She shook her head sadly. "It was a long time ago."

Jenna's stomach lurched. That was the first time her mom had ever said the name *Zyngor* in front of them, and even though they didn't know much about him yet, she didn't like the way it sounded.

"A Sought Six can only destroy Zyngor if all six of them are alive and well," Annabel added, taking Lou's hand in her own. "Once our friends were... well, we couldn't do the job anymore."

The flicker of hope Jenna felt had all but disappeared. She swallowed hard before saying, "Are we going to die?"

"No," Lou said quickly, regaining her composure. "Absolutely not, baby. You know I'd never let that happen."

"But it happened to your team," Jenna argued. "Who's to say it won't happen to us? Nope, I'm not going and you can't make me."

"You don't have a choice," Annabel said rather dully. "I told you: Zyngor has found your school; it's only a matter of time now before he finds your house, too. He's going to try to get you before you can get him. You aren't safe here anymore."

Jenna shook her head. "But we'll be safe in this other world, where he lives? How does *that* make sense?"

"It makes sense because we can protect you in Pawcombe. A Sought Six is the most valuable group of children in our world. Your safety will be everybody's top priority. And besides, we have weapons—" Her eyes went to Lou since she had just spilled the beans about swords—"and buildings where we can hide you in Pawcombe. We can't do that here."

"And you're sure there's no one else who can do this?" Hallie sounded defeated. "Does it have to be the six of us? I mean, there's nobody else who was born on the 18th of a month, or the 11th?"

Annabel nodded. "We're sure."

"I'm sorry, girls," said Lou, blinking away a tear and sniffling. "We all knew when you were born that this day would come. We hoped that, by moving you away from Pawcombe when you were only babies, Zyngor might never find out about you. I guess we should have known better."

Annabel's eyebrows crinkled. "Lou, this isn't your fault."

Lou shook her head. "It's a lose-lose, An. If Zyngor knows about the Sought Six, they're in danger. If he doesn't know about them, Pawcombe falls to ruin because nobody else can stop him."

"I know. I went through it, too, remember?"

"We really don't have a say in this, do we?" said Jenna. She sat slumped in her chair. Her eyes felt heavy with tears, which she blinked away. "I mean, like you said, he's going to come after us no matter where we are. We're going to this other world—to Pawcombe—whether we like it or not, aren't we?"

Lou ran her hand over her forehead as if there might have been sweat there to wipe away. "Yes," she said. "We're going."

CHAPTER 6:
THE ROOT PATH

Hallie

WHEN THEIR BAGS WERE packed and they were ready to leave, they made their way to the backyard. Nobody said a word as they locked the back door and followed Annabel across the yard. It seemed strange to leave the house via the back entrance but, frankly, everything about the day was turning out to be strange. Hallie didn't even bother questioning it, unlike Jenna.

They stopped walking when they arrived at the base of a large maple tree in the corner of the backyard. Jenna cleared her throat. "Why are we standing next to this tree?"

"This tree," said Annabel, patting it with her open palm, "is our road to Pawcombe."

"A tree?" She looked up. "Do we have to climb it or something?"

"And go where, Jenna?" said Hallie. "The sky?"

"No," said Annabel, chuckling, "Pawcombe isn't in the sky. All we have to do is knock on the trunk four times. There are trees all throughout Canada with roots that connect to different trees in Pawcombe. That's how it'll get us there. Trees that can transport you from one place to the other are called Root Paths."

"Root Paths," Jenna repeated. "You're saying we've had one of these things in our backyard all this time?"

"Well, you can't find what you aren't looking for, can you?"

"How many trees can do this transportation thing?"

"Quite a few in Pawcombe, but not as many here."

"How do they work?"

Hallie groaned. "You know, Jenna, I think you only have about fifteen more questions until you get to twenty."

"Shut up," said Jenna.

"*You* shut up!"

Lou, who had been quiet as a mouse since they packed their bags, suddenly snapped. "We don't say 'shut up' to each other!" Her eyes flashed for a moment, almost like she might have really been angry, but she quickly recoiled. "Sorry. Just... An, we should go." She looked nervously back at the house.

"Yes, you're right." Annabel took Jenna's hand in her own and Lou took Hallie's. "Ready?"

Hallie didn't answer; she didn't know what to be ready for.

Annabel and Lou, together, knocked on the tree four times.

The next thing Hallie felt was a punch in her stomach that almost winded her. The only reason she wasn't knocked to the ground was because Lou was holding onto her hand so tightly. She closed her eyes and winced, gulping in a few breaths of air. She could hear Jenna doing the same thing, so something must have hit her, too.

When she finally opened her eyes again, their backyard was gone. Rather than just the one maple tree and a fence, there were dozens of maple trees surrounding them now, and no fences in sight. They appeared to be standing in a forest that stretched for miles, and some of the trees were so huge that Hallie didn't think she could wrap her arms all the way around them. In fact, a few of them were so big that she, Jenna, Alan, Jules, Lindsay, and Thomas could all join hands and *still* not be able to wrap their arms all the way around.

"What's that?" came Jenna's voice from behind her. By the sound of it, her mouth was hung open in wonder.

"That," said Annabel, just as Hallie turned around, "is Maple Cliff."

The forest came to an end where they stood, and across a great green field, there was a giant stone cliff with a sort of castle protruding out from it. It looked like quite a grand castle, too. Even from a distance, it was huge. There were tons of towers and turrets. Some of the windows were beautifully coloured with stained glass.

"That's Maple Cliff? That's where you work?" Jenna was astounded.

Annabel nodded. "That's where I work."

"Okay, hold on," said Hallie, motioning behind her. "What the heck was that? How did we get here? It felt like one of you punched me."

Annabel laughed, but Lou looked sympathetic. "No, sweetheart," she said, "that's how Root Paths work. They pull you into their force to get you from one place to another. It's a strong pull, so most people feel a little winded the first time they use one."

Hallie massaged her stomach. "Yeah, that's one word for it."

They picked up their bags and knapsacks, and walked across the open field, closer to Maple Cliff. Hallie took a good look around. The sky was grey, but not threatening. The air was cool, but not cold. The tops of the trees, far above them, were swaying as if there was a strong wind, but Hallie couldn't feel anything more than a light breeze. A few birds chirped in the distance.

Really, it didn't look much different to any ordinary field or forest back home (except for the giant castle in the cliff).

They walked up the hill and around to the opposite side of Maple Cliff, which looked simply humungous now that they were so close to it. There was a big black iron gate on this side with two guards stationed at it, both wearing violet coats with golden medals at the shoulders. They wore black helmets and black pants, and attached to each of their belts was a sturdy-looking sword.

"Where are we, Buckingham Palace?" said Jenna, chuckling a little at her own joke.

Annabel chuckled, too. "Not exactly, although, security-wise, it's pretty close. It has to be. This is where you guys will be staying." She turned her attention to the guards. "Annabel Scott, Lou Dalmore, Jenna Dalmore, and Hallie Dalmore."

The guards, who so far hadn't moved a muscle, turned to look Annabel in the eye. When they saw that the people before them were indeed the ones Annabel had just named, one of them resumed his position whilst the other unlocked the gate. While he fiddled with the key, Hallie kept looking around.

This side of Maple Cliff, although not exactly protruding from the cliff like the other side, was just as beautiful. There was a cobblestone path that led to the front doors, and it was lined with a lush garden full of red and purple flowers.

At last, the gate gave a *clunk*, and the guard pulled it open. Hallie shivered as she followed Annabel up towards the big wooden front doors.

"Is it, like, really cold or is it just me?" she said.

"No, it's not cold. It's just not thirty degrees like it is in Peterborough," said Annabel. She took off her blazer and draped it over Hallie's shoulders.

When they got to the top of the stairs, there were two more guards waiting for them. They wore the same violet coats and black helmets as the other guards, but these ones ignored them completely. On the left side of the door, there was a large bronze plaque nailed to the stone wall. It had an elegant coat of arms on it, bearing purples and reds, and a rearing white horse. Underneath the coat of arms, there were only two words in block capitals:

MAPLE CLIFF

And just underneath read the following:

Official Address:
1 Forest's Edge Way
Maple
Pawcombe

Jenna, who had also been reading it, looked at Annabel and Lou, confused. "Forest's Edge Way, Maple?" she said.

Lou nodded. "Maple is one of the forests here in Pawcombe. It's sort of like a city. Pawcombe has eight cities: Maple, Birch, Elm, Pine, Ash, Willow, Cedar and Oak."

"Why are they named after trees?" asked Hallie, but as soon as she asked the question and looked around at the hundreds of surrounding maple trees, she knew the answer.

"Each forest—or city—only grows one kind of tree," said Lou, confirming Hallie's guess, "the tree they're named for."

"So, Maple only grows maple trees?" said Jenna, looking around. "Cool!"

Lou allowed herself a smile. "That's important to remember. If you're ever out and you start seeing another kind of tree, you'll know you're entering another forest." She pointed down the hill and towards the trees. "See that pathway there, leading into the forest? That's the rest of

Forest's Edge Way. It comes out way down there, right by one of Pawcombe's lakes, Lake Maple."

"There's a lake, too?" asked Jenna, showing her first real glimmer of excitement.

"Lots of them. Each forest has at least one, but I think Maple's is the prettiest." Lou smiled again as she looked around the world she had grown up in—the world she knew. "Gosh, I can't believe how quickly it's all coming back to me. Everything is exactly like I remember it. It even smells the same." She took a deep breath, taking in the crisp breeze that was beginning to sneak in.

Hallie shivered as it passed through her. "So, um, are we going inside?" She tightened Annabel's jacket around her shoulders.

Without a word, Annabel retrieved a golden key from her pocket. It was small, but it looked heavy. She turned it easily in the lock of Maple Cliff's great front doors, and then turned one of the handles.

Inside, they found themselves in a sort of foyer with hardwood floor, lined with a strip of maroon carpet. The walls were almost covered in portraits of people. Each one was a painting rather than a photograph, and they were all framed in gold. The people featured all looked very important. While Annabel shut and locked the door, Hallie examined the portraits.

"That guy there," said Lou, pointing up at the portrait of an old man, "is Conrad Mugford. He opened the Maple Cliff Library—years and years ago, mind. He even donated its first few books—some historical texts, I think. The Mugford family still runs the library."

"I'm sure Thomas would love to explore it," said Hallie, watching Conrad Mugford's white beard and soft blue eyes, which seemed to follow her down the hall.

"Speaking of our friends, when will they get here?" Jenna asked quietly.

"They're already here." Annabel didn't look at her. "Didn't you notice the other footprints in the dirt by the Root Path we took?"

Jenna looked at Hallie, who also hadn't noticed them.

"Then, where are they?" said Hallie.

"With their parents, I assume, getting settled in. Unlike the two of you, their parents don't get to stay here with them, on account of their lack of Sought Six experience."

"Oh." Hallie took Lou's hand. "That must be hard for them."

Annabel shrugged. "It's protocol. The more people surrounding a Sought Six, the higher the chance of them being found. We certainly don't want that, do we?"

"What about Jules' uncle?" said Jenna. "You said he used to be on the Sought Six team, too, so he's staying, right?"

"Pretty Boy? Yes, he's staying."

They walked down the foyer until they came to a door at the very end of it. This door was also locked, and so Annabel had to fiddle with another key (this time a silver one) before opening it for them.

"Well, here we are," she exhaled. "Jenna and Hallie, welcome—and Lou, my friend, welcome back—to The Tower."

Hallie could barely absorb the grandiosity of the room. The floors were now marble, not hardwood. There were no portraits on the walls in here. In fact, there was no way any portraits could possibly hang because the walls were curved. The entire room was a giant, tall tube. And it sure was giant; from one end of the marble floor to the other, it had to be the length of an ice rink. Spiraling upwards against the wall was an elegant set of stairs. The stairs met up with doors that were placed evenly all the way up. First floor, second floor, third floor, and so on. Hallie dragged her gaze so far up that her head was tilted all the way back. The ceiling was a glass dome, which also happened to be the only window to the outside.

"Keep up," said Annabel over her shoulder as she began walking across The Tower. Hallie jogged to catch up, dragging her knapsack full of clothes behind her.

"Where are we going?" she asked. She glanced at the other people in The Tower, most of whom were also looking at her.

"To meet the people who will be helping you with your job." Annabel kept her eyes forward. "It'll be a quick meet-and-greet—it's already kind of late in the day."

Hallie darted her eyes between the people surrounding them. The ones who weren't looking at them were whispering to one another, but they weren't exactly subtle about it.

"That's them!" one of them exclaimed. "The twins!"

"They're here," another one responded. "The Sought Six is finally *all* here! Can you believe it?"

"Good heavens, the Sought Six is here!" another one added.

In fact, in the time it took to get all the way to the other end of The Tower, Hallie heard the words 'the Sought Six' about a dozen times.

Annabel led them to a door with a gold plaque reading, CONFERENCE ROOM 1. This door wasn't locked, and so she simply opened it and stepped aside to allow them to enter. "In you go, away from the whispers and stares," she said, winking.

Chapter 7:
Old Friends, New Friends

Jenna

THE ROOM HAD SEVEN people in it already. Four of them were spread out on couches surrounding an unlit fireplace, whilst three were standing around a large oval table. The walls were painted dark green and the floor was back to hardwood. It was a cozy room, Jenna thought. Much more like a living room than a conference room.

Jenna zeroed in on the people sitting on the couch, and a wave of relief flooded her body. "Guys, there you are!" she said, just as Alan, Lindsay, Thomas, and Jules all stood up.

"Hey, you're here!" Lindsay exclaimed, rushing towards them. "We weren't sure you were... I mean, we've all been here for, what, about half an hour?"

"About that," said Jules.

"So, then, you guys know?" Hallie said slowly.

"If by 'know' you're referring to our newly appointed jobs as something known as a Sought Six, then yes. We know." Thomas nodded his head. "We were informed by some very polite people upon arriving home today after school, who then promptly brought us here. I assume that's what happened with you guys, too."

"Yeah," said Jenna, briefly glancing back at Annabel, "that's exactly what happened."

She turned her gaze to the other three people in the room, all of them adults. One was a woman, perhaps in her late-sixties, who Jenna only noticed first because her pantsuit was difficult to ignore: it was bright pink. Her silver-white hair was in a neat, low ponytail, and her fingernail polish matched her suit.

The other two were men, both about Lou's age. One of them was tall and skinny with snow-white skin and a mop of jet-black hair. The other one—actually, Jenna recognized him immediately: it was Levi Hopper, Jules' cool uncle. His short brown hair was greying in areas, and the same went for the stubble on his face, but he still had a childish sparkle in his deep, chocolate eyes. He was a strong, solid man, but he wore a joyous smile. It was the kind of smile that told you he was a kind and gentle man; you wouldn't need to know anything else about him.

All three of them appeared to be invested in some papers and file folders laid out on the oval table, but once they saw who had just entered the room, their attention quickly shifted. At first, Jenna thought for sure they were all about to be bombarded with hugs, but it soon became clear which one of them they were fixated on.

"Wow," said the man with bushy black hair, looking Lou up and down. He smiled. "You, um... um... you..."

"You're beautiful," Levi breathed, also staring at Lou.

"Oh, my dear!" the white-haired, pink-clothed woman exclaimed, starting toward Lou. She fanned her face with her hands to stop her tears, but it wasn't working. "Oh, my dear girl! It's you! Oh, it's *you*!"

Levi giggled and darted forward, now giddier than a kid in a candy store. "You're here! I can't believe it's you!"

In fact, all three of them leapt forward and wrapped their arms around Lou. She hugged them back just as happily, lapping up their affection.

"Denny, Levi, Klaus... Oh, I've missed you guys! I've missed you so much."

"Oh, how we have missed you!" the woman—Denny, apparently—gasped. She held Lou tight. "You're home. My dear, you're finally home."

"I want you guys to meet someone—two someones, actually," said Lou, stepping back and reaching her hands behind her. That was their cue, Jenna and Hallie both knew, to take her hands. "These are my girls. Levi, you'll remember them, I'm sure."

"Of course," said Levi, putting them a little at ease with his kind smile. He stepped forward and bent down on one knee so that he was at eye-level. "Now, let me see if I've got this... You're Hallie and you're Jenna?"

They giggled a little because he was wrong. He knew how to tell them apart—he had learned to identify the freckle on the left side of Jenna's face at Jules' sixth birthday party. But since it made them laugh when he got them wrong, he always did it on purpose.

"I'm just teasing," said Levi with a wink. "It's very nice to see you both again. Do I get a hug? I need a hug. Can I have a hug?"

As they hugged him, Denny was simply overcome with emotion. "Oh, merciful heavens," she gasped, clapping her hands to her cheeks. If she wasn't already wearing blush, that slap would have done the trick. "Just look at these two precious gems! It's like seeing you again at that age, Lou. Only double!"

Jenna gulped. "Hi, I'm Jenna, and that's Hallie."

"Yes, you are." Denny smiled wide. She hardly needed any of the makeup she was wearing because her smile lit up her entire face. She wrapped them both in a hug so big and tight that an involuntary squeal escaped Hallie's mouth.

"Oh, my apologies," Denny said rather cheerfully as she let them go. "My name is Denise Cole, but you may call me Denny. Everybody does. I'm the Department Head here at Maple Cliff."

"Department Head? You're the boss?" said Jenna, and even she heard the surprise in her own voice. "I, I mean, I just didn't think... um—"

But Denny simply laughed. "You didn't expect some wacky, pink-clothed old woman to be the head honcho around here, did you?"

Jenna's cheeks became hot and red. Hallie must have sensed her discomfort because she cleared her throat and stepped forward. "Well, um, I like pink," she said. "It's my favourite colour."

"Mine, too!" Denny squealed, adjusting her stance to model her suit for them. "Perhaps we can outfit you with something of the rose variety later."

"Outfit?"

"Weapons, dear."

Hallie's cheeks suddenly paled. In fact, with her white cheeks and Jenna's red ones, they could have been a human Canadian flag.

"Well, we'll have a bit of time before delving into the weapons," said the bushy-haired man, Klaus, after seeing the concern on their faces. He offered them a kind wink. "Don't worry."

"Girls, this is Klaus Vandnav." Lou turned and looked at the other four. "Have you guys met—"

"When we got here," Lindsay interjected for the group. "We met everybody."

Klaus extended his hands and crossed them over each other to shake Jenna's and Hallie's. His hands were bony, which matched the rest of him. Jenna wondered how he would have used the swords they all apparently knew how to use, since it didn't look like he had many muscles.

Klaus smiled at them. "Kind of strange being here, eh?"

Jenna shrugged her shoulders, trying to play it cool. Eventually, she nodded her head.

"I get it," said Klaus. "I remember our first day here. Seems like yesterday."

"Tell me about it," Lou agreed.

"Well, let me get a look at this beautiful sight," said Denny, standing back and holding her cheeks in her palms as she stared at the group. "All six of them. Here again, together. At long last. And so grown up! I just can't believe it."

Alan cleared his throat after a moment of silence. "We're um, we're glad to be here."

"Glad?" Jules said, probably louder than she intended. "We're *glad*?"

Alan exhaled. "Okay, maybe that was the wrong word..."

"We got the sentiment, buddy, don't worry," said Levi, smiling reassuringly. He reached for Jules' hand and squeezed it. "It's going to be okay. We're all here to protect you. We're your mentors. That's our job."

"It certainly is, Levi," said Denny. She twitched suddenly, like she'd just remembered something, and clapped a hand to her forehead. "Goodness me—where are my manners? I suppose four of our dear children haven't met you yet, have they, Annabel?"

Jenna's eyes shot to Annabel. She had been so quiet that Jenna had almost forgotten she was there.

Annabel shook her head. "Not yet." She turned her attention to Jules, Lindsay, Alan and Thomas. "My name is Annabel Scott. I used to be one of you guys, on a Sought Six team. Now I'm Assistant Department Head here."

"My right-hand-woman," said Denny, affectionately pinching Annabel's cheek. "Not to mention the greatest archer in this or that world. You'll not find anyone quicker or swifter with a bow, I guarantee it."

Annabel looked slightly embarrassed. "Thanks, Denny."

"And, Lou, my dear girl," said Denny, opening her arms for another hug, which Lou happily allowed. "The best swordswoman in all of Pawcombe. Why, she and Annabel were quite the team in their day. I reckon they still would be..."

Alan was astounded. "You know how to sword-fight, Lou?" He looked at Jenna and Hallie. "Did you guys know about this?"

"Not until today," Jenna said dully.

"But still," said Alan, looking rather wide-eyed, "that's so cool!"

"Isn't it?" Denny squealed, matching his excitement. "You kids will get to learn it yourselves, soon enough."

"We... we will?" said Alan, excited.

"We will?" said Hallie, worried.

Klaus cleared his throat. "We have a bit of time before we have to focus on that," he repeated. "Not to worry."

"That's right," said Lou, massaging Hallie's tense shoulders, "and when the time comes, we'll train you. You'll be okay."

Hallie opened her mouth to retort, but she didn't get the chance.

"Does anybody have any questions or comments for their new mentors?" Denny looked earnestly between them all. "Don't be shy. Any questions?"

At first, nobody said anything. Jenna figured none of them wanted to be the person who asked questions, but eventually, Hallie broke the silence.

"I'm sorry, I'm not really sure about using weapons," she said.

"Me neither," Jules quickly agreed, like she had been hoping someone else would say it first.

"Aw, come on, guys. What's the big deal?" said Alan. "They said they'd train us."

"For goodness sake, Alan, this is not some stupid video game!" Hallie spat. "This is real life, with real weapons! You really want to end up on the wrong end of a sword? I sure don't!"

"I'm sure it's all just a precaution," Lindsay put in nervously. She played with the ends of her ponytail. "I mean, you guys don't really expect us to fight anybody, do you?"

Nobody said anything—nobody seemed to know *what* to say.

"All I can tell you for sure," Annabel finally said, "is that we will train you, and we'll always be there for you. That's a promise."

Something in the way she said that settled Jenna's mind a little. She didn't know whether it was Annabel's smooth tone or the sentiment in her words, or both. Either way, she relaxed, and so did everybody else.

"I suppose we can look at the bright side of being here," Thomas said suddenly. "I mean, for one thing, look at where we get to live during our stay. I'll be honest—compared to what I was expecting, this place is very nice. From the way it was explained to me at my house, I was expecting our accommodations to be akin to the ones in Middle Earth."

Alan's eyebrows crinkled. "Middle what?"

"It's from *The Lord of the Rings*," said Lindsay, "and I agree. The woman who came to get me at my house mentioned the swords and stuff, so I thought that meant we'd be staying in, like, tents or caves or something."

"Well, I am glad we're *not* staying in tents or caves!" said Hallie, shivering. "They're cold and dirty."

Annabel let out a good laugh, like Hallie had legitimately ticked her funny bone. "Fair enough," she said.

"I've got a question," Alan said, raising his hand as if he were back in Mrs. Schwantz's classroom.

Denny smiled. "Yes, dear?"

"When do we start our weapon training?"

Hallie rolled her eyes and groaned.

"Soon, for sure. The sooner the better," Levi answered. He motioned between himself, Lou, Klaus and Annabel. "The four of us will be teaching you. We'll take you to pick out your weapons, and then we'll start your training."

"We get to pick our own weapons?" said Alan, his eyes becoming even wider.

Levi nodded. "You bet. You need to get the feel for different swords, or if you're like Annabel, different bows."

Jenna's brain felt like it was busting at the seams. She supposed, in the grand scheme of things, it wasn't too much information: a new place to live, new people to live with, and learning new things like sword-fighting. If only each of those things didn't feel like they weighed a thousand pounds in her mind.

"Any other questions?" Denny asked. She waited for what seemed like forever. "No? Alrighty then, that's perfectly fine. We'll have plenty of time to become further acquainted with one another over the coming days. We'll be in each other's company for quite some time. For now, I suggest we all go upstairs and get some shut-eye."

"But I'm not tired," said Alan through a yawn.

Jenna chuckled. "Clearly."

"No ifs, ands or wait-and-sees! Up you all go!" said Denny.

"But we haven't even had dinner yet," said Jenna. Right on cue, her stomach began to growl. She looked up at Lou and lowered her voice a little. "I'm hungry."

"I've made sure each of our rooms has a room service menu for tonight," said Annabel, overhearing. "It's on the house."

Lou squeezed Annabel's hand. "Thanks, An."

"This place has room service, too?" Alan exclaimed. He looked thoughtful. "I might be able to get used to living at Maple Cliff after all!"

Annabel chuckled. "I'm glad, Alan, because, for the foreseeable future, you haven't got much choice."

CHAPTER 8:
POOR OLD WINSTON PEARCE

Jenna

TRUTHFULLY, JENNA WAS BARELY able to keep her eyes open long enough to eat what room service brought up. It was quite tasty, too: pink, juicy prime rib and smooth mashed potatoes. It was such a generous portion that she only got through half of it before falling asleep.

The suites they were staying in were incredible, Jenna had to admit. Just three floors up from Conference Room 1 were apartment-style rooms with fluffy beds, shelves full of books, and great windows that allowed the sunlight to pour in and warm the rooms.

The dining room in which they would eat all their meals was also magnificent. There were two claw-footed tables: one to eat at, and the other offering a buffet of food. The windows, which overlooked a blanket of maple trees, had small stained-glass images in their centres, and multi-coloured sunlight shone through them.

In the morning, everybody made their way up and down the buffet table to get breakfast. One of the butlers standing around the dining room (and there were three) brought Denny the morning mail.

"Thank you, Reginald," she said, lifting the letters and a silver letter opener off the tray he was holding.

Jenna had taken a bit of everything from the buffet; she wasn't sure where to begin. There were eggs prepared three different ways, thick and wavy strips of bacon, fruit salad, assorted pastries, coffee, tea, three types of fruit juice, pancakes, waffles, French toast, and plenty of maple syrup.

"Make sure you don't waste any of that maple syrup," said Levi, watching them all dig in. "It's made fresh from the maple trees here in Maple, and you won't find a tastier syrup anywhere."

Jenna, who was used to lapping up all her maple syrup at home, held up a spoon she had retrieved from the buffet. "No problem there!" she said. Levi gave her a thumbs-up.

"Oh, listen to this, everyone," said Denny, smiling at a yellowish piece of parchment from the mail pile. "Winston Pearce has written."

Instantly, every adult's eyes lit up.

"There's a name I haven't heard in a while," said Lou. She tied her golden hair back into a ponytail, away from her breakfast, and smiled as she thought about this man. "Gosh, he must be in his eighties by now."

"He's still just as sprightly as ever," said Denny, smiling at the letter. "He came up here for tea the other week. Such a lovely man."

"Who's Winston Pearce?" Alan asked. He leaned so far forward in his chair that his chest tipped his plate of fruit salad, sending melon and berries rolling onto the floor.

Two of the butlers promptly got on their hands and knees to pick up the fruit, but Alan stood up as well.

"Sorry, guys," he said. "Here, I can do that."

"Not to worry, Master Alan, not to worry," one of them smiled. "It was an accident."

"Yeah, but I can help..."

"No, no, we wouldn't hear of it," the other one said, plopping raspberries and blackberries into a napkin. "You need your strength. Please, sit. Nigel, please bring Master Alan a new plate of fruit salad."

The third butler in the room—Nigel, apparently—nodded his head courteously and disappeared into the kitchen. Jenna could hardly believe they had butlers to wait on them at Maple Cliff. Being a Sought Six was akin to being royalty, it seemed.

When the butlers were finished cleaning the floor, Alan resumed his seat. His cheeks were a little red, Jenna noticed, but she wasn't sure if it was embarrassment or the delight of being treated like a prince. Probably both.

"So, um, Winston Pearce," he said as casually as he could. "Who is he?"

"Winston Pearce is a dear friend," said Denny. "Not just to me but to the first Sought Six as well. Why, he protected you during one of your trips, didn't he? Gave you food and a place to stay?"

"Yes, he did," Annabel nodded sadly. She took a spoonful of her own fruit salad. "We stayed with him during the last trip we made as a team of six, if memory serves me correctly."

Everybody stopped eating and turned to look at Annabel just as Nigel emerged from the kitchen with two plates of fruit salad. He gave one to Alan and one to Hallie.

"I noticed your plate was becoming sparse, Miss Hallie, so I took the liberty of bringing you some more," he whispered.

"Oh, um, thank you," said Hallie.

"The... um, the last trip you made as a team of six?" Jenna repeated slowly.

"As I mentioned: two of our team members were killed before we could finish the job," said Annabel, staring at her plate. Then she shot her eyes up and darted them between each of them. "You were all informed of that, yes? You should have been..."

Everybody nodded, but nobody spoke.

"Well, it doesn't matter much now," Annabel continued, sniffling. "The point is, Winston Pearce is a kind, good man. And he's written to us, Denny?"

Denny started suddenly, as if Annabel had roused her from a deep sleep. "Yes," she said, "he has, and he's invited us to his house for dinner tonight. He wants to personally wish the new Sought Six good luck in their journey."

"Oh," Lindsay said thoughtfully, "well, that sounds nice."

"It sounds *very* nice." Denny smiled and folded the letter. "Winston makes the best pot roast you'll ever eat, and he's got such a lovely cottage here in Maple. It's only a stone's throw from here. We'll walk there later. That way, you kids can get some fresh Pawcombe air into your lungs."

"Walk?" Jules gulped. "Aren't we... I mean, aren't we being, you know, hunted?"

"Oh, you're perfectly safe here in Maple, dear," Denny said sweetly. "Zyngor and his followers reside in Oak. That's a forest all the way on the other side of Pawcombe. And we have many allies within the forests between Maple and Oak."

"Not to mention you've got us," Levi added, ruffling her hair and giving a cheery, reassuring smile. "We won't let anything happen to you guys, kiddo."

Jules paused. "Well, okay, then. If you're sure."

"Come on, Jules, it'll be an adventure," said Alan, mouth full of berries. "We never get to explore the forest."

"Never get to? We only just got here."

Hallie made a disgusted face. "Yeah, and close your mouth while you chew."

Denny laughed delightedly at their banter. "Well, that settles it! I'll send a message to Winston informing him that we'll be prompt at 6 o'clock sharp."

The rest of the day passed by pretty quickly. Annabel and Klaus had separate errands to run, and so they were both gone for most of the morning. By the time they got back to Maple Cliff shortly after lunch, Alan was chomping at the bit to go outside. They had been in Maple Cliff for less than twenty-four hours, but he had never spent so long indoors in his life. Even when it was raining back at home, he'd be the kid out on Metcalfe Street splashing about in the puddles.

Levi sympathized with him; he said he was the same way growing up, with everybody else attesting to that.

"Levi? Indoors?" Annabel had said upon arriving back from her errands. "Please. If he didn't spend at least two hours a day outside when we were kids, he'd get cranky."

Levi scoffed. "Cranky? You make me sound like a two-year-old!"

"Nothing wrong with being an active boy." Annabel gave his cheek a light slap with her palm, and while Levi pretended to react, she turned her attention to Alan. "Don't worry, we'll be leaving soon."

Soon couldn't come soon enough for him, though. In fact, Jenna and Hallie got dressed and ready to go to Winston Pearce's house two hours before they had to leave, simply because Alan was so eager. He followed them into the suite they shared and helped them pick out their outfits. Well, he called it helping; *they* called it annoying.

"For crying out loud, Alan, you're acting like you've been cooped up inside for weeks," said Jenna. She sat on the end of her bed, waiting on Hallie in the bathroom. "It's only been a few hours."

"Twenty-two hours, actually."

"You're counting?"

Alan groaned. "I'm just so darn bored. They won't let us explore Maple Cliff because they think we'll get lost."

"Have you seen the size of this place? We *will* get lost."

"We can't even go outside without the adults."

"Outside is even bigger than inside! You do the math." Jenna sighed. "Look, there must be something you can do. What's Thomas been doing?"

"Reading. We're not even in school anymore and he's, like, doing homework." He plopped himself into the soft leather chair next to the big window. Like most other windows in Maple Cliff, it overlooked a spread of maple trees. Alan pointed to the bookshelves on the other side of his chair. "He's been reading all the books on the shelves in our room. He says he wants to be well-informed."

"What does *that* mean?"

"Dunno," said Alan. "It means no time for laundry soccer, apparently."

Jenna paused. "Laundry soccer?"

"Tie up some socks into a ball and play soccer," Alan explained, as if it was obvious. "I thought we could try to score on each other in the hallway just outside, but he said he wanted to finish reading about the reptilian beasts of Pawcombe."

Jenna almost asked what he meant by *reptilian beasts*, but she didn't; after all, he wasn't the one reading about them. Still, even if he was, she didn't think she wanted to know anyway.

Hallie appeared from the bathroom suddenly, and Jenna groaned.

"About time," she said, standing up with her outfit to change into. "What did you do, re-decorate in there?"

"No," Hallie said simply, smoothing the body of her pink blouse. "I couldn't decide which shirt I wanted to wear."

Alan looked at her over the back of the chair. "That's the one you chose, then?"

Hallie suddenly looked mortified. "What does *that* mean?" she exclaimed. "Is it awful? Does it look bad?"

"What? No!" said Alan, leaping to his feet.

"Tell me the truth!" Hallie slapped Jenna's arm. "Do I look good or bad?"

"First of all, *ow!*" said Jenna, holding her arm, "and second of all, you look good! I don't think Alan meant anything by it."

"I didn't!" said Alan, holding his hands at his defense. "I swear! I only meant—"

"Well, that's that. I'm changing," Hallie huffed and sped back into the bathroom.

Alan followed her and shouted through the closed door. "Hallie, come on! I'm sorry! I didn't say you looked bad!" he pleaded. "You don't have to change—you look nice!"

Jenna fell back onto the bed and groaned. She had a feeling she'd be waiting for the bathroom for a while yet.

When it was finally time to leave, everybody gathered in the front foyer downstairs. They did some last-minute tidying of their clothes and hair. They tied their shoelaces and picked jackets from a selection offered to them by Maple Cliff's uniform department (all of them adorned with Maple Cliff's purple and red emblem).

The adults were also equipping themselves with something else: weapons. Swords in holster-belts, a quiver of arrows nestled at Annabel's back and a bow over her shoulder, and even a dagger here and there. For Jenna, the weirdest thing by far was seeing Lou with a sword. The image just couldn't compute in her mind. It was a good-looking sword, as far as swords go; the blade was silver steel and the handle was gold, like buried treasure. Lou wore it on her belt so naturally that it almost didn't look strange at all. Except that it did.

"I still don't understand why you're even bringing those," said Jules, fidgeting by the front doors. "I thought you said we'd be safe in Maple."

"We are, kiddo," Levi replied, combing the stubble on his face with his fingers, "but Rule Number One around here is: never leave anything to chance."

"Especially where a Sought Six is concerned," Lou added. "Leave absolutely nothing to chance."

Lindsay lifted the curtain from the window next to the door. "Denny?"

"Yes, dear?"

"Didn't you say dinner was at 6?" She checked her watch, confirming that it was only 5 o'clock now. "And didn't you say Winston Pearce lives in Maple?"

"Yes, dear." Then her face brightened in realization of Lindsay's true question. "Oh, well, Maple is a large forest. It'll take us at least half an hour to get there on foot, and it's not polite to arrive late."

"Speaking of arriving, are we going now?" said Alan. He pranced on his toes at Maple Cliff's giant front door, which had to be about twice his height.

"Yes, yes, indeed we are!" said Denny, ushering everybody towards the door.

As they walked down the grassy hill toward the start of the forest, Jenna thought a lot about how much things had changed in just the past twenty-four hours—*exactly* twenty-four hours. It had been 5 o'clock yesterday evening that they arrived in Pawcombe, a whole other world they didn't even know existed.

"I bet this all looks really pretty in the fall," said Hallie, gazing up at the green maple leaves as they walked.

"Oh, the prettiest of pretty," Denny nodded. "Pine in winter is another very pretty sight."

Lindsay tilted her head. "Pine is another forest here, right? The one with only pine trees?"

"Right!" said Denny, clapping her hands. She was thrilled that they appeared to be getting the hang of things.

With each step they took further into the forest, it got darker—and not just because the sun was setting. These maple trees were the thickest trees Jenna had ever seen. It was a good thing the dirt path was clearly marked by years of wear and tear, or it might have been much easier to get lost. There were trees as far as the eye could see, and some of them were so big around that small houses could have been built into their trunks.

"Which forest is next to Maple?" Alan asked, picking up a fallen leaf off the dirt path and twirling it in his fingers.

"On one side, it's Willow," answered Klaus, "and on the other side, it's Cedar, which is where I live."

"Where you live? You don't live here?"

Klaus shook his head. "I mean, part-time, I suppose I do. But my house is in Cedar. We were all given estates once our time as a Sought Six was over; sort of a 'thanks for your service' kind of thing. You guys should come see my place one of these days. It's beautiful, if I do say so myself. I've got a first-edition copy of *The Hobbit*. You've read some Tolkien, right, Thomas?"

Thomas' eyes nearly popped out from behind his glasses.

Jenna looked at Lou. "Did you get a house, Mom?"

"I had one," said Lou, "with a waterfront view of Lake Maple, but I left it when we moved to Peterborough."

Jenna suddenly felt guilty. She and Hallie were the reason Lou had to move away from Pawcombe, after all.

"Sorry," said Hallie, practically reading her thoughts. "I guess that was our bad."

Lou shook her head. "I wouldn't have had it any other way. I had the two of you, and that was all I needed."

They continued walking and Jenna made sure to fill her lungs with all the fresh air. Denny might have been onto something when she suggested they walk to Winston Pearce's house. There was something different about the air in Pawcombe. It seemed fresher somehow.

With each inhale, Jenna could feel her body relax, which made her realize just how tense she had been since they arrived yesterday.

At last, they reached a fork in the dirt path. There was the dancing glow of a fire ahead of them; at first, it made everybody nervous, but when they focused on it, they could see it was just the flame from a torch mounted to the stone of Winston Pearce's house.

"Isn't it rather dangerous to have a flame in the middle of a forest?" asked Thomas.

"Well, there isn't any electricity here. We're lucky Maple Cliff has running water." Annabel shrugged. "People here are just used it. You know, keeping an eye on fires."

"Winston must have lit that one for us, so we wouldn't miss the place," said Levi, pointing ahead at the house. Jenna looked and saw the torch—but that wasn't all she saw. In fact, at exactly the same time, everybody saw the same things.

The front door was ajar, but the entire house was dark. The front window was broken, like someone had smashed it in. The whole place was silent as a graveyard; even the wind around them had stopped whistling.

Thomas tilted his head. "Is Winston Pearce not that great of a housekeeper?"

"Shh!" Jules hissed, afraid to disrupt the silence.

"Come on," said Levi, walking forward. He had a very serious look on his face. Everybody followed him, some of them willingly, but most of them reluctantly. Levi took the torch off the house and pushed open the door.

From the moment they entered the house, Jenna could hear a strange buzzing sound, but it was so dark that she couldn't see where it might have been coming from. They appeared to be in the living room, but it was hard to tell. Most of the furniture was overturned and the whole house was generally a big mess. But all of that was nothing compared to the awful stench. The air smelled like raw meat and farts.

"Oh my—what *is* that?" Jenna exclaimed, holding her nose.

"Beats me," said Lindsay, also holding her nose. "I'm not sure I want to know."

"I don't like this," said Lou. She spoke softly but nervously. She barely took more than two steps in the door. "Let's go home. We'll send investigators back here."

"Mom," said Jenna, tugging at her sleeve. "What is it?"

"I've smelled this odour before," she said, darting her eyes around what was left of the living room.

"We all have," said Annabel, "and I'm with you, Lou. Let's just go."

"What odour? What is that smell?" Jenna persisted.

"In here!" Levi called from the next room. Jenna was so focused on the mess and the smell that she hadn't even realized he had gone in further ahead of them.

Lou groaned as she stomped into the next room. "Levi, for heaven's sake, there's nobody here."

"Not anymore," Levi replied. Just as Jenna walked in, he shone the torch in the direction of the corner. An old man was sitting straight up against the wall, his legs spread out before him. He was dead. There was an arrow in his chest, and a trail of blood descending from the wound. Flies were buzzing all around him.

"Oh, Winston," Lou gasped, clapping her hands to her mouth.

"Merciful heavens!" Denny exclaimed. Her entire body tensed, and she grabbed the hands of Lindsay and Alan, who were closest to her.

Thomas gulped. "Well, that explains the buzzing sound."

Jules turned around and suddenly threw up all over the floor. Klaus consoled her, but it didn't do much good. She was shaking from head to toe.

"What... what happened?" she managed to say.

Annabel knelt and pulled the arrow out of Winston's cold chest, which also unpinned him from the wall. His body fell over like an overdone spaghetti noodle. Luckily, Klaus covered Jules' eyes or she might have thrown up again.

"Oak wood," she said after examining it. "It's Zyngor."

"It was a set-up," said Levi, already turning around to leave. "Whoever did this knew we were coming here. They're probably still in the forest somewhere. Making their rounds. Waiting for us to show up here. We have to leave."

His urgency and franticness shook Jenna's stomach as if it were on its own little trampoline. She clung to Lou.

"But, is it... I mean, is it really Zyngor?" she said quietly.

"If it's not, then it's one of his followers," Annabel replied, tossing the arrow away, "which isn't much better."

"They must have known that Winston sent us that letter," Klaus added.

"How?" said Levi. He rushed over to take over consoling his niece. "To get from here to Maple Cliff, the letter never left Maple. It's not like it had to pass through Oak."

"Maybe... um, maybe Zyngor has spies," Alan suggested.

"Of course he has spies! I just didn't think any of them were in Maple," said Annabel, and for the first time since they met her, she looked worried. Sincerely worried. Jenna didn't like it.

"It's incredibly risky, I admit," Denny agreed. "With all the protection around Maple Cliff, especially now that there's a Sought Six living there, I never thought any of them would dare settle in Maple."

Jenna thought for a moment. "Zyngor must be desperate to end this, then. He must be desperate to kill us." She tightened her grip on Lou, who tightened right back.

"Quite right, everyone. We must leave," said Denny, starting for the door. "Come, come. We'll find a Root Path. We might not have much time before the perpetrator comes back."

"Hang on a minute," Annabel said, holding her arm out in front of her. "Look around. Aren't we missing a kid?"

Everybody looked at each other, counting in their heads. Jenna knew straight away who was missing without even needing to count.

"Oh my God," said Lou, frantically whipping her head all around. "Where's Hallie?"

CHAPTER 9:
SPIES IN THE DARK

Hallie

WHILE EVERYBODY ELSE WENT off the path toward Winston's house, Hallie heard a strange voice coming from the opposite direction. At least, it *sounded* like a voice. She supposed it could have been an animal of some sort. She wasn't sure which one she would have preferred.

Either way, the sound had caused her to freeze. She simply stood there, watching and listening. She only realized nobody else had heard the sound when she turned back around to see them all entering Winston Pearce's house. She almost followed them. Truly. If something was out there, she didn't want to be left alone in a strange forest to deal with it.

Clunk! Swish!

Something was rustling around in the leaves somewhere off in the distance. The only problem was it was much too dark for her to see what it might have been.

"Well, I know where they are," she mumbled to herself, glancing back at the house. "I won't go far..." She shook her head. She couldn't believe she was even considering going to investigate the noise. Anything could have been out there. Then again, it could have simply been the wind in the branches. More than anything else, she wanted to prove to herself that the latter was true. So, she began to walk slowly off the path.

Crunch! Snap!

Hallie gasped at the noise, but it wasn't the same sound as before. Then she realized it was her own shoes stepping on twigs. She huffed. "Pull yourself together," she mumbled. Then she rolled her eyes. "And stop talking to yourself."

She walked a little further. Eventually, she stepped out of the leaves and twigs, and onto another path leading who-knows-where. It was next to impossible to see much of anything. She still hadn't come across anybody else in the forest, but—

Clunk! Swish!

She gulped. There was a large tree next to her, just off the path. She darted behind it. There appeared to be a low fog surrounding some of the treetops. Surely that didn't mean anything bad—perhaps it was going to rain soon. Still, it made this nighttime forest even creepier. She strained to hear any other rustling noises, but there was nothing. A rush of cool wind blew past her, which made her skin jump in goosebumps. She tightened her jacket around herself.

Crunch! Crunch! Snap! Snap!

Hallie gasped, and immediately held her hand against her mouth. She hoped nobody heard her.

Crunch! Snap!

It was getting louder. Hallie's heart was like a hamster on a wheel. She squeezed her eyes shut and held her breath.

Suddenly, someone grabbed her wrist. She yelped and her eyes snapped open.

"Jeez, Jenna," she hissed. She held her chest. "Don't do that!"

"Sorry," said Jenna, but she didn't sound sorry. "What are you doing all the way over here? Everyone's looking for you and Mom's having a panic attack."

"I got lost," said Hallie, tilting her head and straining to listen for the clunking-swishing noise again.

Jenna looked in the direction her head was tilting. "What are you doing? Is someone over there?"

"Shh! I don't know."

Jenna tensed. She lowered her voice to a whisper. "What do you mean you don't know?"

Hallie rolled her eyes. She kept listening and she peered into the blackness of the forest. Some tree branches blew in the wind, and... and something was scurrying through the leaves. It sounded like it was only a few feet away from them.

"What the..." Jenna muttered as she took Hallie's hand and backed away.

The scurrying through the leaves got louder and closer. There was one last moment of noise, during which Hallie thought her heart had come to a stop, before a squirrel appeared in front of them. It, too, didn't know anybody else was around, because as soon as it noticed them standing there, it scurried off in another direction.

"Oh, it's a deadly little squirrel," said Jenna, pretending to bite her nails.

Hallie exhaled. "I guess the coast is clear," she said, but she still thought she heard something further in the distance. "It's probably just the wind in the trees. Okay, let's just get out of here."

Jenna nodded. "Good plan."

"Hang on, Jenna, I know why I'm over here, but why are *you* over here?"

"They, um, they sent me to find you."

"Yeah, right."

"Okay, so I snuck off to find you when we realized you were missing. I'm your twin sister. We have telepathy. I'd find you the quickest."

"You know twin telepathy isn't real."

"Maybe not in the reading-each-other's-minds kind of way, but we can still sense things and you know it."

But Hallie wasn't listening anymore. She heard something rustling in the leaves again, and it wasn't another squirrel; it didn't sound frantic enough. It wasn't the wind in the tree branches, either; it was too low to the ground. She looked down the dirt path within the trees, where a few crunchy leaves were dancing around in the wind. She couldn't see anybody coming toward them, but something inside her knew there was indeed something—or some*one*—there.

"Hello?" said Jenna, rather loudly, waving her hand in Hallie's face. "Earth to first-born-twin!"

"Would you shut up, please?" Hallie hissed. She kept her eyes glued to the path. There was definitely something coming towards them now. She could see its shadowy figure emerging from within the trees. It was far too big to be a person, though.

"Is that... is that a bear?" Jenna gasped.

"It's too tall to be a bear," said Hallie.

"How do you know? Maybe the bears in Pawcombe are giant."

But it wasn't a bear. A sudden, sharp whinny and a hoof pawing at the earth told them exactly what it was.

"A horse?" said Jenna. "But it's too tall... Oh, somebody's riding it! There's somebody there!"

Hallie was frozen. Denny said they'd be safe in Maple. Annabel said it. Levi said it. Klaus said it. Lou said it. For heaven's sake, had they been lying? No, they couldn't have been. That meant whoever this was couldn't possibly be someone nice.

"Hal!" Jenna whacked Hallie sharply on the arm. "We've got to get out of here! Come on!" And with that, she took off running. Hallie turned around. The horse reared and took off down the path, directly at them.

Hallie yelped and sped after her sister.

"Come on!" said Jenna, ducking behind a bunch of bushes. "Hide here, quick!"

Hallie joined her. The bushes were tall, about their height. They were also thick. Nobody coming down the dirt path would see them behind there, surely.

A low whinny from a horse made them jump. Jenna grabbed Hallie's hand. They ducked down. The mystery rider and his horse slowed to a walk, and eventually a halt, opposite the bushes. Hallie peeked through a tiny gap in the leaves. She couldn't see this man's face, but it was definitely a man. He was pivoting in his saddle, looking all around. He truly didn't know where they had gone.

Swish.

He had a sword. Great.

Thud.

He slammed his feet into the ground as he dismounted. Hallie squeezed her eyes shut. When she opened them again, Jenna was staring at her and pressing her finger against her lips. As if she didn't already know to be quiet.

The bushes rustled. They each took a step backward as quietly as they could. The rider had to have been right there, sifting through the leaves.

Go away, Hallie thought, holding her breath. *Please just go away.*

Jenna slowly bent over and picked up a stick. Right when Hallie was about to shoot her with a piercing stare, silently asking her what the heck she was doing, she tossed the stick as far down the path as she could.

The rider heard the commotion as the stick landed away from them. Quicker than he had caught up to them, he was back on his horse and galloping back down the path.

Hallie looked at Jenna. "That was clever."

"You sound surprised," Jenna said wryly. "Come on, let's get out of here before he comes back."

Hallie shivered as they tip-toed out of the bushes. "How far are we from Winston Pearce's house? We should probably warn him that someone's out here."

Jenna looked sad.

"What?"

"Winston is dead."

Hallie's head began to pound. "He's... he's what?"

"Dead," Jenna repeated. "His house was torn apart when we got there. We found him with an arrow made from oak wood in his chest."

Hallie's mouth had suddenly gone dry. "Why does the kind of wood matter?"

"It means it was Zyngor or one of his followers that killed him. Zyngor lives in the forest called Oak, remember?"

Hallie nodded, but she couldn't find any more words.

"Levi and Denny think that whoever killed him is probably still hanging around somewhere." Jenna looked behind them, but nobody was there. "They think Zyngor has a spy in Maple, and that they killed Winston because they're trying to get to us."

"A spy?" Hallie gulped. "Do you think it's..." She pointed behind them.

"I don't know, probably," said Jenna. "That's why we have to—"

"Ha!"

The mystery rider appeared in front of them suddenly, sword drawn. His horse, black as the night, neighed loudly. A sharp, sickening laugh shot from the rider's mouth. Unsettlingly, his mouth was all they could see; it was so dark. So much for their diversion.

Hallie screamed. Jenna almost lost her footing. The rider lifted his sword high above his head, and Hallie pulled Jenna's sleeve, speeding off the path.

Swish!

The sword cut through the air, but that's all. The rider grunted, angry that they had run, and kicked his horse's sides to follow them into the mess of maple trees.

"Where do we go?" Hallie asked, panicked.

"Mom!" Jenna yelled in no particular direction. Hallie almost snapped at her for being so loud, but there was no use pretending the rider couldn't see them. "Denny! Annabel! Levi! Alan! Lindsay!"

"What the heck are you doing?!"

"They're out there somewhere! Someone's got to answer sooner or later! Mom! Annabel! Jules! Thom—"

"Jenna!" It was Lou. Her voice was high-pitched and frantic. "Jenna, where are you?"

Hallie's heart gave a leap. "We're here!" she shouted.

"Hallie?" Lou's voice now sounded elated as well as terrified.

"Come on, it's coming from over here!" Jenna pointed up ahead, but Hallie couldn't see anybody when she looked. All she could see were maple trees and the blackness of the night.

She looked behind her. The rider was still chasing them, albeit slowly because he was having to weave through all the trees. He had his sword ready to strike. Hallie was suddenly glad he didn't have a bow instead.

"Oomph!" Hallie grunted. She ran right into a tree. She crashed to such a quick stop that her knees buckled, causing her to fall into the leaves and twigs on the ground.

"Ha!" the rider spat. The horse's thundering hooves shook the ground beneath her. He was right above her now.

Hallie spun around, rolling herself sideways to avoid his incoming sword. She scrambled back to her feet just as the rider yanked his sword from the dirt. He lifted it again, ready to swing it, but Hallie started to run. She looked all around for Jenna, but she was gone.

"Jenna!" she called. "Where'd you go? Jenna!"

And that was when she saw it: an orange glow up ahead. It looked like fire. She ran towards it as quickly as she could, even though the prospect of a forest fire terrified her. It didn't terrify her as much as being sliced in half, though.

"Hallie?" she heard someone call. It sounded like Alan.

"Hal!" That was definitely Jenna. Nobody else called her Hal.

"I'm here! I'm here!" she called back, but she didn't know where anyone was. All she could do was follow the fire light. "Is the forest on fire?!"

The point of fire light began to move all around as if someone was waving it like a flag. Then, Levi's booming voice shouted out, "Do you see this?"

"Yes!"

"Come to it!"

Hallie ran, but she could still hear the hooves pounding behind her. She continued to weave in and out of the trees, making it harder for the rider to keep up with her. At last, she came to a clearing in the trees and she leapt onto another dirt path. She ran as fast as her legs would carry her, and didn't dare look back again.

She rounded a bend on the path. At last, she saw Jenna and Lou, and everybody else. They were all prancing on their toes, waiting to see her. Now that they did see her, they looked happy. Very quickly, however, their smiles faded into terrified expressions, and Hallie knew exactly why.

The horse neighed behind her. The rider grunted and yelled, urging the horse to go faster. Jules screamed in terror. Thomas and Lindsay became very pale.

"Run, Hallie!" Alan screamed, lunging forward as if he planned on taking on the horse and rider by himself.

The next few seconds happened so quickly: Hallie heard the sharp, steel swishing of the sword being swung. She couldn't bring herself to think just how close to her the rider was.

"Help!" she exclaimed, and just as she did, Annabel stepped forward. She had her bow on her arm and it was loaded with an arrow.

Thwip!

The rider grunted and yelped loudly. He fell from his horse and into the dirt, but Hallie kept running. She sped into Lou's open arms and, at last, turned around. The horse was galloping away in another direction now, probably spooked by the removal of his rider, and the rider was lying on the ground, covered in dirt and blood. He was squirming and writhing.

"You... you..." he gurgled, but it was unclear to whom he was speaking. Klaus took the liberty of pulling out his sword and ending it. He stabbed his sword down into the man's chest, making an awful squishing sound.

"Well, that takes care of him," said Klaus, sheathing his sword again. He noticed the rather green expression on Jules' face, and added, "Sorry you had to see that." Denny, whose hand was covering her mouth in horror, extended her arm and wrapped it comfortingly around Jules.

"What are you doing?!" Annabel exclaimed. She grabbed Klaus' shoulder and pulled it so he was facing her. "I didn't take the kill shot for a reason, Klaus! I wanted information from him."

Klaus made a face. "We know he was working for Zyngor. It's obvious. What other information did you want?"

"Information like which one of Zyngor's right-hands let him into Maple, genius," Annabel sneered. "This guy was clearly an assassin, not a spy. The spy's still out there somewhere."

"Wait a second, who is that?" said Jenna. She made a move to step toward the dead body to get a better look, but Lou stuck her arm out and stopped her. Hallie clung tightly to Lou's other arm. She felt like a frightened toddler.

"I think Annabel might be right," said Levi, bending down next to the body. He gave the lit torch to Thomas to hold, and then he pressed his finger against one of the eyes to lift the eyelid. There was something strange about it that Hallie almost didn't notice right away. The entire eye was jet-black. It looked like this man didn't have a pupil or any eye colour. All of it, including what should have been the white of the eye, was black.

"Ugh!" Hallie exclaimed. "What's wrong with his eyes?"

"Curious," said Thomas, adjusting his glasses and leaning forward to see. "Could he have been a heavy smoker, perhaps?"

"This is what happens when humans become hunters for Zyngor. They're stripped of everything light and good, leaving them with just darkness." Levi shut the eyelid.

"So, this is the guy who killed Winston and who was going to try to kill us?" said Alan. He looked up at Annabel. "And the spy, who's still out there, let this guy into Maple?"

"Seems like it," said Annabel, breathing deeply. She was furious, but not at him.

Klaus lifted his eyebrows. "This complicates things a bit."

"I'll get an urgent bulletin out at once," said Denny, still rubbing Jules' back. "I'll have everyone on the hunt for any spies. We'll even bring people in for questioning. Don't worry, kids. We'll find the person responsible for sending this man."

"And one more thing," said Annabel, practically through gritted teeth. "Alan, you keep asking when you guys are going to start your weapon training, yeah? Well, you're in luck. It officially starts tomorrow."

CHAPTER 10:
BELLE

Hallie

A s SHE EXPECTED, HALLIE didn't sleep a wink that night. When they finally got back to Maple Cliff, after finding a Root Path, most of the employees seemed to know something awful had happened. A whole flock of them were waiting in The Tower.

What Hallie *didn't* expect, however, was that she'd have just as much trouble sleeping the next night—especially since Annabel had stayed true to her word and started their weapon training that day. She was exhausted—they all were—and, yet, she was still wide awake as the grandfather clock in the hall outside her suite chimed. She lay there, staring at the wooden beams on the ceiling, counting each chime. Twelve.

She got up to go to the bathroom. Lou's suite was adjoined to hers and Jenna's by the bathroom, so Hallie quietly opened the connecting door and listened. Lou's deep breathing let her know she was indeed asleep. She closed the door. She then stepped back into her suite and listened for Jenna's breathing. It was deep and steady, just like Lou's.

She tip-toed out of the suite. A thick stream of white moonlight was streaming in through the wall-length window at the end of the hallway. To her surprise, there were already two people sitting on the window-seat.

"What are you guys doing up?" she asked, approaching Jules and Alan.

They jumped at her voice. "Hey," said Alan. "Um, the same reason you're up, I guess."

"We can't sleep," Jules added. "We're tired, but we can't sleep."

"Yeah, me too." Hallie sat next to them. "I keep thinking about being chased around by that spy."

"Assassin," said Alan.

"Whatever."

"I keep seeing Winston Pearce's dead body," said Jules, going rather pale. "Each time I close my eyes, that's all I see." Hallie was glad she couldn't agree with her.

"What's going to happen to him?" she said.

"His body will be buried and his house will be cleaned." Alan shrugged. "That's what Klaus said. It's such a shame. If only we had gotten there sooner."

Jules cleared her throat. "Denny said we'd eventually learn to embrace our *what-happeneds* instead of dwelling over out *what-ifs*." She paused. "What was it like, Hallie? Being chased through the forest like that...?"

"I would rather be back up in front of the class talking about invertebrate sea creatures," Hallie replied, resting her elbows on her knees and cupping her face with her hands. "I'm going to have nightmares for weeks."

"How can you have nightmares if you never go to sleep?"

Everybody jumped at this voice, and they turned around. Once they saw who it was, however, they relaxed.

"Annabel," said Jules, "what are you doing up?"

"I should be asking you the same question," she said. She joined them on the window-seat. "Actually, I came to check on you guys, so try to imagine my panic when none of you were in your beds."

Hallie stared at her lap. "Sorry."

Annabel said nothing. She sat there with them in several moments of silence. It was the kind of silence that Hallie could tell was not going to be broken by the adult. She was waiting for one of them to lead the conversation.

"We could have died, Annabel," Jules blurted out, right on cue.

Annabel exhaled. "I know."

"Somebody tried to kill us. And what's worse is that someone in Maple betrayed us."

Alan tilted his head. "How is that worse?"

"Because it means that not everybody is here to protect us, like we were told," Jules replied. She picked at a loose string on the cushioned seat and held back her tears. "We aren't safe anywhere."

"Yes, you are," said Annabel, stroking her hair. "You're safe here at Maple Cliff. You're safe with all of us. You're safe with me. You know that, right?"

Everybody nodded. Hallie had to admit that she did feel safer when the five adults were around. Even as she was running away from Zyngor's rider, she couldn't deny the wave of relief she felt when she saw them all on the path waiting to defend her.

"Come on, back to bed," said Annabel. She stood up, which prompted everyone else to do the same. "Even if you can't sleep, you need to rest."

"I don't know how my mom and my sister are doing it," Hallie sighed. "They're both sleeping like babies."

"Lou?" Annabel sounded surprised. "She hasn't slept as much as two winks since you guys got here. A nervous mom thing, I guess."

"But she was sleeping when I came out here," said Hallie, looking down the hall at her closed suite door. "I heard her deep breathing. That means she's asleep."

"Pure exhaustion, then," Annabel concluded. "You can only lie awake for so long before you just pass out."

Hallie walked back to her suite uneasily. Still, Annabel was right: you can only lie awake for so long.

She hoped that would ring true for her when she climbed back into bed and listened to Jenna's low breathing next to her.

~*~

The next thing Hallie knew, she was squinting at a ray of sunlight streaming in through the suite's big window. She felt refreshed—more refreshed than she had in days.

"I guess I slept after all," she muttered, rubbing her eyes.

"Yeah, and you took all the covers," Jenna said next to her. Hallie turned over and saw her identical hazel eyes glaring at her. "You're lucky I can still sleep when I'm cold."

Hallie sat up right into another beam of sunlight. She brought her hands to her face. "Who needs an alarm clock when the sun shines right in your eyes?" she yawned.

There was a sudden knock at their bathroom door, which meant it could only be one person—the person whose suite shared their bathroom.

"Mom?"

The door opened and Lou smiled at them, which somehow made the room seem even brighter. "Oh, good. You're awake." She came and sat on the end of their bed. "Did you sleep?"

Hallie shrugged. "More or less."

Jenna sat up. "Did you?"

"I think I did," said Lou, sounding impressed with herself. She seemed much more relaxed than she had in the past couple days. In fact, for the first time since arriving in Pawcombe, she was looking like her old self. "Well, look, I'm glad you're awake because I want to take you somewhere and introduce you to someone."

Jenna shook her head. "I think we've had enough meet-and-greet excitement for a while."

Now Lou shook her head. "No, nothing else like that. We aren't even going to leave the property."

Hallie squinted again in the sunlight. "What do you mean?"

"Get dressed," said Lou, standing up and heading for the door. "Then come down for breakfast. We'll go after that."

"Go where?"

Lou tilted her head and winked at them. "Trust me."

Breakfast was delicious, as usual, and Hallie totally stuffed her face. A much-needed night's sleep struck up quite an appetite. When everyone was finished, Lou led Hallie and Jenna outside. The grass in the sweeping field was dewy, and it sparkled in the sun. Lou was leading them out the back of Maple Cliff, straight for a big red barn and paddocks with white fences. Hallie couldn't believe she hadn't noticed it the day they arrived. It was quite large.

They walked inside and Hallie immediately brought her hand to cover her nose.

"It smells like manure," she said in a nasally voice.

Lou chuckled. "Well, that makes sense. There's plenty of it to go around. Follow me, she's just down this way."

"Who is?" said Jenna, eagerly following at her heels. They stopped in front of a stall, where a beautiful white horse stuck its head out to greet them.

"This is Belle," said Lou, extending her arms and allowing Belle's entire head to rest against her chest and stomach. "She was my partner in battle when I was a Sought Six."

"Wow," said Hallie, watching as Lou turned around to let Belle use her back as a scratch post for her face. "She's... she's..."

"Big," Jenna finished. "I thought horses would look smaller than this up close."

"I was going to say she's beautiful," said Hallie, glaring at Jenna.

"Oh." Jenna nodded. "Well, yes. That, too."

"She certainly is," said Lou. "That's why her name is Belle. It's French for *beautiful*."

Hallie was so entranced by Belle that she almost forgot what Lou had said when she introduced her. "Wait... did you say she was your battle partner?"

"Yes, I did." Lou reached into her pocket and pulled out a carrot, which must have come from the kitchen inside. "We never knew what we were going to run into on the job. Riding was sometimes necessary because of how far we had to travel. See that black horse, a few stalls over? That's Nuit. He was Levi's. Belle's always been mine. She's nearly thirty years old by now, which is pretty old for a horse back home. In Pawcombe, though, not so old. Animals age slower here. Belle's in no worse shape than I am."

"You know how to ride?" Jenna sounded amazed. "Can... can you teach us?"

Lou smiled, but she had the same look on her face that she got when she was going to say no to something. "It's been so long since I've ridden," she finally said. She bent and picked up a wooden box that had different brushes and combs sticking out of it. "She does need a good grooming, though. You can help me with that, if you want."

"Grooming?"

"Brushing."

"Oh. Okay."

They walked into the stall. Belle looked even bigger now that her entire body was in view, but she was calm.

"Hold your hand flat, palm up," said Lou.

"Why?" said Jenna.

"Just do it."

Jenna did. Belle perked up, seeing her hand, and she stretched her neck to reach it. She seemed to be looking for treats, and Jenna almost asked Lou for another carrot. After a few moments of sniffing, Belle's long pink tongue stuck out and licked Jenna's palm.

Jenna giggled, drawing her hand back. "Horse kisses!"

They each picked a brush and began to smooth her snow-white hair. Hallie took one that looked like her own hairbrush.

"What's this for?" she asked.

Lou looked. "Her mane and tail. You're good at getting tangles out, Hallie. Would you mind doing her tail?"

"Her tail?" Hallie looked at the brush in her hand at then at Belle's back end.

"She won't kick you. She's a sweetheart, just like you," said Lou. "Stand beside her, not behind her, and bring the tail to you. But be careful—you know how tangles can hurt."

Hallie walked tentatively toward Belle's tail.

"It's okay," Lou went on. "Goodness, you look so nervous."

"I am, but not about this," said Hallie.

"I don't—"

"I'm nervous just being outside. What if somebody attacks us again?"

Lou paused. "They won't."

"You said they wouldn't the other night, too."

Lou adjusted her stance. She danced around her words before speaking again. "I know what I said. Believe me: none of your mentors are more shaken up about what happened than I am." She sighed. "Listen, Zyngor having a spy in Maple is a one-in-a-million thing. He knows full-well that spy will eventually be found and killed, just like the assassin was the other night."

"How do we know this spy won't let another assassin into Maple?" said Jenna.

"If you were Zyngor, would you risk losing another one of your followers to a plan that already failed?"

Jenna stared at her shoes.

"Sorry, baby, I didn't mean to snap," said Lou. "Pawcombe is a good place, girls, and it's full of good people. I know it doesn't seem like it right now, but there are more good people than there are bad. That's partly why I wanted to introduce you to Belle. She's not a person, I know, but she's good."

Hallie kept brushing Belle's tail. She couldn't believe how thick each strand of hair was. They were almost like wires, but they were so silky and smooth in her fist. Suddenly, there was a knock on the stall door. Hallie looked over her shoulder to see Klaus standing there.

"Room for one more?"

Lou nodded. "Of course. Come in."

Klaus gave Belle a few pats and then sat down on a bale of hay. "How are you guys?" he said.

Hallie huffed. Jenna shrugged. Lou forced a smile.

"I think we're okay," Lou answered for all of them. Belle nuzzled her face, and Lou gave her a kiss on her velvety nose. Klaus watched her, smiling.

"Somebody's sure missed you," he said.

"I missed her," Lou replied. "I missed everything about Pawcombe. Well, most of it. You know what I mean."

"I do," said Klaus, and then added rather wryly, "there's no place like home, right?"

Lou looked briefly between Hallie and Jenna before nodding. "That is what they say."

Klaus cleared his throat. "Well, the reason I came out here is to ask you all something. I've already made my rounds to the others. How would you like to join me for a dinner party at my house in Cedar tonight?"

Lou smiled at the thought, but she looked at Jenna and Hallie for an answer first.

"A dinner party?" asked Hallie.

"Just a casual gathering," Klaus retracted. "Supporters of the Sought Six over the years. All friends."

"Well, that could be fun..." Jenna began. She swallowed. "Would we have to... walk there?"

Klaus shook his head and smoothed his thick black hair. "Cedar may be next door to Maple, but it is still much too far away. We'll take a Root Path." He leaned forward and rested his forearms on his knees. "I know you guys have been pretty spooked since the night we found Winston."

"The night we were chased and nearly killed, you mean?" Hallie added dully.

Klaus exchanged looks of concern with Lou, but he quickly composed himself. "I totally understand. It's scary. I just want you guys to see the good places and good people that Pawcombe has to offer. Lou, I'm sure you feel the same."

"Actually, I was just saying the same right before you came in," said Lou.

Klaus nodded, satisfied. "I thought a dinner party might be a nice way to get everyone together. But if you guys aren't feeling up to it—"

"No," said Hallie. She looked at Jenna and Lou for agreement, which she got. "No, it does sound nice. We, um, we'd love to come."

"Thank you, Klaus," said Lou, reaching forward and squeezing his hand. "This is really sweet of you."

Klaus shook his head. "It's nothing. Anything I can do to make things easier."

"So, tonight?" said Jenna. She reached for Lou's wrist and lifted it so she could see her watch. "We still have a few hours, then."

"Oh, quite a few. Seven, to be exact," said Klaus, standing up. "I won't expect you until 6 o'clock. How does that sound?"

"It sounds like there's lots of time for a riding lesson before we go," said Jenna. She looked eagerly back up at Lou. "Please, Mom?"

Hallie groaned. "Jenna, really?" All the same, she also looked at Lou for the answer. "But... can we?"

Klaus chuckled and stood up. "Well, that's my cue. I'm off to my place in Cedar. Lots to do to prepare for this evening. I want to make sure it'll be a special night. Oh, I almost forgot: I'm planning a little surprise for you kids as well, so start practising your 'surprised faces'!"

"A surprise?" said Jenna, looking excited. "What kind of surprise?"

"It wouldn't be much of a surprise if I told you," said Klaus. "But I promise you, it'll be one to remember."

"We're looking forward to it!" said Lou. "Aren't we, girls?"

Hallie nodded her head while Jenna smiled. Belle nickered softly and pawed at the hay on the ground.

"Sorry, Belle, I don't think you're allowed to come," said Hallie, giving her a pat.

"Well, I'm off, then. I'm so glad you can come. It'll be loads of fun, I promise. See you all at 6." With that, Klaus left the barn.

"Another dinner invitation," said Hallie. "This better not be like the last one."

"Stay on the path this time and it won't be," Jenna mumbled. Hallie slapped her on the arm. "Ow! Mom, she just hit me!"

"Girls, behave," Lou said, continuing to brush Belle's back, "or no riding lesson."

Neither of them said another word after that.

CHAPTER 11:
VANDNAV HALL

Jenna

THE ROOT PATH TO Cedar was only a short walk from Maple Cliff, and the punch-in-the-gut journey from Maple to Cedar was much smoother than the one from Peterborough. Perhaps it was because it wasn't as far to travel. What took time was the walk from there to Klaus' house, and although Jenna was constantly looking over her shoulder, she was excited to finally see one of Pawcombe's other forests. Just like how Maple only had maple trees, Cedar had had only cedar trees. The air smelled so strongly of cedar that it was almost overwhelming, but everybody was used to it after not too long.

Jenna ran her fingers along the waxy cedar branches as they walked. Her silver-and-gold sword—just like Lou's—kept bouncing against her legs, even though she was sure she secured her holster properly. The adults had insisted they all bring their weapons with them, even though they were just going to see friends. Never leave anything to chance, they had all repeated.

"This thing keeps falling," Jules muttered, adjusting her bow on her shoulder. "Why did we have to bring them again?"

"Wouldn't you rather have it and not need it than need it and not have it?" asked Annabel, eyes forward.

"Well... I mean... I guess so."

"I, for one, feel quite confident having Bloodstain at my side," Thomas said, puffing out his chest as he walked.

Alan, who was a few steps ahead of Thomas, stopped walking and turned around. "Dude, are you really going to keep calling it by its name?"

"Of course." Thomas grinned. "You should, too. You've been using Wind Rider all week. You, of all people, can't deny it's aptly named."

Alan shrugged, but he admired his own sword, embedded with sapphires on the handle. "It does glide around pretty smoothly."

Hallie whipped her head to her left when a crow cawed in the distance. "How much farther until we get there?"

"Not much. Vandnav Hall is just around that corner down there, at the end of the path."

"Vandnav Hall? Klaus named his house after himself?"

Annabel lifted her eyebrows. "Charming, no?"

Eventually, they came to a big iron gate, much like the one at the front of Maple Cliff. Beyond, there was a red-brick house—actually, it was more of a mansion— with a black roof. Every window shone with yellow light.

"Wow," said Jenna, pressing her face against the bars of the gate. The front garden was beautiful. It had flowers of nearly every colour. Jenna figured Klaus must have hired someone to do his gardening for him, because the neutral-coloured clothes he always wore were no indication of these brightly-coloured flowers.

"This is Klaus' house?" said Alan, joining Jenna at the gate. "The one Maple Cliff gave him?"

Levi nodded. "This is it." He yanked at the violet tie around his neck. "Why did I have to wear this thing?"

"It's a nice dinner party, dear," said Denny, taking his hand away from his neck and fixing his tie herself. "Heavens, you're just as fussy as you were when you were a boy."

Alan nudged Jenna in the arm. "Good thing we didn't have to wear anything fancy, eh?"

Jenna looked down at her blouse. "I think we all look nice."

"Well, yeah," said Alan, "but Thomas and I didn't have to wear ties. And you girls didn't have to wear dresses."

"Would you rather I wear a dress?"

Alan shook his head. "Nope."

After unlocking the front gate with a special key Klaus had given them earlier in the day, they made their way to the front door. Denny lifted the brass lion-head doorknocker and tapped it sharply against the wood. Almost immediately, somebody opened the door. It was a tall man with hair as red as Thomas', only it was slicked back with far too much oil. He was wearing a fancy black tuxedo and white gloves.

"Welcome, everybody. Please, come in," he said, smiling as he stood aside. "My name is Mr. Keele, and I am the butler here at Vandnav Hall."

"Wow, this house is really nice," said Jules. They all looked around at the stone tiled floors and wood-panelled walls of the front foyer. Jenna noticed a couple leather tub chairs—each with a fancy letter 'V' sewn into the backs—and a small table between them.

"Please wait here," said Mr. Keele, "and I will inform Mr. Vandnav of your arrival." And with that, he turned and walked out of the foyer.

"This place is amazing," Jules repeated, peeking out the foyer and down the hall. "It's like one of those old mansions in TV shows."

"Indeed," said Thomas. "I wasn't aware Klaus was this wealthy."

"He isn't," Annabel said, staring into the wall-mounted mirror above the small table and fixing her hair, "Maple Cliff is."

"Are these the kind of houses all of you were given?" asked Hallie. She looked at Lou. "Was yours as big as this one?"

Lou nodded. "Maybe we'll move back in there someday. Would you like that?"

Neither Jenna nor Hallie answered her. As cool as it would have been to live in a mansion on a lake, it wasn't home. Not to them, at least.

Just then, they heard footsteps tapping against the hardwood floor in the hallway. Jenna was about to peek around the corner again when Klaus arrived in the foyer. He smiled as he checked his watch.

"Oh, wonderful, you're right on time!" He was wearing a fancy black suit with a black cape over his shoulders. He adjusted his burnt-orange tie at his neck. "Burnt-orange is Cedar's official colour, you know. Just like how eggplant-purple is Maple's. Come with me, I'll take you straight to the dining hall."

Everybody nodded their heads, and Klaus guided them out of the foyer and down the hallway he had just come from.

"The cape's a little small on you, eh, Klaus?" said Annabel, lifting the bottom of the black cape on his shoulders, as if she were carrying the train of a wedding dress. "Is this the same one you've had since you were thirteen?"

"Oh, well, we're honouring the Sought Six tonight, so I just thought I'd wear something from our time as... I mean, I thought it went with the ensemble," he said, pulling it out of her fingers and looking rather embarrassed. He cleared his throat and turned his attention back to the whole group. "First off, I'd like to welcome you to my home, kids. I hope you'll remember that you all are welcome here anytime."

"Thank you," Jules answered for everybody. "I was just saying it's a nice house."

"Well, thank you for saying that. It's served me well over the years."

When they turned the corner, they were faced with yet another hallway. This one was lined with doors, all big and made of dark-stained wood. There were thick, green potted plants in between each door. Jenna was about to ask if they were real when she suddenly got a strong whiff of soil. She figured they were.

"The dining hall is just around the corner over there," said Klaus, pointing to the end of the hall.

"There sure are a lot of doors," said Lindsay, darting her head from side to side. Her blonde ponytail almost whipped Hallie in the face, but she ducked. "Where do they all go?"

"Just any old places that all houses have," said Klaus. "My living room, one of my bathrooms, my study, my library—"

"Where does *this* door go?" asked Alan, pointing to one next to a particularly lush potted plant. He ran his hand along the wood grain. He touched the golden handle, but immediately snatched his hand back. "Whoa, this handle is freezing!"

Klaus turned around to see Alan touching the door and his eyes went wide as golf balls. "No!" he exclaimed, grabbing Alan's wrist. Everybody stopped and stared.

"Okay, sorry," said Alan, pulling his arm out of Klaus' white knuckles.

"Forgive me, but that's... that's my basement," said Klaus. "Nobody must go down there. It's a mess, and its unfinished. I'm afraid that's what comes with owning an old manor like this."

"Just a basement?" said Lindsay, peering at the door.

"Well, sure," said Klaus, "but I can't say there aren't rodents and mold down there."

"Gross," Hallie muttered.

"Indeed." Klaus cleared his throat. "Follow me. Everybody can't wait to see you all."

"Quite right, let's make our way to the dining hall," said Denny, clapping her hands together. She guided them away from the door, practically bouncing in her step. "There's a wonderful view of the cedar trees through the window in the dining hall. And when Klaus opens that window in the summertime, oh, the smell is heavenly. Cedar wood is such a nice smell, don't you think?"

She kept talking about the views and the general grandiosity of the house as she walked, and everybody followed her.

Everybody except for Jenna and Alan. Alan stayed put at the door and Jenna watched him, waiting until everybody else was out of earshot.

"What are you doing?" she whispered.

"Why can't we go down there?" said Alan, massaging his wrist. "Feel the door handle, Jenna. It's freezing."

Jenna reached out and touched it. It felt like ice. But still, she shook her head.

"Well, Klaus just told us it's a basement. They're usually cold."

"You really think that's all there is to it? I mean, he snatched my hand away pretty hard. If it really is just a basement, what's the big deal?"

"I... I don't know."

"Maybe he just told us it's a basement because he doesn't want us to know what's actually through this door."

"You watch way too much TV."

"I'm serious, Jenna."

Jenna groaned. "Is it locked?"

Alan turned the handle. It clunked so loudly that Jenna froze for a second, worried that someone might have heard. When nobody showed up to bust them, she relaxed a little and watched as Alan slowly pulled the door open.

"Ugh," she said, holding her nose. It smelled musty and damp, and overall rancid. It was dark, but she could clearly see a set of stone stairs leading downward. "Sure looks like a basement to me."

"Nuh uh, look at it," said Alan, pointing at everything. "The stone stairs, the stone walls, the cobwebs—"

"The smell," Jenna added, turning away. "It smells like something died down there, Alan. Shut the door."

"Exactly. Jenna, it's not a basement. It's a dungeon."

"A dungeon? Why would Klaus have a dungeon in his house? For crying out loud, Alan, shut the door."

He shut it. Then, he took off his watch and nestled it in the soil of the potted plant next to the door. "Later on, when nobody's watching us, we'll come back and check it out."

"Why are you leaving your watch here?"

"So we'll know it's the door next to this plant," said Alan. "All the doors look the same in this hallway. We need some way to tell."

"Oh," said Jenna. Then she shook her head. "This is nuts, Alan. Even if it *is* a dungeon, we have no reason to assume anything bad. I mean, it was probably built into this house before Klaus even got it, and he probably doesn't want us to go down there because there's toxic mold and stuff, like he said."

"I hope you're right," said Alan, "but my wrist still hurts where he grabbed it. The look in his eye when he saw me touching the door... it was weird, you know?"

Jenna glanced down the hall again and listened. She couldn't even hear Denny's high-pitched, excited voice anymore.

"Fine, we'll come back later. Can we just go now, though? I don't want to have to lie about where we've been."

"I hate to say it, Jenna, but now that we're a Sought Six, I think lying and secrets are in our job description."

CHAPTER 12:
THE DUNGEON

Jenna

KLAUS STOOD AT THE head of the dining hall, before about two hundred guests, with his wine glass in one hand and a knife in the other. He gently tapped the glass with the knife and everybody quieted down in a matter of seconds.

"Welcome, friends, to my humble abode," said Klaus, emphasizing the word 'humble' because everybody could see his house was far from humble. As he hoped, the entire dining hall laughed along with him. He took a sip from his wine glass. "We are at the start of a very special time in Pawcombe. A time when peace is once again on the horizon. A time when hope is something we have, not only dream of having. And we owe it all to six children. Come on up here, kids."

With that, everybody in the room turned to look at them. Jenna could feel her cheeks redden. Lou gave her a slight push forward and she walked to the front of the room. People moved aside to make way for them. Klaus winked at them, probably a way to ease their minds, as they arrived next to him.

"May I officially present to you," said Klaus, ready to hover his hand over each of their heads as he said their names, "Master Thomas, Miss Lindsay, Miss Julie, Miss Hallie, Miss Jenna, and Master Alan."

Jenna was impressed that he didn't confuse her with Hallie. Everybody erupted in applause, which made Jules jump. Either that, or she was still stumbling over Klaus calling her by her full name. She tried to hide herself behind Thomas, who had gone beet-red at the eruption from the crowd.

Jenna suddenly felt dwarfed by the people in that room, not because they were all bigger than she was, and not because of how many of them there were. It was because of their hopes. They looked at the six of them with beaming eyes, wide smiles, and adoration. All of these people knew they were the ones with the task of stopping Zyngor—and they were treating them like royalty because of it.

"Don't they look wonderful?" Klaus went on, clapping with the crowd. "Bright-eyed and stable. Outfitted for combat, too! Just like any Sought Six worth their salt."

Jenna swallowed hard. What if they *weren't* worth their salt? What if they failed at their task? The people probably wouldn't hate them or shun them, because Lou, Levi, Annabel and Klaus failed to free them from Zyngor's clutches, and everybody still looked at them with the highest respect and esteem. But still, in that moment, with everybody clapping for them, Jenna felt the pressure much more than she had so far.

"And now," Klaus went on, holding his hand up as a way to silence to crowd, "please continue with your conversations and your drinks, and later I will announce the surprise I've been hinting at all evening."

Everyone looked excited about this plan, and they resumed their conversations like he had said. Jenna wasted no time in hurrying back to Lou's side, who welcomed her with an open arm.

"Kind of crazy, eh?"

"I don't know how you did this, Mom."

"You get used to it," said Lou, but she didn't even sound convinced. "How about you go get something to eat? You haven't had any dinner yet."

Jenna looked over and noticed Alan standing at the hors d'oeuvres table. Maybe this would be their chance to slip out for a bit.

"Okay," said Jenna, forcing a smile. "I am a little hungry." She walked to the table and caught Alan's eye. He was holding a plate full of finger sandwiches and pastries.

"Want a shrimp puff?" said Alan, his mouth full with one.

"You're not seriously eating this stuff, are you?"

"I'm hungry," Alan responded, shrugging. "It's no slice of pizza, but it's not horrible. Seriously, you want one of these? I took too many."

"Forget about the food, Alan," Jenna hissed. "I think now's our chance."

Alan's eyes lit up. He looked around for a place to put his plate. As if he had snapped his fingers and commanded it, one of Klaus' manservants appeared at his side and offered to take his plate from him.

"Thanks," said Alan.

"Of course, Master Alan," said the servant, and he walked away towards a door Jenna could only guess led to the kitchen.

"Master Alan," Alan repeated with a sly grin. "I could get used to that."

Jenna snapped her fingers in his face. "Focus, *Master*, we don't have much time."

"Right, sorry. Okay, I don't think anybody's looking. Let's go."

They slipped out of the dining hall unnoticed and found the correct hallway without a problem, but it was a good thing Alan had left his watch in the plant, or they would have had a hard time finding the correct door.

Alan brushed the soil off his watch off and fastened it back on his wrist. "Okay, it's 7 o' clock now. What do you say? Twenty minutes?"

"Make it fifteen," said Jenna. "Any longer and they'll come looking for us."

"With all those people in there, they probably won't even notice we're gone."

"My mom will."

Alan couldn't argue with that. He set a timer on his watch for 7:15. Then, he opened the dungeon door.

It clunked very loudly again, and the smell hit Jenna in the face like a frying pan.

"Ugh, gross," she said, wafting the air in front of her. "I can't believe I'm doing this."

"Hurry up," said Alan. He had already started down the stairs. "We've only got fifteen minutes. You got your sword?"

"Yes," Jenna gripped the golden handle at her hip. "Why?"

"Just in case. Come on."

The closer they got to the bottom, the darker it became. Right when Jenna was starting to wonder how they were going to explore if they couldn't see anything, she noticed a glimmering orange light in the distance.

"Alan, look!" she said, pointing. "It looks like... I think the dungeon is on fire!"

"Come on, let's go check it out!" Alan exclaimed, picking up his pace. Jenna had to break into a trot to keep up with him. They turned a corner.

"Well," said Jenna, staring at the stone blocks of the wall, "it is a fire." There, mounted on the wall, was a torch with a dancing flame the size of both Jenna's fists.

"And if there's one here, there are probably others around," said Alan, looking beyond it down the hall. "At least we'll be able to see where we're going."

"How far exactly do you want to go?" said Jenna. "What time is it? Should we head back?"

"Relax, Jenna, it's only been a few minutes."

"Relax? Here? In Klaus' dungeon? Yeah, right. Good one."

They walked a bit further and, sure enough, they came to another wall-mounted torch. This flame was even bigger than the last one. As far as Jenna could tell, there was nobody in the dungeon besides the two of them, but that then begged the question of why the torches were even lit at all.

Every so often, they passed a cell with big iron bars, but there were only bits of hay and rusty chains lying in them. Jenna shuddered to think of someone trapped in those chains.

"Any signs that people were tortured down here?" Alan asked, practically reading her thoughts.

Jenna stopped and examined the cell they were passing. She touched the bars, which were wet, and sniffed inside. She coughed. "There's no one in here." She ran her hand down the bars and, to her horror, felt something hairy. She jerked her hand back and a squeal escaped her mouth.

"Shh!" Alan hissed. "Quiet! You want to get caught?"

Jenna peered closer at the bars. "Hey, this is horse hair," she said. She tried to pull it out, but it was stuck in a hinge. "From a mane or a tail. It feels like Belle's hair. It's got to be from a horse."

"And look in the back," said Alan, pointing to the back corner of the cell. "Are those horseshoes?"

"Oh, don't tell me Klaus kept horses down here. This is no place for a horse to live." She felt herself welling up at the thought. She'd hate to see Belle or Nuit or any of the other horses in a place like this.

Alan shrugged and opened his mouth to respond but didn't get the chance. Someone was behind them now, and whoever it was grabbed their shoulders.

"Yargh!" Alan shrieked, leaping five feet in the air. Jenna spun around and tried to unsheathe her sword, but it slipped from her fingers and fell with a *clank* to the stone floor. If she had truly needed to defend herself, she would have been dead meat. Thankfully though, all she saw was her identical face glaring at her.

"What the heck do you two think you're doing?" Hallie demanded. She stared at Jenna's sword on the ground. "Were you going to stab me, Jenna?"

"I thought you were... well, you scared me!" Jenna picked up her sword and nestled it back at her hip. "Give me a break. You know we've only had a couple lessons."

"Yes, I know, and we aren't in a lesson now, so you shouldn't be using it," Hallie scolded. "What are you even doing down here? This isn't your house. You can't just explore anywhere you want."

"Yeah, no kidding," said Lindsay, behind her. Jules and Thomas were there, too. "Klaus already told us this was a basement. You needed proof?"

"Well, you didn't have to give us heart attacks," said Jenna, clapping her chest with her hand. "Hold on, let me get it going again."

"Quit being so dramatic," said Hallie. "You're the one who messed up. You shouldn't even be in the basement."

"Hal, look around," said Jenna, pointing at the stone walls, the cobwebs, and the torches. "This is clearly a dungeon, not a basement."

Hallie sneered. "What's the difference?"

"There are plenty of differences, really," said Thomas, stepping forward. "Firstly, basements are found under houses, and dungeons are found under castles. I'm no expert on homes, but I'd say Klaus' home is much closer in size to a castle than a house. Secondly, basements act as another room in one's home, and dungeons act as prisons. Look around—I see jail cells, don't you? Thirdly, basements, even the unfinished ones, aren't as damp and dark as this place is."

"Yeah, um, exactly," said Jenna. "So, don't you think it's a little bit weird that Klaus has a dungeon in his house?" She widened her eyes a little.

"Maybe he's really into the whole *Dungeons and Dragons* thing," suggested Lindsay. "He certainly strikes me as that nerdy type."

Thomas cleared his throat. "Excuse me?"

Lindsay blushed, remembering Thomas liked to play *Dungeons and Dragons*. "I didn't say it was a bad thing..."

"Did anyone follow you guys down here?" said Alan, trying to look past them but not seeing anything in the darkness.

"No," said Hallie, "but if we don't leave now, someone is going to find us and bust us. Klaus already said we weren't supposed to come down here."

Jenna grinned. "Then why did you?"

"Because *you* did!"

"Guys, if we stay down here, we're going to miss the surprise Klaus has planned," said Jules, shifting sideways when a water droplet fell from the ceiling, "so can we go back upstairs now? Please?"

Boom. Boom. Boom. Boom.

Suddenly, the whole dungeon shook with the steady pounding of what sounded like a drum. Only, it couldn't have been a drum. The pounds were much too loud.

"What was that?" Jules shrieked, looking around every which way.

Boom. Boom.

"It's coming from behind you guys!" Jenna hissed.

"Great," said Lindsay, spinning around. "That's where the stairs are! We're going to have to find another way out of here!"

Boom. Boom. Boom.

This time, it was accompanied by laughter. Only, not happy laughter. Villainous laughter. And it didn't sound even remotely human. For a moment, Jenna thought there might be a pack of hyenas loose in the dungeon.

"Come on!" Alan exclaimed, pushing and pulling them away from the noise. "We've got to hide somewhere!"

They found an open cell with a few bales of hay in it, just big enough for them to duck behind. They huddled together, holding their weapons close. Hallie sat down on the stone floor, but immediately got back up.

"Oh, disgusting!" she shrieked. "I just sat in something wet!"

"Quiet!" Jenna hissed. "They're going to hear us!"

"Who?"

"Whoever!"

Just when everybody settled behind the hay bales, there were thumping footsteps rounding the corner. The footsteps were joined by snorting, grunting, and a few cackles. They sounded like pigs. Jenna peeked out in front of the hay bales. All she could see clearly were shadows dancing in the torch's gleam. Whoever it was, they had to be close.

Then, a pair of legs stomped their way into Jenna's line of sight. And just as she expected, they weren't human legs. They were green. They were slimy. They were hairy. The feet quite resembled a pig's. Whatever this thing was, it appeared to be wearing something made of brown leather and steel. Then, the blade of a sword slammed down next to the legs with such force that it stabbed the stone floor.

Jenna snatched her body back behind the hay and squeezed her eyes shut. Just then, one of these creatures spoke.

"The brats aren't here," it said. The voice was extremely rough and crackly. "They must have left when they heard us coming."

Another one snorted. "I told you we should have been quieter."

"Quieter, bah! We're nilbogs of Oak, not fairies of Birch."

Jenna stumbled over that entire sentence. She knew Oak and Birch were two of the forests, or cities, in Pawcombe—the ones that only grew oak trees and birch trees. And fairies—well, they knew by now that Pawcombe was home to many different creatures. But nilbogs? She had never heard that word before, and if they lived in Oak...

"The Master was sure of his plan," said another one of these creatures—the nilbogs. This nilbog's voice was so deep and booming that it sent a shiver up Jenna's spine.

"The Master said that boy, one of the new Sought Six boys, wouldn't be able to resist a warning to stay out of the dungeon."

"We're well aware of what the Master said," said the first voice.

Jenna jerked her head to Alan. "Zyngor!" she mouthed. He took her hand and squeezed.

"We'll go back to our den," said the booming voice, "and have our dinner."

"But the Master said we could eat the children for our dinner," another one whined, "after we got them to tell us where the Sterling Cone is."

Jenna wasn't sure why, but those last few words rang out like a bell. Everybody perked up and darted their eyes between each other.

Jules gulped. "The *what*?" she mouthed.

"Well, we can't *eat* the children if we can't *find* the children," said another. Then, it sounded like he slapped him. "Use your head!"

"But the Master is certain that the brats know where the Sterling Cone is," the nilbog kept whining. "He said they're keeping its location a secret."

"We all know what the Master said!"

"The Master told us children are unpredictable," said the first nilbog in a calm voice. "He will have another plan."

"Very well. We'll hunt some rats on the way back. Not much meat, but better than nothing."

And with that, they all hobbled back where they came from. After a few minutes, Alan stood up and carefully peeked above the hay bales.

"I think it's safe," he whispered.

Lindsay lifted her eyebrows. "Not if you're a rat."

"What the heck were those things?" said Jules. Her eyes were as wide as golf balls.

"Nilbogs, apparently," said Thomas. He took off his glasses and cleaned them with his shirt. "I read about them in that book I found in our suite, Alan. 'Reptilian Beasts of Pawcombe'...? A very interesting read, but it made sure to mention that nilbogs are the primary minions of Zyngor."

"Zyngor?" said Hallie, going rather pale.

"That's who they must have been talking about when they said 'Master'," said Jenna. "Zyngor must be using Klaus' dinner party as a way to get to us."

Hallie groaned and ran her hands down her face. "Will we ever just have a quiet dinner in Pawcombe?"

"What's more puzzling," Thomas began, scratching his head, "is something they said: The Sterling Cone. Anyone have any knowledge of that?"

They all shook their heads.

"Must be important, though," said Jenna. "If their master—I mean, Zyngor—wants this Sterling Cone thing and he thinks we know where it is, it sounds like we're in trouble."

"*Where* it is," said Jules, shaking her head. "We don't even know *what* it is."

Beep! Beep! Beep!

Everybody jumped and gasped. They froze solid. Alan's watch was beeping. It was the timer he had set for 7:15.

"Turn it off!" Jenna hissed. She even reached over to try and turn it off herself.

"Shh! Did they hear it?" Jules whispered.

They listened.

More snorts. More cackles. More footsteps, but this time they were coming back.

"What was that?" one of the nilbogs said.

"The little brats are here!" shrieked another.

"Run!" Alan exclaimed, leaping out from behind the hay bales. "Quickly, before they corner us in here!"

They left the cell and sprinted down the dark hallway, only having their way lit every so often by the torches on the wall. The footsteps and cackles were gaining on them, and since they couldn't see more than ten feet in front of them, they couldn't see an exit. They could be going in circles for all they knew.

They ran until they came face to face with another wall. They were running so fast that they almost crashed right into it. They pranced from side to side, looking for a corner to turn, but there wasn't one.

"Oh no," Jenna heaved. "It's a dead end!"

"Great! What do we do now?" Hallie shrieked.

Alan reached up and grabbed the torch on the wall. He pulled as hard as he could, even lifting his legs off the ground to use his entire bodyweight, and it snapped off. He swung it in front of them, and what they saw there made them all freeze again.

The nilbogs had caught up to them, and now, in the torchlight, they could seem them clearly. They were all green and slimy. Some were tall and others were short, but they were all wearing brown leather and steel clothing. It looked like some sort of poorly-designed armour. They were all carrying swords, too. Their faces were the ugliest things Jenna had ever seen. Their noses were pushed in and wrinkled, and their mouths were as wide as their faces. Their teeth (and each nilbog only had about six or seven) were yellow and sharp. Their tongues, black as night, slipped in and out of their mouths like snakes' tongues. One thing was certain: they were definitely not human.

Alan held the torch firmly in his hands. Jenna wished he had grabbed his sword instead.

"Get back!" he shouted. He waved the torch in front of him like a shield, which seemed to keep the nilbogs away. Their eyes, although dark and cloudy, flashed with fear at the sight of the fire.

"L-l-leave us alone!" Jules exclaimed through a fearful sob.

Lindsay copied Alan's actions, seeing that the fire was a better defence than their swords. She took the torch off the wall opposite and pushed past them all so that she could stand next to Alan. She looked fierce, but Jenna could see her arm shaking.

Thomas pulled out his sword. "I'm sure glad the adults made us bring these," he muttered, holding it at the ready. "Bloodstain, don't fail me now!"

Upstairs, Klaus was at the head of the dining hall once again, tapping his wine glass and getting ready to announce to everyone that the surprise was about to be revealed.

CHAPTER 13:
NILBOG AMBUSH

Hallie

ALAN AND LINDSAY STOOD on their toes, holding the torches as steady as they could. Everybody else stood behind them in a state of panic. The nilbogs had no interest in coming anywhere near the fire, but that didn't stop them from threatening to. They snorted and squealed horrible sounds; piercing, screeching, growling. Without a shadow of a doubt, they were not happy that there were waving flames between them and their dinner.

"We need a plan, you guys!" Lindsay said over her shoulder, without taking her eyes off the angry nilbogs, "and we need one now!"

"Working on it!" said Jenna, pounding on the stone wall with her fists. Hallie could hardly believe what she was seeing.

"What are you going to do, punch us out of here?"

"Maybe there's a secret passage somewhere," said Jenna.

"Splendid notion!" exclaimed Thomas, and he and Jules joined her.

"Seriously?!" Hallie felt the hysteria bubbling up from within her. "Where do you think we are, in some spy movie?"

"You got any better ideas, Hal?"

The nilbogs' grunts and screeches were getting louder and angrier by the second. Some of them even tried to jolt forward—until Lindsay and Alan waved the torches at them.

"Come on, guys, hurry up!" Alan exclaimed.

Hallie didn't hesitate any further and she helped punch the stone wall. After what seemed like an eternity of Alan and Lindsay waving the torches at any nilbog who dared to take a single step toward them, Jenna punched a stone that crumbled away from the wall. She reached into the mess of stone and cement, brushed it away, and then she appeared to feel something else.

"Guys!" she said, but only loud enough so that Hallie, Jules and Thomas could hear her. "There's something in here... it feels like some kind of latch."

"What are you waiting for?" said Jules, hope leaking from her voice. "Pull it!"

Jenna did. There was a loud *thud* and a *clunk* that made everybody jump.

"What was *that*?" asked Alan, turning his head to look at them.

He shouldn't have done that.

One of the nilbogs took its opportunity and lunged forward. It grabbed Alan's wrist and squeezed so tightly that Alan had no choice but to let go of the torch. He struggled to free himself, but it was no use.

"Hey, let me go! Help! Help me!"

Lindsay wasted no time. She turned her own torch into a baseball bat and swung it directly at the nilbog's head. It leapt back, its head ablaze, screeching and flailing around the other nilbogs. It got so close to some of them that they lit on fire, too.

"Whoa!" said Alan, now that he was free. He stepped backward, massaging his wrist. "Look how fast their skin is catching on fire!"

Thomas nodded. "Highly flammable..."

"Boys, for heaven's sake! Pay attention!" Hallie shrieked at them. She pointed to the area of the stone wall where Jenna had pulled the latch. The wall was gone, the latch having loosened all the stones from their positions and crumpled them into a dusty pile. Through the fresh hole, there was another long hallway—a secret passageway.

The nilbog with its head on fire—actually, its whole body was on fire by now—fell down dead in front of them. It landed in a pile of old hay on the ground, which was immediately set alight as well. The rest of the nilbogs were panicking, trying to stay away from the fire. Luckily, that also meant they were staying away from the new hole in the wall.

"Now's our chance," said Lindsay, still holding her torch. "I'm going to throw this at them."

"No, keep it!" said Hallie. "What if it's dark over there?"

"Good point."

Everybody climbed and jumped their way over the pile of stone rubble and ran as quickly as they could down the hallway. As Hallie predicted, it got darker the further they went. They rounded so many corners that they couldn't turn back now even if they wanted to, and each new hallway looked exactly the same as the last: stone.

"Ow, guys, stop!" said Jules, slowing down. She was clutching her side and heaving. "Cramp! Cramp! Can we stop?"

Everybody stopped running. Hallie listened. She couldn't hear anything. Had they really run so far away from the nilbogs that they couldn't even hear the screeches anymore?

"Yeah, I think we're safe," said Hallie after a moment.

Jenna scoffed. "For now, anyway."

"So much for being protected in Pawcombe, like everyone said we would be!" Lindsay sighed with exasperation. She switched hands to hold the torch and gave her arm a shake. "This is ridiculous. Who can we trust around here?"

"We can trust Mom," said Jenna.

"Yeah, and Uncle Levi," Jules added.

"And the others, too," said Alan. "Imagine how Klaus feels right now. All he wanted to do was give us a nice dinner party, and Zyngor crashed it! Or, he tried to, at least. The party is probably still going on upstairs, eh?"

"Upstairs," Jenna said thoughtfully. "Let's not forget, guys, that we're technically still in Klaus' house. This dungeon is in his house. Those nilbogs are in his house."

"So—what?—Zyngor is using Klaus' house as a hideout for some of his nilbogs?" asked Hallie, shaking her head. "I don't think so. I find it very hard to believe Klaus wouldn't have known about that."

"That's my point," said Jenna.

"Well, now, hang on. Klaus did say he never comes down here because of rodents and mold, remember?" said Thomas. "Perhaps he truly doesn't know what's down here."

Lindsay squeezed her eyes shut as though she had a headache. "We have got to find a way out of here," she said. "When we get back to Maple Cliff, I'm going straight to bed and sleeping for a week."

"Yes, I agree," said Thomas, looking back where they came from, "Perhaps there's another secret passage somewhere."

"So, you want to start pounding away at the walls again?" said Hallie. "Face it, we just got lucky before. And even if we do find another secret passage, how do we know it won't lead us to more nilbogs?"

Jules' eyes widened, almost like she hadn't considered the possibility that there were more nilbogs in Pawcombe than the ones they just left in the fire.

"Yeah, you've got a point, Hallie," said Lindsay. "Maybe we should just stay put until someone comes and finds us."

Alan squinted. "No way. What if more nilbogs find us first?" He squeezed the handle of his sword but didn't take it out. "We've had—what?—two lessons? Three, max? We can't fight an army of those things alone! We have to find a way out."

Boom! Boom! Boom!

"Oh, not again!" Jenna exclaimed, looking in every direction. Her heart began racing and she stared at Alan. "You were saying?!"

Boom! Boom! Boom!

"Where are they?" said Hallie, also looking around everywhere.

The stone hallways echoed with the same sinister laughter they had heard before. They heard a few squeals and grunts, but no English words this time. The echoes were so loud that it was impossible to tell exactly where they were coming from.

"Run, guys!" Alan exclaimed, pushing them.

"Run? Where?!" Jules shrieked.

"Anywhere! Just run!"

And so, they ran. Lindsay's torch was their only source of light, and they still had no clue where they were heading. The nilbogs' cackles were getting louder and echoed down every hallway.

They came to a clearing and rushed into a large room with a high stone ceiling. It was very poorly lit with only a few torches on the walls, but it was light enough for everyone to see the room wasn't empty. Lindsay, leading the way with her torch, stopped so abruptly that everybody crashed into her. Somehow, she kept her stance. Everybody else collapsed onto the cold stone. When Hallie regained her footing, she nearly fell over again at the sight.

There was a group of nilbogs spread out in the room—dozens of them. A few of them had large bellies that could barely be contained by their brown leather garments, and which even seemed to hinder their balance as they turned to notice the six kids in the doorway. Not a single one of them looked happy—and they all had swords in their hands. Their wide, snake-like mouths were gaping, and some were even hissing. Most of them, however, simply snorted like angry pigs.

Everybody backed up against the wall, and Jules began hitting Lindsay's arm.

"Throw the torch!" she shrieked. "Throw the torch!" Lindsay did throw it—right at the head of one of the nilbogs—but it dodged the flames. The torch landed with a deafening *clunk* on the ground. The nilbogs all cackled at the fact she had missed, while a few of them spat on the torch. Then they raised their swords and started toward them. Hallie squeezed her eyes shut, and then—

Thhhwwitttt!

One of the nilbogs jolted sideways into the stone wall. It took a few seconds for everybody to realize why. There was an arrow in its head; it was hit with such a strong force that its head had become skewered on the arrow and stuck in the wall.

Just as the other nilbogs grunted in shock at what had what just happened, Hallie's stomach began churning as she watched a line of blood drip down the wall from the nilbog's head (only the blood was green, not red).

"Who shot that arrow?" Jenna cried, looking all around. "Who's there?"

Then, three people—one with a bow and two with swords—arrived, positing themselves between the children and the nilbogs. It was so dark down there that Hallie couldn't tell where these people had come from, but her heart gave a leap when she saw who one of them was.

"Mom!" she exclaimed happily, watching as Lou stood with a tight grip on her sword, protecting them. Oddly, the nilbogs appeared to recognize her. They looked at her with a strange sort of familiarity in their cloudy eyes. Some looked frightened, while others looked furious. They all rushed forward on their stumpy legs with their swords. Lou's shoulders relaxed—so much so that, for a moment, Hallie was afraid she wouldn't be able to fight them off. However, once she successfully dodged their first swipe, the rest appeared to be easy for her.

Clang! Clang! Squish!

Her shiny silver blade was splattered all over with green nilbog blood. As many nilbogs as there were, Lou was doing well—very well, in fact. Hallie couldn't believe what she was seeing.

"Did you know she could do that?" Jenna whispered in Hallie's ear.

"Did *you*?" Hallie answered. They had seen her use her sword in their combat classes, but not like this. This was quick. This was precise. This was angry. It was strange for Hallie to see her so fired up. This must have been what Denny meant when she said Lou was 'the best swordswoman in all of Pawcombe'.

They watched as Lou continued to move swiftly and successfully around the angry nilbogs. Some of them came close to hitting her, but she either dodged them or hit them first. A clang here, a slice there. An angry scream. A vicious growl. And not just from Lou—from Levi, too. Levi was the second person at their rescue, and he was quite evenly matched with Lou, so none of the nilbogs were succeeding in hitting him, either.

"Uncle Levi?" Jules exclaimed in absolute wonder as she watched him fight. "Oh, watch out! Duck! Oh—oh no! Behind you!" Her cries were going unheard because of all the commotion, but Levi hardly needed the help. He was always one step ahead of Jules' advice.

Clang! Squish!

Hallie was afraid those squishing noises would haunt her dreams that night but, more importantly, Lou and Levi appeared to be unbeatable. Still, there were far more nilbogs than there were people, and right when it looked like one of them was going to join another and gang up on Lou, an arrow pierced its head. It was dead before it hit the wet stone ground, its sword landing beside it with a loud *clang-clunk!*

"Again with the head!" Hallie muttered, swallowing a lump in her throat. This time, she turned in the direction the arrow had come from.

And there was Annabel, their third rescuer. Not having a sword made her a prime target for the nilbogs, but it didn't matter. She was so quick and so spot-on with her bow that the nilbogs had arrows sticking out of their faces if they dared to take even one step toward her or anyone else.

"Hey!" Lou gasped, finishing off another one with a clean slice. She looked at Annabel, and then at the nilbog she just saved her from. "What'd you do that for? I could have fought them both!"

"Yeah, I know you could have," Annabel replied, releasing an arrow into another nilbog, who gave a high-pitched snort before falling. She looked right at Lou. "Duck."

Lou did, and Annabel shot another arrow into a nilbog who had been trying to sneak up on Lou. Then, Annabel turned her attention to Hallie, Jenna, and the others. Her face was energized and her eyes were flashing.

"You guys going to just stand there and let us have all the fun?"

Jules gulped. "Can't we?"

Another nilbog snorted its way over to them, sword raised. It didn't get more than a few steps, however, before Annabel's arrow pierced its body. The squeals the nilbogs made as they were struck down were ear-piercing.

"Come on! Let's go!" said Annabel, much louder and more urgently than before.

Everybody pulled out their swords and Jules loaded her bow but, for a few seconds, no one moved. Then, Alan and Thomas started yelling out battle cries as they lunged toward the nilbogs, which made all four of the girls almost jump out of their skin. Nonetheless, they followed them.

Even with only a few lessons under their belts, they all managed to defend themselves. Either that, or the nilbogs weren't very skilled fighters. Perhaps their fat bellies were causing them to be off-balance, or perhaps the fact that their eyes were cloudy also meant their vision was cloudy. Whatever the reason, Hallie and her rose-gold sword (conveniently named Rose) were doing quite well.

When she had a moment, she spun around. There was a nilbog who had zeroed in on Jenna, and although Jenna was giving it a run for its money, she couldn't seem to strike it down for good. Then, it grabbed her sword arm with its slimy hand and dug its black claws into her skin. Jenna let go of her sword and tried to pull her arm free, but she couldn't. Her eyes flashed with fear.

Hallie ran toward them, and practically squeezed her eyes shut as she aimed for the nilbog's back.

Squish.

Her pinkish sword was completely covered in greenish blood, and the now-dead nilbog fell to the ground in a heap.

"Oh my..." she began, hardly believing her own actions. She stared at the blood-caked blade of her sword. "What did I just... why is it green?!"

"Hal, duck!" Jenna gasped suddenly. Hallie ducked without even thinking, giving her sister room to lunge toward an incoming nilbog as tall as Levi. She swung her sword and sliced it right across its belly. It screeched and gurgled as it stumbled backward. The contents of its stomach (whole fish and rodents mixed with stinky stomach bile) spilled out onto the stone floor. Hallie thought the contents of her own stomach might join the slimy fish and rats.

"Oh, gross!" Lindsay shrieked. She was catching her breath after using her white-gold sword (a sword as soft yellow as her hair) to stab a nilbog that had been giving her a hard time. "Don't they chew their food?"

"Hard to chew when you have as many teeth as they do! Or rather, as few..." Levi heaved, skewering two nilbogs on his sword at once. "Nilbog shish kebab!" He pulled it out of them with a high-pitched *swish* and they fell.

"Uncle Levi! Look out!" Jules yelled from across the room. Levi turned, but there was a nilbog less than a foot away from him, its sword raised high and its toothless mouth bared. Levi couldn't have defended himself even if he tried. Lou, who was on the other side of the room, also turned when she heard Jules' scream. Her eyes widened and she started to come over, but she had to get past two other nilbogs before she'd make it to Levi.

Just then, an arrow hit the nilbog's face and pierced through both cheeks. It was hit with such a strong force that it flew sideways against the wall, away from Levi. At first, Hallie was sure Annabel had done it—Annabel had saved Levi's life—but when she looked across the room, she saw which archer's bow was aimed in that direction.

"Jules?" said Hallie, impressed. Annabel also looked very impressed.

"Nice shot!" she grinned, shooting down yet another nilbog without a hitch.

"I was aiming for his chest," said Jules.

The nilbog hit by Jules writhed in pain on the ground, not dead yet. It swung its sword at random, as if the arrow through its cheeks had somehow impaired its vision even more. Hallie tripped over her own feet as she jolted away to avoid the thrashing blade, and Alan, seeing the commotion, rushed over.

"Allow me," he said, stabbing his sword through the nilbog. It made an ugly grunting noise, and its slimy green body finally stopped moving. Alan sheathed his sword. "I think I'm getting the hang of this."

"Gee, I'm so glad." Again, Hallie felt like she might be sick.

Lou arrived at Levi's side, having fought her way through the other nilbogs. By now, most of them were dead. The only people left fighting were Annabel, Thomas, and Lindsay, and only one nilbog apiece.

"Are you okay? I'm sorry," Lou gasped, taking the sides of Levi's neck in her hands. "I tried to get over here faster, but..."

"I'm okay," he said. He gently pushed a piece of her golden hair from her face. "Thanks to Julesey, I'm okay. Turns out, our kids are quite the fighters after all. And you were so worried about them."

"I'd hardly call us fighters!" Jules mumbled, wrapping her arms around Levi's waist.

Hallie scoffed her agreement. "Yeah, we just got lucky." She made a face at the green smears all over her sword. Lou knelt next to her.

"That wasn't luck," she said. "That was impressive. We didn't fight our first battle like this until we had—I'm not even sure—maybe a dozen lessons?"

Levi thought. "Fourteen. But close enough."

"If it makes anybody feel better, I'd much rather have waited until we had fourteen lessons," said Jules. Levi kissed her forehead.

"If you can save my life after only a couple, I'm not worried, kiddo."

The remaining nilbogs had fallen, and the dungeon was quiet once again. Annabel made her way around the room with a loaded bow, in case any nilbogs weren't completely dead yet, to make sure the coast was clear.

Hallie looked around, counting in her head to make sure there were indeed six kids and three adults still alive. "Where are Denny and Klaus?" she said after a moment.

"They stayed upstairs," said Lou. "Somebody needed to keep everybody else calm while we came and looked for you."

"When did you realize we were missing?" asked Thomas.

"When Klaus wanted to announce his surprise," answered Levi, wiping a few beads of sweat from his face with the back of his hand. "We went to find you guys so you wouldn't miss it, and we couldn't find you."

"Mom?" said Jenna, suddenly. She sounded upset. Lou whipped her head around.

"Yes? What's wrong?"

"Does this stuff clean?"

Hallie noticed Jenna was giving her bloody sword (and hers was very bloody) a disgusted look.

Lou smiled, but more out of relief than anything else. "Yes," she said, "it cleans." She opened her arms and gave them both a hug and a kiss. Hallie could feel her heart pounding out of her chest as she held them close.

Lindsay sat down on the stone floor, just narrowly missing a puddle of nilbog blood. "Zyngor used Klaus' party to get to us," she said, breathing deeply. "That's why the nilbogs are here. He sent them."

"So, you do know what these slimeballs are," said Annabel, finishing her inspection and arriving at their side. She knelt next to Lindsay and examined her face and limbs for any cuts. "I wondered. We hadn't told you about them."

"I read all about them in a book from our room," said Thomas, looking pleased with himself.

"And we heard them say they were from Oak," Jenna added, "so we knew Zyngor must have sent them to kill us."

"I'm sorry, guys," said Alan, also collapsing into a seated position on the ground. He was sweaty and dirty. "This is all my fault. If I hadn't been so keen on exploring down here, none of this would have happened."

"Yes, it would," said Annabel. She shifted so she could examine Alan's eye. She herself didn't appear to have a scratch on her. In fact, compared to everyone else, she only looked slightly dishevelled. Even her chestnut hair was still shiny and bouncy. "This would have happened whether you came down here or not. If Zyngor wanted to get to you, it wouldn't have mattered where you were. Trust me."

Thomas' eyebrows crinkled. "But that doesn't make sense. If that's true—if Zyngor could have attacked us, say, in the dining hall—then why did the nilbogs say their master knew Alan wouldn't be able to resist a warning to stay out of the dungeon?"

"Yeah," said Jenna, her eyes narrowing. "Yeah, that's true. It was like their plan to kill us depended on at least one of us coming down here."

"Maybe Zyngor wanted to isolate us," Lindsay suggested. "Separate us from the group so the adults wouldn't know what happened to us...?"

Annabel shook her head. "He doesn't care about that. In fact, he likes when people watch his killings." She said that last part with a sneer that made Hallie uneasy. She was becoming more and more afraid to come across Zyngor with each mention of his name.

"I hate to say this," said Jules, "but are we sure it was Zyngor who sent the nilbogs?"

"Who else would they have called their master, though?" said Lindsay.

Boom! Boom! Boom!

The pounding echoed throughout the room. Now that Hallie thought about it, the pounding sounded like dozens of stumpy nilbog legs marching in a rhythm, not the beating of a drum.

"Oh, you have got to be kidding!" Jules moaned. "There's more?!"

"There are more nilbogs in Pawcombe than there are people," Thomas stated. "At least, that's what 'Reptilian Beasts of Pawcombe' said."

"Get up," said Annabel, though she was looking wildly around the room rather than at any of them. "Get up, right now. Up! Come on!"

Everybody stood up and readied themselves with their swords and bows.

Boom! Boom!

There were high-pitched squeals and cackles and then, through the doorway they had all entered the room earlier, there came another ambush of slimy, green nilbogs. Annabel immediately shot the first one with an arrow, and then she reloaded her bow so quickly that Hallie almost missed it. The shot seemed to surprise the skin off the next few that followed. Their gaping mouths stretched open across the width of their faces and they screeched with shock, or perhaps it was anger; Hallie couldn't tell. Either way, their sharp, yellow teeth were bared as they hissed and snorted. She gripped the handle of Rose tighter.

As Annabel loaded her bow and shot another arrow, Jules shot her first. It hit a nilbog square in the face. Again, Annabel looked impressed.

"You're on fire today," she chuckled.

Jules huffed as she loaded another arrow. "I was aiming for the chest again."

The nilbogs would have come through the doorway and into the room much faster if the entrance wasn't as small as it was. At the rate they were able to waddle their awkward bodies and their swords into the room, Annabel and Jules were shooting them down.

Lou whipped her head all around the room, as if she was looking for something. Hallie followed her gaze across the carpet of dead nilbogs on the ground, up and down the dark stone walls—and then Lou's sapphire eyes stopped moving. They practically sparkled with relief. Hallie saw what she was looking at, and she hadn't even noticed it until now: it was a ladder. It appeared to be hanging from the ceiling, but when Hallie peered closer, she noticed a hole in the ceiling leading who-knows-where. She didn't care where it led, though. That ladder—that hole in the ceiling—was a way out of there.

"Get ready," Annabel said calmly over her shoulder as she fired another arrow. "They're starting to come in too fast."

And with that, part of the stone wall next to the entranceway burst apart. A few nilbogs came forward with the broken bits of stone, as if they had been using their bodies to crash through and make the doorway bigger. Levi wasted no time and bounded forward with his sword. Lou, however, chose a different path of action. She grabbed Jules' shirt before she could load another arrow, and then she pushed everyone else toward the ladder.

"Go, all of you!" she yelled over the nilbogs' shrieks and snorts. "Go! Up! Up the ladder! Now!" Her eyes were wider than Hallie had ever seen them. As much as she didn't want to leave her, the urgency in her voice made her listen without question.

Jules and Lindsay went first, scurrying up the ladder as fast as they could without slipping on the slimy iron rungs. Hallie didn't even want to think about exactly why they were slimy. Thomas took one last swing at a nilbog, who had gotten past Annabel and Levi, and then sheathed his sword. He climbed but only got about halfway before another nilbog got through, leapt up, and grabbed hold of his leg.

"Hey!" he exclaimed, hanging from the bars and using his other foot to kick the nilbog. "Get off me! Help! Lou!"

Quicker than a snap, Lou revealed a dagger that had been nestled in her belt. She threw it with the precision of a professional darts player, and it speared the nilbog clean through its neck. Thomas' cheeks went pale as he watched the nilbog fall off his leg and down to the ground below him, but he quickly regained his balance and continued his climb. Jenna began her climb, followed immediately by Alan.

"Come on, hurry!" Lindsay urged from the hole at the top. She and Jules were lifting Thomas through.

"Climb faster!" Alan exclaimed, constantly knocking his head on Jenna's heels.

"I'm going as fast as I—" And with that, Jenna's foot landed on a large spot of slime and slid right off the rung. She let out a yelp, holding on with her hands for dear life.

"Hold on, hold on!" said Alan, reaching out with one of his hands and grabbing her ankle. He guided her back onto the ladder, where she steadied herself.

Hallie turned and looked back one last time. Lou, Levi, and Annabel were doing quite well keeping the nilbogs at bay, but this group of nilbogs was even bigger than the last one.

"Hal!" Jenna called out. Hallie turned and looked up just in time to see Alan bonk his head on Jenna's foot again. "Let's go! What are you waiting for?"

Hallie didn't hesitate. She rushed up the ladder two rungs at a time. Luckily, everybody else had wiped most of the slime away with their feet and hands.

"What about Uncle Levi?" Jules shrieked as Lindsay and Thomas lifted Jenna through the hole. "And Lou? And Annabel? What about them?"

"They're fine," Alan grunted, hoisting himself up after Jenna. "They actually know how to fight, remember?" Hallie hoped and prayed he was right.

"Hallie!"

She turned around on the ladder to see Lou staring up at her urgently.

"Mom?"

"Two rights and then a left," Lou heaved. She spun around in a rather balletic turn and sliced a nilbog that was making its way toward her. Hallie gulped, trying to ignore the gurgle-squeal it gave as it fell.

"Two... um, two lefts and a right?"

"No! Two rights and then a left," said Lou. "Remember that, sweetheart, it's really important. Pawcombe's dungeons are built that way. Two rights and then a left. When you get to the clearing, stay there. We'll find you."

"But what happens if we—"

Lou wasn't paying attention because she had already gone back to help Levi fight off a trio of nilbogs. Hallie continued her final steps up the ladder, trying not to look down at the dead nilbog with Lou's dagger in its neck. Once she was up, Alan and Thomas found a large piece of broken stone and pushed it over the opening.

"That ought to hold it," said Alan, picking up smaller rocks and piling them on top as well.

"Yes," Thomas agreed, "The nilbogs lack the bodily proportion that will allow them to push this aside and keep their footing on the ladder."

"What do we do now?" asked Lindsay, looking around. Hallie looked, too. They were in what looked like an attic, but everything was made of the same wet stone that was everywhere else. There was a loud dripping sound coming from somewhere Hallie couldn't see. The ceiling was much lower here than it was in the dungeon below. Parts of the wall had crumbled in areas and there were crumbly stone pillars spread out in every direction. Aside from the commotion down below them, it was silent up there.

"I'm surprised the ceiling hasn't fallen down," said Jenna, also noticing the withered stone.

"Should we just start walking?" Lindsay tried to look across the room, but it was too dark to see anything. "Where are we supposed to go?"

"Two rights and then a left," Hallie blurted out. She paused, hoping she was remembering it correctly. "Yes. Two rights and then a left."

Jenna gave her a look. "What?"

"That's what Mom said before I got up here," said Hallie. "She said take two rights and then a left. We'll find a clearing, and we're supposed to wait there for them."

"A clearing?" Jenna looked all around, like she expected it to be in plain sight. "What kind of clearing?"

"Somewhere out of this place, I would guess," Lindsay replied, also looking around.

"Good, let's get going, then," said Jules. "This place gives me the creeps."

"Hal," said Jenna, pointing her arm up ahead. "You lead the way."

"Two rights and then a left," Hallie repeated to herself, and she began to walk.

CHAPTER 14:
THE TRUE SURPRISE

Jenna

THEY WALKED FOR WHAT seemed like an hour. They took their first right turn almost as soon as they started walking, but now the room stretched as far as they could see. There were so many pillars holding up the crumbly stone ceiling that every step looked exactly the same as the last. The room's only redeeming quality was that it wasn't completely dark, which meant there had to be light coming in from somewhere.

"Are you sure Mom said two rights and a left?" said Jenna. She looked around, not seeing any corners at all—just lots of pillars, and puddles of water on the floor. Where the water had come from, she didn't know.

"Yes, I'm sure," Hallie huffed. She swallowed. "I mean, I'm pretty sure..."

"I think we might be lost," Lindsay mumbled. "This place is a ghost town."

Jules gulped and reached for her bow. "Ghosts?"

"Our next right and left turns must be somewhere," Thomas said as confidently as he could. "Lou wouldn't have told us to come this way if it didn't lead anywhere."

"That's right," said Hallie. "She wouldn't have. So, let's just keep walking."

Jenna groaned. "My feet are starting to hurt."

"Oh, I'm sorry," said Hallie, turning on her and staring. "Would you rather stay here and take a cat-nap?"

Jenna rolled her eyes. "Jeez, Hal, calm down."

"Don't tell me to calm down! We're in a dungeon, Jenna. In a foreign country—no, a foreign *world*! I was calm when we had people to protect us, but now, well, once again, we're by ourselves. We're exposed."

"But, Hallie, we held our own," Alan said carefully. "I mean, we weren't totally useless down there. We each killed a few nilbogs."

Hallie scoffed. "You sound proud of that."

"Well, I am," said Alan. Everybody stopped and looked at him, and he continued. "They aren't human. They're evil creatures who work for an evil, bad man, and they were sent down there to kill us. Eat or be eaten, right? We were defending ourselves, we were defending the honour of the Sought Six, and we were defending Pawcombe. So, yeah, I'm proud."

Someone began clapping slowly from a few yards ahead of them. The sound echoed off every single pillar. They all jumped at the noise and Alan pulled out his sword.

"Who's there?" he demanded. The clapper emerged from behind one of the pillars. It was Klaus.

"Eloquently put, Alan," he said, still clapping. "You've got a way with words, I must say. You should think about becoming a writer when you grow up."

"Klaus!" they all exclaimed, relaxing with relief. Hallie and Jules hugged him, but he didn't hug them back.

"Man, are we glad to see you," said Alan, sheathing his sword.

"What happened up at the party?" Hallie asked. He was still dressed neatly in his suit, tie, and cape. "Is everyone okay?"

"They're fine. Nothing like a few mishaps to liven up a party."

"Listen, Klaus, I'm sorry I came down here," said Alan. "This isn't anybody else's fault. It's mine. I didn't listen to you."

Klaus looked strangely affable. "Not to worry, although the nilbogs were expecting different results, I'm sure."

Lindsay shook her head. "You... you knew those things were down there? You knew about the dungeon?"

"Of course I knew about the dungeon in my own house," he said, a smile playing at his lips. "Where else was I going to put the nilbogs? In the front foyer? Hire them as manservants in tuxedos?" His tone caused everyone to take a small step back.

"What's going on?" Hallie asked timidly. "You're— you're being weird."

"Klaus, the nilbogs tried to kill us!" said Jenna. She didn't know why, but her heart was beginning to speed up. "We're the Sought Six... we can't do our jobs if we're dead."

Klaus nodded. "Those are the rules, yes."

Jenna swallowed hard. "So, why would you let creatures who are working for Zyngor... I mean, why would you let them live here if they want to kill us?"

Klaus scoffed. "The nilbogs only do what they're told. They aren't the brightest of beasts, but there are a lot of them in Pawcombe. So, for the sake of numbers, it's good to have them here."

"I... I don't understand..." It took everything Jenna had to steady her breathing. "The nilbogs tried to kill us, Klaus."

"For crying out loud, children, wake up!" Now, Klaus' face became angry—so angry, in fact, that everybody took another step back. His voice dropped a tone. "The nilbogs were only following orders. And since this is my house, *I* gave those orders. *I'm* the one who tried to kill you. Me. Now do you understand?"

"What... you..." Jenna swallowed. "Why?"

"But you're supposed to be helping us!" said Jules, practically in tears already. "You're on our side. Aren't you?"

"Aren't I?" Klaus said, almost sweetly. It gave Jenna chills. "On a mission as important as annihilating the Sought Six, wouldn't it be smarter for The Great Zyngor to use a spy that Maple Cliff already knows and trusts?"

Hallie leaned close to Jenna and whispered, "The *Great* Zyngor...?"

"Spy?" Thomas' eyes blinked fast behind his glasses. "Then... then *you're* the one who let the assassin into Maple the night Winston Pearce was killed!"

"Very good, Thomas," said Klaus, mock-clapping, "but that good-for-nothing assassin the Master chose couldn't seem to do his part!"

Jenna held her stomach. Her gut wrenched hearing him refer to Zyngor as 'the Master'. She gulped. "His... his part?"

"He was outrun by two little girls. The only thing he did right was eliminating that useless, withered old man, Winston Pearce—whose pot roast isn't even that good, by the way. I've certainly had better. I don't know what that batty old Denny was talking about."

"Don't talk about Denny like that!" Jules exclaimed, finding a moment of nerve.

"Wait a second," said Hallie. "When the assassin was dying on the ground after Annabel shot him off his horse, he started talking to someone. He said '*you*', like he was mad at someone, and... he was talking to *you*, wasn't he, Klaus?"

Klaus looked impressed. "I must say, you're a smarter Sought Six than we were, back in the day. At times, it seemed I had to carry the lion's share of the brains and leave the brawn to Dewey-Eyed-Levi." He scoffed. "If that dopey jock paid half as much attention to you kids as he does to Picture-Perfect-Lou, you might not even be in this mess right now. But, sadly for you, that isn't the case."

Jules bounded forward suddenly, her hands in fists. She punched Klaus' body a few times before he grabbed her arms and shoved her onto the cold, wet ground, not at all gently.

"You're all so pathetic," he sneered as they knelt to help her back up. He fixed his suit and tie. "Why Maple Cliff would entrust you with the location of the Sterling Cone is beyond me."

Everybody perked up.

"Ah," said Klaus, noticing, "my suspicions are confirmed! You *do* know about the Sterling Cone!"

Alan shrugged, trying to act casual. "What do you care?"

"I care because the Master cares," Klaus growled. He seemed to stand taller in this room than he ever had before, maybe because the ceiling was so low, but more likely because he was being so nasty and brooding. "The Sterling Cone will grant the Master his wish to make Pawcombe a better place. The last thing he needs is six little brats standing in his way."

Jenna scoffed. "A better place? How exactly? By ruining it? And anyway, *we're* the Sought Six! It's our job to stand in his way!"

Immediately, she wished hadn't spoken. Klaus was calm for a moment, but then he swung his arm across his body and gave her a backhanded slap across her face. Instantly, her eyes filled with tears. The sound of the slap was sharp; her ears were ringing as she brought her hand to her cheek, now flaming and reddening.

"Klaus, stop!" Alan pleaded as Hallie comforted Jenna. "We don't know where the Sterling Cone is! We don't even know *what* it is! We swear!"

"Oh, what a load of bull!" Klaus spat. He pointed a bony finger at them. "You've all been briefed about it. I know you have, and Maple Cliff is leaving me out of it."

"Well, you can forget it, Klaus," said Jules, still riding the wave of her nerve. "Even if we knew where the Sterling Cone was, we wouldn't tell you. Not when you're working for Zyngor! Not when you've betrayed us and the others!"

Klaus sighed. "I was afraid you'd feel that way. That leaves me with no alternative." He pulled out his sword and his upper lip twitched. "Oh, how the Master will reward me."

"Run!" Alan yelled loudly, so loudly that everyone else followed him without even thinking. The right side of Jenna's face was still stinging, and she could barely see out of her right eye. Still, she ran. She heard the swipe as Klaus' sword swung after them.

"You think you can outrun me?" he shouted. Jenna looked over her shoulder and, even though her eye was sore and fuzzy, she could see he wasn't chasing after them.

"This is my domain, kids! Just try to escape me."

"What do we do?" Hallie shrieked. "Where do we go?"

"Keep running!" said Alan, pushing their shoulders. "We're still going in the same direction as before—our next right turn must be around here somewhere!"

Just then, a big puff of smoke burst from the ground in front of them. In the middle of it, there was Klaus, sword still at the ready. Everybody stopped running. Jules and Hallie squealed in a start.

"It's pointless to run." He adjusted his cape on his shoulders and dusted off the smoke, looking oddly proud of it. Then Jenna understood. The cape was magic.

"Your... your cape..."

"I can go anywhere I want in the blink of an eye. Clever, no? The Master bewitched it for me when I pledged my loyalty to him."

"He... he can do that?" Jules mumbled.

"He can do anything."

Jenna didn't like the way he said that.

"Listen, kids, this can all be over with very quickly," Klaus went on. "Tell me where the Sterling Cone is, and I'll leave you alone. It's that simple. You'll have to find your own way out of here, of course, but I'll leave you in peace. And alive."

"Yeah, until Zyngor ruins Pawcombe," Lindsay sneered. She took a deep breath. "Forget it, Klaus. We're done with you."

Klaus grinned at first, amused by her boldness. Then he just became angry. He lifted his sword high above his head and threw it down in front of him. Everyone separated; four of them jumping to the right and two of them jumping to the left, all of them managing to avoid the strike.

Jenna lifted herself off Thomas, who had jumped to the left with her. As they got to their feet, Klaus was looking between the two groups, knowing he couldn't chase them both. It only took a fraction of a second for Thomas to work out their solution.

"Separate the lock from the key," he said, nodding to the others. "Go, you guys! Split up!" And with that, he took Jenna's hand and ran away from Klaus. Jenna heard Klaus growl in frustration as, no doubt, the other four ran off in the opposite direction.

"Behind here, quickly!" said Jenna, pulling Thomas around a dusty pillar. "Is he following us?"

Thomas looked. "No, it doesn't look like it. He must have gone after the others."

She sighed. She hoped they'd all be okay. She leaned against the pillar, trusting it wouldn't crumble from her weight, and held her sore eye.

"Is it bad?" Thomas asked in a whisper.

She nodded. "It feels like it's twice its normal size."

"Let's see."

She brought her hand down and turned to face him. Instantly, he winced.

"What?" she gasped.

"Nothing."

"You don't wince for nothing, Thomas!"

"Well, you've almost certainly got the beginnings of a shiner," he said, peering closer, "and it does look a little swollen. That's probably why it feels larger than normal. We'll need to get some ice on it as soon as possible."

Jenna wanted to cry, but she held her tears in and steeled herself. "How could Klaus do this? How could he betray us? Mom, Levi, Annabel, Denny... they're his friends."

Thomas shook his head. "If there's one thing about Pawcombe I think we need to understand, it's this: not everybody is good. And anyway, human beings are fickle creatures. Perhaps Klaus was frightened into siding with Zyngor."

"Frightened away from everything he knew? Everyone who loved him and would have protected him if he had just asked?"

Thomas shrugged. "What do you think he looks like?"

"Who? Zyngor?"

"Yes."

"Well, he's... I mean, probably..." Jenna paused. She hadn't given it much thought. All anybody had said about him so far was that he was an evil, bad man. That put an image of a monster in her mind, but no details. She almost preferred it that way, especially since she saw with her own eyes what happened to Winston Pearce back in Maple. She didn't want to even imagine the face of the person who arranged that.

"I think he's big," said Thomas. "I don't know why. I just think he's larger than the average man. Oh, and with black hair."

"So, like a bigger version of Klaus?"

Thomas thought. "Perhaps."

"As if we need two of them." Jenna sighed again. "I still can't believe he could do this. Do you think my mom and the others know?"

"Hard to say. Surely they would have mentioned it down in the dungeon. Something like this doesn't exactly make for a slow news day."

"AAARRRRGGGHHHH!"

Jenna and Thomas jumped and ducked closer to the pillar. Klaus' deep, booming scream was so loud that it echoed multiple times off each pillar and wall.

"Where are you, you little brats?!" he shouted. There was a swishing sound of a sword slicing through the air, and then a crashing sound of the blade hitting something. Then they could hear the crumbling of stones. He must have broken a pillar or part of the wall.

Jenna gulped. She took Thomas' hand.

"I know you're here somewhere," Klaus' voice echoed. It seemed to be getting closer. "You can't hide."

Jenna forced herself not to think of the reasons Klaus was now coming this way. He had either lost the others within this mess of pillars and darkness, or he had... he had... She gulped again.

"I will find you," Klaus went on. The angry, eager sound of his voice made Jenna imagine he was tip-toeing around with his hands up and his sword ready, like a villain from a fairy tale. "I *will* find you! I know you're in here."

Jenna briefly considered moving out from behind the pillar and finding another one. As if he read her mind, Thomas squeezed her hand and mouthed, "Don't move."

"I wish you would see reason," Klaus' voice echoed. "Just tell me what you know about the Sterling Cone. Tell me what Maple Cliff is keeping from me, then we can all go home."

After a few moments, they could no longer hear his footsteps. Jenna squeezed her eyes shut and tried to think of something to say about the Sterling Cone—whatever it was—if he found them. Maybe they could just make something up. They could tell him it was in one of the other forests. Oak, maybe. No, Zyngor lived in Oak. If it was there, he'd have found it by now.

Thomas nudged her arm gently and she opened her eyes. "Do you see him?" he mouthed.

Jenna swallowed hard. She tip-toed closer to the edge of the pillar. She peeked around. There was nobody in sight. In fact, the only things around were the bits of broken stone all over the floor. She looked back at Thomas and shook her head, but just as she did—

"BOO!"

Jenna yelped and Thomas jumped out of his skin. They both fell backward as Klaus stood over them, laughing at their fear. He lifted his sword above his head.

"You're mine," he growled.

"Come on!" Thomas urged, scrambling back to his feet and pulling Jenna to hers. "Run!"

They ran out from behind the pillar just as Klaus swung his sword at them. He meant to slice them, but he ended up slicing clean through the pillar. It crumbled down to the ground behind them.

Jenna looked behind her, the broken bits of pillar rolling after them. "Jeez! How sharp is his sword?!"

"I'm not sure I want to know!" said Thomas, taking her hand. "Just run!"

They had turned around so much that they didn't know where they were going. For all they knew, they could have been running back the way they came. All the pillars made it easy for them to zig-zag around the room, which also meant Klaus had a harder time hitting them. Even still, he wasn't following them very quickly. He seemed to be enjoying the chase more than the idea of catching them.

With a loud grunt, he swung his sword through another one of the pillars, causing it (not to mention the part of the ceiling it was holding up) to come crashing down to the ground. Thomas pulled Jenna's hand and dodged sideways to avoid being hit, but they kept running. Klaus laughed manically and loudly. He sounded like he had lost his mind.

"Give it up, kids!" Klaus shouted, slicing another pillar. This time, one of the falling bits of stone bounced off the back of Jenna's leg.

"Ouch!" She almost fell forward, but she kept running.

"He knows you have it! He will take it from you!" Klaus was beginning to sound hysterical. Jenna didn't like that; it probably meant he was going to start chasing them faster. "One way or another, he'll get what he wants. And when he does, you'll all be very, very sorry!"

"Where do we go?" Jenna shrieked, looking around and seeing nothing but pillars. "There's no way out!"

Klaus sliced through another pillar, causing that chunk of the ceiling to crash down as well. The room was falling apart more and more by the minute.

Thomas took Jenna's hand and coughed in all the dust. "This way!" he said, pulling her and running around a group of pillars. At first, Jenna had no idea where he was leading her, but then she saw what he must have been seeing: light.

"Get back here, you little monsters!" Klaus' voice boomed. In his anger, he sliced through two more pillars. The entire room was beginning to make deep cracking noises that Jenna didn't like one bit.

"He's going to make the entire room come crashing down on us!"

"Then we'd best not be in this room!" Thomas replied, picking up the pace. They ran so fast toward the light that they thought their legs might fall off.

"Why isn't he using his cape?" Jenna looked behind them to where Klaus was chasing them, albeit slowly because of all the fallen stones in his way.

"He doesn't appear to be wearing it," said Thomas, also looking behind them. "Let's not question it! It's our saving grace at the moment!"

The light was getting closer. It appeared to be coming from a giant hole in the wall, through which there was either a bonfire or some torches—Jenna didn't really care which.

"AAARRRRGGGHHH!" Klaus yelled, noticing how close they were to escaping. They heard his sword cut through another pillar, and a huge part of the ceiling crumbled down with it.

They practically jumped through the opening once they got there. Jenna didn't even realize until she completely crashed into people that they weren't alone in the huge clearing. Hallie, Alan, Jules and Lindsay were all there, waiting for them.

"Jenna!" Hallie exclaimed, catching her and stopping her sprint. She held her tight. "We could hear the stones breaking and crashing from out here. We thought maybe you guys had... well..."

"Where's Klaus?" asked Lindsay, taking Thomas' shoulders in her hands. "Where is he?"

"He's been knocking down all the pillars!" Thomas exclaimed, spinning on his heels to face the opening in the wall. "He's gone mad!"

Jenna also turned around. She could see a shadowy figure heading toward the opening, and the shiny silver gleam that was most certainly a sword. The cracking and crunching sounds of falling stones behind him were unyielding, and finally...

The whole place shook as if there was an earthquake. Several of them wobbled on their feet and fell to the ground. Jenna forced herself to look over at Klaus. He, too, had fallen over, right before the opening in the wall. He was about to gather himself up, but that's when the entire wall shifted. The ceiling inside the stone opening came crashing down at last, creaking and almost wailing as it did. Enough pillars had fallen in there that the weak stone could hold its own no longer.

Jenna kept her eyes on Klaus, lying flat on his back. He looked up toward the falling chunks of stone, a fierce look on his face, and—

That was it, because then Jenna closed her eyes.

CHAPTER 15:
THE SEWER EXPRESS

Hallie

EVERYBODY STOOD TOGETHER IN a huddle against the wall, protecting one another from the collapsing pieces of stone. Luckily, the clearing they were in was big enough that they were able to stay out of the direct path of any incoming rocks. The dust that flew up from the ground made it impossible to see anything for quite a while—not that Hallie was particularly keen on seeing Klaus' dead body once it settled, if it wasn't buried under the broken pieces of the wall and ceiling.

"Well," said Alan, swallowing hard, "that's the end of him!"

"I hope the adults aren't too upset," said Jules.

"Unlikely," said Thomas, in his matter-of-fact tone. "Death is horrible, of course, but Klaus was a traitor. A liar. A murderer, even."

"He didn't kill us," said Hallie, but she didn't know if she was trying to reassure the rest of them or herself by saying that.

Thomas cleaned the dust off his glasses with his shirt. "That's true, and he allowed Zyngor's assassin to kill Winston Pearce rather than doing it himself, but with all that in mind, it's possible he could have committed murder elsewhere at another time. And don't forget, this was definitely a *him or us* scenario. One of us was going to die in here, if not more than one."

Hallie shook her head. "Can we talk about something else, please?"

Jenna swallowed. "What happened to his cape? He wasn't wearing it when he was chasing me and Thomas."

"I ripped it off before we got away from him," said Alan. He gently stroked her sore eye with his thumb. "Man, he really got you."

Jenna winced. "Careful!" she snapped.

"Sorry."

"How did you rip it off?"

"What?"

"The cape."

"Oh. Well, I'm wicked-fast."

Jenna stared at him. "Wicked-fast?"

He sighed. "Luck. I got lucky, okay?"

Hallie groaned. "That seems to be our mantra tonight."

"Guys, do you see what I see? Or, rather, what I *don't* see?" asked Lindsay, looking around the dusty clearing. "If this is the clearing we were supposed to find, where are Lou, Levi, and Annabel?"

"Hey, yeah!" said Jenna. "They said they'd meet us here!"

"Oh, you don't think the nilbogs... you know..." Jules muttered as she began to bite her nails.

"No," Hallie said quickly. "No. Maybe this just isn't the right clearing. We got all turned around when Klaus was chasing us. Who knows where we are right now!"

Jules huffed. "That isn't exactly comforting."

"Maybe we should just start walking," Lindsay suggested. She pointed to a threshold out of the clearing. Hallie looked into the dark hole in the wall, and that was when she heard something. She strained to listen. It sounded like a strong wind, or maybe even flowing water.

"But if this *is* where we're supposed to be," Jenna continued, "shouldn't we wait here for Mom and the others to find us?"

Alan shook his head. "What if more nilbogs show up after hearing the place collapse?"

"We could also run into more nilbogs if we start walking," countered Jenna.

"Well, what do you want to do?"

"Guys!" Hallie snapped. She pointed toward the threshold. "Listen! Do you hear that?"

Everyone listened.

Thomas nodded his head. "Yes. It sounds like water." Then, his eyes lit up behind his dirty glasses. "Hey, you don't suppose that way leads outside, do you? Perhaps near a lake or, more likely, a riverbank?"

"It might," said Hallie. "I say we go check it out. We have our weapons if we need them. Besides, part of this place has already crumbled into pieces, and I don't want to be around if the rest of it decides to do the same." She looked up at the high stone ceiling, already full of cracks.

"Yeah," said Jules, looking up and gripping her bow. "Alright, let's just go."

The hallway through the threshold was narrow. They had to walk in single file. As they got further away from the clearing—away from Klaus' dead body—Hallie felt a chill run up her spine. How could Klaus have fooled Denny and the rest of Maple Cliff for so long? Had he always been a traitor, or had he become one after his time as a Sought Six member? Those types of questions consumed her thoughts until they found themselves close to the rushing water sounds, then all she could think about was finding the river or lake, or whatever it was.

Eventually, the hallway they were taking led out to another clearing; this room was lined with wall-mounted torches. They appeared to be on some type of mezzanine; there was an iron railing over which they looked down to a rushing stream of dirty water. It was probably a fifteen- or maybe even twenty-foot drop. And the room stunk, too—it was just like sewage.

"Ugh!" Hallie held her nose. "Where are we? A sewer tunnel?"

"Hey!" Jenna exclaimed, whacking Hallie in the arm. "It's Mom! Mom! Mom, over here!"

Hallie looked across the river to another mezzanine, identical to the one they were standing on. Sure enough, there was Lou. She was standing with Annabel and Levi, and they all looked incredibly worried.

"Mom!" Hallie yelled, waving her arm. Lou took one look at them all standing there and collapsed to her knees, covering her face. They couldn't hear her because the stream below them was so loud, but she was surely happy-crying. Levi held her shoulders and comforted her as Annabel waved at them.

"The bridge!" she yelled.

Hallie looked at the others. "Huh? What bridge?"

Thomas pointed further down the railing. "*That* bridge, I assume!" he said. There, connecting the mezzanine they were on to the mezzanine the adults were on, was a rickety old bridge. It appeared to be made only of pieces of rotting wood and frayed rope.

"You have to take the bridge!" Annabel yelled, slowly and clearly.

Hallie couldn't believe what she was hearing. "Oh, I don't think so! It looks to be older than all of us combined!"

"Yeah," said Lindsay. "Have they even looked at that thing? It's got 'death trap' written all over it!"

Jules cupped her hands. "Isn't it dangerous?" she yelled.

"It's the only way across!" Levi called. "It'll be fine! Just go slow and steady! Don't bunch up! Keep moving so your weight doesn't settle!"

"In other words, it might break," said Hallie. She crossed her arms. "Nope. No way."

"I agree," said Thomas, walking down the line to examine the bridge. "It looks like it's had years of damp eating away at it, and... oh, and there's a possible sign of termite infestation."

"If Uncle Levi says it's okay, then it's okay," Jules said firmly as she started to cross the bridge. Her very first step caused the bridge to squeak and sway, but she kept on walking. Alan followed her lead, and the two of them were across in no time. The bridge made a lot of noise, but there was no sign of breakage.

"It's not so bad," Alan called. "A little shaky, but alright."

"Shaky," said Hallie, her stomach churning. "Fantastic."

"Come on, let's just get it over with," said Jenna, looking over her shoulder at Hallie, Lindsay and Thomas. "Would you rather stay here?"

Thomas followed without delay. Lindsay groaned loudly but followed as well. Hallie couldn't quite bring herself to step onto the planks.

"Come on, sweetheart!" Lou called. She was so earnest; her eyes were flashing so much that Hallie could see their blue hue from where she was. "Please! It's the only way!"

Hallie sighed. "I can't believe I'm doing this," she muttered, and she stepped on.

"That's it, just take it easy," Lou was saying. "You've got it. Keep moving." For a few moments, everything seemed alright. The bridge was holding up just fine, and they were almost there. Then—

Snap! Crack!

"What was that?" Hallie shrieked, her eyes darting around every which way.

Snap! Snap! Crack! Crack!

Lou seemed to know what was going to happen before it even happened. Her eyes went wide and she

177

yelled at them to hurry off the bridge, but it was too late. The weak wood underneath their feet cracked and splintered, the bridge collapsed, and the four of them fell, the broken bits of wood falling through the air as they tumbled down into the rushing sewer water below.

Hallie didn't dare open her mouth or her eyes until she had come up from under the water. It smelled putrid and felt slimy against her body. The sound of it rushing was much louder now that she was in it, but the loudest sound by far was Lou screaming from above them.

"Swim!" she was saying. "Swim to the side! Swim hard!"

Hallie tried, but it was no use. Lindsay coughed as she tried to fight against the rushing water, but she couldn't muscle her way through it. Lindsay was arguably the most athletic of the four of them; if she couldn't fight it, Hallie knew there wasn't much chance of her, Jenna, or Thomas being able to.

"The current!" Thomas yelled, spitting out a rush of water that had just splashed into his mouth. "It's too strong!"

"Guys!" Jenna exclaimed in horror, splashing about. "Up ahead! Look!"

Hallie did look. There was an opening in the stone wall ahead of them, and it led into a small dark tunnel. All the water was rushing so quickly toward the opening that Hallie wondered if some sort of suction was pulling everything in.

"Swim!" Lou kept yelling as the group made their way down the mezzanine to the side of the water. Hallie looked back briefly and saw all of them, panic-stricken, rushing along the edge. A splash of water slapped against her head suddenly, but it wasn't only water. It was sticky and slimy. She thought she might throw up.

Jenna gasped as she inched closer and closer to the dark tunnel. She could see how small the tunnel was versus how much water was rushing into it. There was hardly any room for air, if any at all.

"Hold your breath!" Jenna yelled. She had just enough time to take a big gulp of air before submerging under the water and into the tunnel.

"Jenna!" Lou screamed, much louder than the water. "No! Jenna!"

Hallie turned and tried once again to swim to the side, but she couldn't. Thomas and Lindsay drifted quickly into the tunnel after Jenna, and Hallie had just enough time to take a breath before the current pulled her in, too.

CHAPTER 16:
THE GRYPHON EXPRESS

Jenna

JENNA BURST THROUGH THE water's surface and heaved a breath of air. She barely had enough will left in her arms and legs to keep her afloat, but luckily the water wasn't too deep anymore. She had used up all her strength trying to fight the current in the small dark tunnel, which was useless. It rushed them all very quickly, submerging them fully under the slimy sewer water, to the clearing where they were now.

Jenna crawled out of the water and onto the cold wet rock just as the others burst up out of the water. They coughed and gulped the air, which smelled very musty, Jenna noticed. She looked around. They appeared to be in a cave of some sort, where the only exit was the small pool of sewer water from which the tunnel had just spit them. There was nobody else in there with them, but there was an area of the stone wall that was blocked off by large iron bars, like a cage. She couldn't see who or what might be locked behind them, though.

There was an echo of a crow cawing, and when Jenna looked up to find it, that was when she saw the hole. It was an opening in the rock far above them through which Jenna could see the moon. If she didn't know better, she might have thought they were sitting inside some sort of mountain or volcano that towered high above the forest floor, but the trees were also visible from the bottom up through this hole. They were still underground.

Hallie pulled herself out of the slimy water and whimpered in disgust. She wanted to wipe the sludge off her body but she couldn't decide where to start, so she just stood there and trembled.

"My glasses!" Thomas exclaimed, digging and splashing through the water. "They fell off! Where are my glasses? Can you guys help me? Oh, here they are! Never mind!"

"Whoa, look at that cage," said Lindsay, noticing the same cage Jenna had noticed. "Do you see what's in it?"

"No," said Jenna, peering across at it. "I can't see. What is it?"

"They look like..." Lindsay walked a few steps further, and then jolted backward once her suspicions had been confirmed. "Whoa! Yes! They're gryphons! Gryphons! Honestly! I swear, Pawcombe just keeps getting stranger and stranger."

Jenna rushed forward. Sure enough, behind the bars, were two very large, very frightened-looking gryphons. They had brown feathers on their eagle top halves, and golden fur on their lion bottom halves. Their eyes were the same sapphire blue as Lou's, and equally as kind.

"What are they doing here?" Jenna wondered aloud.

"Klaus must have captured them. Look at the initials on the padlocks. VH. Vandnav Hall, maybe?"

"This underground volcano-cave thing is part of Vandnav Hall?" Jenna looked around yet again. "I guess it's all connected to his dungeon, but still. This is crazy."

"Speaking of which, where exactly are we? You think we're still in Cedar?" Lindsay looked up through the hole. She cupped her hands around her mouth and shouted, "Hello?"

"Shh! What if someone bad hears you?" said Jenna.

"How else are we supposed to get out of here? Look, there aren't any other holes or pathways. Just solid rock."

"Oh, this is just great! Look at my leg!" Hallie exclaimed, throwing her arms up in anguish. "It's bleeding! Look at it!"

Jenna looked. The bottom half of Hallie's right leg had a cut the length of her finger, and it had a fair bit of blood around it.

"How did that happen?" said Thomas, staring at it interestedly.

"I don't know... Something in that sewer must have cut me. I might have rabies now. Or scurvy." She groaned loudly. "This is the worst thing that has ever happened to me."

"Hallie, it's going to be alright," Thomas said gently. "It isn't bleeding too much, and the slime from the water doesn't appear to have contaminated it."

"That's not what I meant... but, gross!" she shrieked. "I'm talking about *this* place! Look around! We're trapped! We're trapped and nobody knows where we are!"

"Hallie, calm down," said Thomas in a soothing tone. "Breathe in, breathe out. In and out."

"I don't want to calm down!"

"But you're panicking."

"Well, I think this is an appropriate time to panic, don't you?!"

"Guys, stop it. We have to try to think positively," said Lindsay. She massaged her temples with her fingertips. "Right now, we have to focus on getting out of here. Let's just think this through. We can't go back the way we came." She looked at the pond of sewer water and crinkled her nose.

"Yes," Thomas agreed, "I wouldn't trust our lung capacities against the current. It's much too strong, and that tunnel wasn't exactly short."

"But there must be some other way out of here." Lindsay looked up at the moon way above them. "I mean, Klaus got out of here somehow after he locked up the gryphons, right?"

"Yeah," said Jenna, looking around, "good point."

"We're missing something," said Lindsay. "It's probably right in front of our faces and we just can't see it."

"The cape," said Thomas, his face sinking. "Klaus' stupid cape."

"What about his stupid cape?" said Hallie.

"It allows him passage from one place to another. That's what he told us."

Jenna's legs gave out and she fell to a seated position on the rocks, which seemed to startle one of the gryphons because it squawked. Her heart began pounding in her ears.

"So, you're saying after Klaus locked up the gryphons down here, he just snapped his fingers and left in a puff of smoke?" she said, pointing upward.

"Most likely."

"I knew it," said Hallie. "We are trapped down here."

"Wait," said Jenna. She stared thoughtfully at the gryphons, gnawing at their bars. "Wait a second. I think I have an idea."

"Jenna, I'm sorry, but I do believe Hallie is right," said Thomas, sitting down next to her. "Humans are incapable of such transportation unless we have a Root Path or the proper cape, evidently. What do you propose?"

"We can free the gryphons," said Jenna. "Then we can fly them out of here."

Thomas leapt back to his feet, as if he had some renewed energy. "I stand corrected." His eyes lit up with excitement.

"Hold on," said Lindsay, stepping forward. "Let's not get carried away. Think about it. How are four kids supposed to burst through those iron bars and padlocks? And even if we could, what makes you think the gryphons won't just fly out of here the second we get the doors open? We'd still be trapped. For all we know, they're Klaus' pets or something. And even if all of that wasn't a problem, how do *we* fly gryphons? Unless you've all been having secret flying lessons..."

Jenna looked at her wryly. "Is there a better idea?"

"Jenna's right," said Hallie suddenly, and Jenna was tempted to ask her to repeat herself. "Even if they do fly away or something, we'd be no worse off than we are now."

Lindsay sighed and shrugged her shoulders. "Okay, so the bars... How do we—"

"Pardon me, ladies," Thomas said suddenly, hobbling past them with a large rock, much larger than he looked capable of carrying. He aimed it at the padlock on the bars. The gryphons' blue eyes widened and they backed away.

Jenna stood up. "Thomas, what on earth are you—"

Smash!

The padlock snapped clean off the bars as he threw the rock down against it. The cage door, although it didn't move on its hinges, was free.

The gryphons were squawking in alarm, but neither of them made a move to test their exit yet.

Thomas looked quite proud of himself as he adjusted his glasses on his face.

"It took an IQ of a million to figure that one out," Lindsay muttered to Jenna and Hallie in disbelief. They all walked over to the cell, where Thomas was already trying to befriend the gryphons.

"Here now, gents," he said. He started making kissing noises. "It's okay. We won't hurt you."

The gryphons were obviously cautious because they stayed close to the back of the cage.

"Should we go in?" said Lindsay, reaching for one of the bars.

"No," said Hallie, taking her hand. "We should probably wait for them come to us. If we walk up to them now, we'll be cornering them."

"Here you go," said Thomas, reaching his arm past them through the bars. He had a dead rat in his hand.

"Ugh!" Hallie shrieked, leaping back. "And where the heck did you find *that*?"

"On the ground, obviously," Thomas said. "It's not like I carry dead rodents around in my pocket." He adjusted his voice again to talk to the gryphons. "Here you go. Look what I found for you. Are you hungry?"

Apparently, they were. Both the gryphons bounded forward and squawked their appreciation. The girls leapt backward, but Thomas stayed put and tossed the rat to them. They caught it—one on each end—and very quickly tore it in half with their beaks, making a crunching sound. As they began munching happily on their own halves, Hallie turned around.

"Okay," she said, scrunching her face and holding her stomach, "that was the grossest thing I have ever seen."

"They sure like that rat," said Jenna, watching them swallow the last few bits. "Maybe there's another one around here somewhere."

"Here," said Thomas, bending over and scraping some mud off another one. "This one's fatter. They'll like this one."

"Why are there so many dead rats in this cave?" Lindsay moaned, checking the ground around her feet.

Thomas shrugged. "Want to feed them? It's easy."

Lindsay scoffed. "Pass."

"Okay, I'll do it," said Jenna. She reached out to take the rat, but Hallie shoved her arm in front of Jenna's.

"Jenna, please," she said. "It's a rat. A *dead* rat. A disease-carrying dead rat."

"Hal, relax. It's not like I'm the one eating it," said Jenna. She reached past Hallie and took the rat from Thomas. It was very cold and slimy and much heavier than she thought it would be.

"Your sister is not wrong, Jenna," said Thomas. "We'll need to wash our hands as soon as we can. Rodents carry a plethora of diseases."

"Fine, we can do that once we're out of here," said Jenna. "I, for one, would like to make sure we actually do get out of here. That means we need these gryphons to like us."

Hallie groaned. "Fine, just be careful. I'm not going to be the one explaining to Mom why your hand was bitten off."

Jenna rolled her eyes as she walked toward the bars. The gryphons perked up as she held out her hand. She tossed the rat to them, which they happily caught. Hallie covered her ears when they ripped this rat in two.

"You think they understand English?" said Jenna.

"Jenna, they're animals, not humans," said Hallie.

"Yes, I'm afraid it is highly unlikely," Thomas agreed.

Jenna tried anyway. "Hey, guys. I, uh, I hope you liked those rats. Listen, um, we need your help. We need to get out of here. Can you help us do that?"

The gryphons swallowed the last of the rat and looked right at Jenna. They blinked their sapphire eyes very slowly. Jenna took that as a 'yes'.

"Can you fly us up through that hole?" she went on, pointing up. "Like, you know, can we ride on your backs?"

Again, the gryphons blinked slowly.

Jenna looked back at everybody else, who were all watching her in disbelief.

Thomas shrugged, looking impressed. "I stand corrected once again."

"Okay, there's two of them and four of us," said Lindsay, stepping forward. She looked unsure of this plan, but since they had no other options, she wasn't going to spit on it. "That means two of us will ride one, and two of us will ride the other."

One of the gryphons squawked quietly, non-threatening. It knelt on its eagle legs as its lion tail swished. It looked at Jenna and Lindsay.

Jenna stepped forward and opened the cage door. She tentatively gave the gryphon a pat on its neck. Its feathers were smooth like silk. Despite being trapped in a cold cave, its body felt warm.

"Good gryphon," she said. She swung her leg around and sat on its shoulders. "Linds, come on, sit behind me."

In the time that it took Lindsay to approach the gryphon, say hello to it, make sure it was okay with her presence, and sit down behind Jenna, Hallie and Thomas had already mounted the other gryphon.

"How do we make them go?" asked Hallie, focusing hard on sitting still.

"Well, they seem to understand what we're saying," said Thomas. He cleared his throat. "Excuse me, gents, I believe we're ready to go now."

The gryphons both squawked rather happily and began prancing on their eagle talons.

"Hold on!" Lindsay shrieked, grabbing Jenna's waist. Jenna reached forward without hesitation and gripped the smooth feathers on the gryphon's neck.

The gryphons waltzed out of the cage. Their gait was very smooth. They both took a few deep breaths and spread their wings. Jenna was amazed at how large their wingspan was—it had to be at least ten feet on both sides. They flapped their wings for a few moments but made no move to fly.

"What are they doing?" said Thomas, looking down at the one on which he was sitting.

"Stretching, probably," said Jenna, watching her gryphon. "They've been stuck in that cage for who knows how long."

Just then, the gryphon stood up on its lion legs, rearing happily. It squawked again before bounding off the ground with such a force that Jenna was afraid she and Lindsay might slide right off, but they didn't. The gryphon's wings kept on flapping, keeping them in the air, and then Jenna realized her eyes were closed. She opened them.

"Hey, we're flying!" She looked behind her to see Lindsay looking relieved that they were indeed on their way out of there. The other gryphon holding Hallie and Thomas was following closely behind. Hallie was holding on for dear life, but Thomas was quite enjoying the view with the wind blowing through his ginger hair.

"This is marvellous!" he shouted. He let go of the gryphon's neck and held his arms out to the wind. "Absolutely marvellous!"

"What are you doing? Don't let go!" Hallie shrieked, slapping his middle.

Jenna couldn't help but laugh as she looked up at the sky, seeing the moon get closer and closer. Soon enough they were flying twenty, maybe thirty, feet above the topmost branches of the cedar trees. The gryphons levelled themselves in the air, making it much easier for everyone to stay sitting on their backs.

After what must have been twenty minutes of whizzing over the cedar trees, a new scent filled the air. Jenna recognized it immediately.

"Pinecones," she muttered. Then she raised her voice: "Do you guys smell that?"

"All I smell are farts," Hallie called out in a nasally voice because she was holding her nose. "Our gryphon is farting."

"Yes," Thomas agreed. "Perhaps those rats aren't quite agreeing with him. You alright there, sir?" He gently patted the gryphon's neck, but the gryphon looked quite happy to be passing gas in the air.

"Guys, look," said Lindsay, pointing forward past Jenna. Jenna looked ahead at the carpet of trees before them. They weren't cedar trees anymore. Lindsay squeezed her waist excitedly. "Pine trees!"

Jenna tightened her grip on the gryphon. "This must be Pawcombe's city called Pine!"

"But why are they taking us to Pine? Shouldn't we be going back to Maple?" Lindsay leaned slightly forward over Jenna's shoulder so she could speak to the gryphon. "Excuse me, are we going to the right place?"

Both gryphons squawked delightedly in response but made no move to change their course. Quite the contrary, they flapped their wings to quicken their pace onward.

"They seem to know where they're going," Jenna shrugged.

"I guess." Lindsay held Jenna's middle tighter. "Better to ask questions once we're safe on solid ground, anyway."

Jenna closed her eyes and breathed in the scent of pine (although, she was now starting to get a faint whiff of farts as well), let the wind blow her sandy-blonde hair every which way, and feel the gryphon's warm, strong body beneath her, knowing it would safely guide her through the forest. She thought it unfair that not everybody would get to experience this feeling at least once in their lives. It was truly terrific.

At last, the gryphons began to lower themselves in amongst the pine trees. Everybody held on closely and hoped they would avoid any prickles from the branches on the way down. When they landed, much smoother than any of them had been anticipating, they noticed pine needles scattered all over the forest floor.

Jenna leaned forward and gave her gryphon an appreciative pat on the neck. "Well," she said, looking around, "welcome to Pine, guys."

CHAPTER 17:
NEEDLE MIST

Hallie

HALLIE BARELY KEPT HER balance as the gryphons knelt so they could all slide off their backs. As soon as her feet hit the ground, her legs buckled and she fell forward onto her knees.

Jenna chuckled at her. "What, did the flight give you jelly legs?"

"No," Hallie huffed as Jenna helped her up. She brushed herself off and looked ahead. There, before them, was a large cottage-type building made of stone and wood. It wasn't nearly as big as Maple Cliff, but it had to have been the size of the Rec Centre back home in Peterborough where Alan and Thomas played hockey.

"What *is* that?" said Jenna, also staring at this building.

"The sign says Pine City Centre," said Lindsay, pointing to a wooden sign stuck into the ground. "Maybe we should go inside. Someone in there might be able to help us."

"That must be why the gryphons brought us here," said Thomas, smiling at them. "They must have brought us somewhere we can get help. Thank you, gents." One of the gryphons cleaned its feathers with its beak, while the other one sat back in a dog-like position and scratched behind its ear with its back paw.

"Ugh," said Jenna, lifting her arm and sniffing herself. "Man, you can really smell the sewage now that we're back in fresh air."

"Perhaps there's a lake around here somewhere," said Thomas, looking around. "A rinse in clean water would be better than nothing."

"I hope so," said Lindsay. She lifted her T-shirt to her nose and almost gagged. "We reek."

A creak from a door opening around the side of the building made them all jump. A gleam of yellow light that brightened a streak on the grass shone outward, and a few shadows began filling the light. Suddenly, Alan and Jules appeared from around the building.

"No way!" Alan exclaimed happily, running toward the four of them. "I knew it was you guys! I knew it! I told them I heard something outside just now! I knew you'd find us!"

"Whoa," Jules exclaimed, noticing the gryphons. She had been following Alan with just as much excitement until she saw them there. "What... what..."

"They're gryphons, of course," said Thomas, reaching up to pat one of them. "They're very nice creatures."

"Man, you guys stink!" Alan said suddenly, wafting his hand in front of his face. He looked amused rather than bothered, though. "Wow! You smell like swamp water and manure."

"Gee, thanks," said Jenna, sticking her tongue out at him. "You would too if you had ridden the sewer express with us."

"Oh yeah, where did you guys end up? Even Denny didn't know where that sewer led," said Alan, stepping closer to them, instantly forgetting about the smell. "Or, as she put it, she hadn't the foggiest of inklings."

"Denny?" said Lindsay, squeezing some of the slime out of her ponytail. "Denny's here?"

Alan nodded. "She was waiting for us here when we got here. The first thing she asked was where you guys were. So, where were you?"

"It was kind of like a cave, but the only way out was up," said Jenna, pointing to the sky. As a reflex, Hallie looked up to where Jenna was pointing, but when she looked back down her heart gave a leap.

Lou was outside now, in the stream of light from the building's open door. Her face was blank as she slowly walked toward them all, like she wasn't believing her own eyes.

"Mom!" Hallie exclaimed. Her voice sounded like a double-tone, which made her realize Jenna had said the same thing at the same time.

They both ran toward her. Lou's legs gave out and she collapsed onto her knees on the grass. As they took their respective shoulder (Hallie on her right, Jenna on her left) and hugged her, Lou didn't speak a word. She couldn't have even if she wanted to; it looked like she was using every ounce of her concentration to steady her breathing and keep from bawling. Hallie felt her arm hugging her back, feeling her body up and down to make sure everything was still intact. She assumed the same thing was happening to Jenna on the other side.

"Oh my God," Lou exhaled as she tugged at their shirts, inviting them to step back. She looked them up and down, and then came the tears. She pulled them back into a big, tight hug and kissed them all over. "Oh my God, oh my God..."

"It's okay, Mom," said Hallie, looking across Lou's back at Jenna.

"Yeah," said Jenna, meekly. "We're fine."

Denny, Levi, and Annabel had joined them among the pine trees by now, all of them looking practically sick with relief.

Annabel exhaled heavily. "Thank God you guys are alright. Lou, easy, you're suffocating them." She may not have been vocalizing her relief quite like Lou was, but the shine in her eyes spoke volumes.

"Merciful heavens, thank goodness!" Denny exclaimed, throwing her arms around Lindsay and Thomas, neither of whom were expecting it. "My dear children... Thank goodness."

"I see you guys brought some new friends with you," said Levi, nodding his head at the gryphons.

"That's how we got out," said Hallie. "They were trapped down there, just like us."

Levi walked over without a stitch of fear and examined them. "They're skin and bones, poor things. Klaus probably had them there for at least a month."

Lindsay looked horrified. "You mean Klaus not only kidnapped a pair of gryphons, but he kept them locked up without food? That's despicable!"

"That's one word for him," said Levi, shaking his head. "I prefer to call him a—"

"Levi!" Lou warned, standing up straight but not letting go of Hallie or Jenna for anything.

"Sorry, but after he betrayed us all, what do you expect me to say?" Lou couldn't argue that. Levi now looked sorrowfully at the gryphons. "Besides, anyone who hurts a helpless animal is just sick. How did the four of you get them to help you? You flew them here, I assume?"

"Yeah, once we got them out of that cage. I think they understand English because they agreed to help us when we asked," said Lindsay.

"Yes, gryphons are smart," said Annabel, making her way between the four of them to examine their faces and limbs for any injuries. "But how did you get them to trust you?"

"We offered them some food," said Thomas. "Rats. Common brown rats, if my skills in animal identification are serving me correctly."

"Yeah, dead rats," Hallie added disgustedly.

"Which reminds me," said Jenna, holding her hands in front of her. "Thomas and I need to wash our hands."

"I think you all need to wash more than just your hands. You stink." Annabel chuckled, looking at their damp, swampy bodies. She nodded her head to the building behind them. "The showers are down the first hallway on the left—Oh, Hallie, your leg!"

"Huh?" Hallie had almost forgotten about her leg, but as soon as Annabel mentioned it, she felt it start to sting again.

"Oh, sweetheart," said Lou in a wavy voice, bending down to get a better look at it. The bottom half of her leg was almost covered in dry blood, and the cut itself was still oozing a bit.

"Oh, yeah," said Hallie. "I think that happened in the sewer tunnel. We got to the cave and it was just there."

Lou hugged Hallie again. "My poor girl... Denny, do you have some—"

"Yes, absolutely, just give me... one second here..." Denny began rummaging through the many pockets of her pink overcoat for something. Hallie shook her head.

"It's okay, I don't need a bandage or anything," she said, trying to convince them that it was no big deal. "I know it's a lot of blood, but the cut isn't even that big."

"Got it!" said Denny, pulling out a small vial full of what looked like pale green sand. She pulled out the tiny cork and walked toward Hallie. "Now, we'll just sprinkle some of this on there and you'll be good as new."

"Whoa, whoa, whoa!" said Hallie, leaning back and pushing her body against Lou. "What *is* that stuff? Mom?"

"It's okay, it's just medicine," said Lou.

"Is it going to hurt?"

"Not a bit." She knelt on one knee and invited Hallie to sit on the other one. "Just hold still for Denny, okay?"

"Yes, everybody, gather 'round," said Denny, speaking to the other five. "I reckon you've never seen or heard of Needle Mist before, eh?"

"Needle what?" said Alan.

"Needle Mist," Denny repeated. She held out the vial of greenish sand for everybody to see. "It's a specialty of Pine, made by grinding up the pine needles that are dropped by the trees." She waved her arm at the forest floor around them, covered in pine needles.

"Wow," said Thomas. He adjusted his glasses, which took a moment because the sewage goop had stuck them to his face. "Do the people back home know about this stuff? Our doctors might find it incredibly beneficial."

"I'm afraid not, Thomas, and it wouldn't do them any good," said Annabel, placing her hand on his shoulder. "Needle Mist only works on injuries suffered in Pawcombe. And besides, it takes thousands of pine needles to create that tiny vial of Needle Mist."

"Yes, quite right," said Denny, nodding along to what Annabel was saying. "Now, watch closely, everyone. I'm going to sprinkle a bit of the Mist onto Hallie's leg, just like this. That doesn't hurt, does it, Hallie?"

Hallie shook her head. "It tickles a bit."

"Good, good, that means it's working," said Denny. "Now, watch everybody, because here's the whopper-dooder. Look how fast it works."

Hallie almost asked Denny what on earth a whopper-dooder was, but her eyes were glued to her leg, as were everybody else's. As if by magic, her cut was getting smaller and smaller by the second. Eventually, it was gone entirely, and all that was left on her leg was the dried blood.

"Cool!" Alan exclaimed.

Hallie stood up and walked forward a few steps. Her leg felt as good as new.

"Thanks," she said, smiling at Denny.

"Oh, of course, dear," said Denny, returning the smile. "Does anybody else have any cuts or scrapes?"

Jenna raised her hand. "I've got a black eye. Well, I mean, it'll probably become one by morning."

Everybody else's heads dropped when they remembered how she got it, but all four adults were both confused and concerned.

"Klaus. He, um, he hit me," Jenna explained. "He found us once we were up the ladder and chased us all around. You, um, you know what happened to him, right?"

Denny nodded rather sadly. "Alan and Jules filled us in, dear. They told us everything."

"He *hit* you?" Lou asked, gently running her finger across Jenna's eye. She was trying not to start crying again as she looked at the swelling. "Oh, baby, I'm so sorry."

"I don't suppose needle mist works on bruises?" Jenna asked hopefully.

"I'm afraid not," Denny sighed, "but there's plenty of ice inside."

"Speaking of inside, can we go wash up now?" said Hallie. She could hardly stand the stench anymore.

"Yes, yes, of course," said Denny, holding out her hands for them to take. Hallie took one and Lindsay took the other. "Come with me, kids, I'll show you where to go." Hallie looked behind her instinctively to see if Jenna was following, and she was. Thomas, however, was still with the gryphons.

"They are rather thin, aren't they?" he said sadly. "Is there enough food here for them?"

Levi nodded his head. "Tons. I'll make sure they're fed, don't worry. You go get washed up, bud, okay?"

Thomas gave the gryphons another few pats and then jogged off to catch up with the others, just as they entered the building.

CHAPTER 18:
THE STERLING CONE

Jenna

JENNA RAN THROUGH THE forest. She was running so fast that she couldn't even tell what types of trees were around her. The only thing she knew for sure was how enormous they all were. She felt like a tiny little bug.

She looked over her shoulder. There he was, hot on her trail. The same man who had been chasing her since... well, she didn't know exactly how long. He was a very large man, too. He had to be at least seven feet tall. He was far enough behind her still that his face was in the shadows, but she didn't need to see his face to know who he was.

"Leave me alone!" she shouted. "Leave me alone, Zyngor!"

But he didn't let up. If anything, he ran faster. Jenna tried to retaliate—to run even faster—but she tripped over a root sticking out of the ground. She landed face-first into the dirt and leaves. Just as she turned around, Zyngor caught up to her and pulled out the biggest and sharpest sword she had ever seen. It was hard to tell, but it looked like the entire sword from the handle to the tip of the blade was jet-black in colour.

"No! Leave me alone!" she shouted.

Zyngor pointed the sword at her but he didn't say a word. He held out his other hand, like he was waiting for her to give him something.

"I don't have it!" she shouted. "I don't have the Sterling Cone!" She covered her eyes with her arms. Then, she felt someone's hands on her. Someone was shaking her, but it wasn't Zyngor. It was Hallie.

"Jenna! Come on, wake up!"

Jenna sat bolt upright in her cot. She was safe and sound in Pine City Centre. She rubbed her eyes just as someone holding a lit candle rushed to her bedside.

"Ahhh!" she screamed, hiding herself under the covers.

"Jenna, for heaven's sake," said Hallie, pulling the covers off and allowing Jenna to see that the candle-holder was only Lou. Lou put the candle gently on the bedside table and opened her arms. Like a reflex, Jenna bounded forward into them.

"It's okay," Lou whispered into her hair. "It was only a dream."

Jenna stayed there for a few moments, comfortable on Lou's shoulder. She probably could have gone back to sleep right there, but then she remembered her dream. Her eyes snapped open and she sat back.

"It was a bad dream," she said. "I saw... I saw Zyngor."

Hallie made a face. "What do you mean, you *saw* him? How could you tell? We've never seen him or even a picture of him."

"Well, I didn't see his face," said Jenna, rubbing her eyes again, "and he didn't talk to me. But I knew it was him. I don't know how I knew. I just knew."

"It probably *was* him," Lou practically whispered. Everyone was sleeping in the same room—a long room lined with cots. Nobody else had been awoken by Jenna's bad dream and Lou wanted to keep it that way.

"What do you mean?" Hallie asked nervously.

"The birthdate connection you guys have with him is a powerful one. Even though you've never seen him, deep in your minds, you probably already know what he looks like." Then, she dropped her head and added, "Just like he probably already knows what you look like."

Jenna didn't even want to think about that. "Mom, are you sad about Klaus?" she said instead.

Lou's back stiffened. "I'm sad that he chose to turn his back on us—on Pawcombe." She sniffled. "But after what he tried to do to you guys... no. I'm not sad. Maybe that's wicked of me, but I'm not."

"He was your friend."

"Yes, but you're my kids. Nothing comes above that." Lou paused for a moment. "You two aren't upset, are you?"

Jenna shrugged. "Only because we saw it happen."

Before Lou could react, Hallie added, "We didn't *see* it happen, Jenna. We hid our eyes."

"Whatever," said Jenna.

"Well, either way, he can't hurt you anymore," said Lou, stroking their hair. "I promise. Nobody will ever hurt you. Not while I'm around."

Jenna closed her eyes, but all she could see in her mind was the shadowy silhouette of Zyngor holding out his hand. She shook her head so violently that Lou reached forward and held her face in her palms.

"Jenna, what is it?" she said.

"He wanted the Sterling Cone," said Jenna. She looked at Hallie. "In my dream, Zyngor wanted me to give him the Sterling Cone."

Lou released Jenna's face as her own face became rather pale. "I was wondering when you would mention the Sterling Cone. Alan and Jules already asked about it when the rest of you weren't here yet."

"What even is it?" said Hallie, sitting down next to Jenna on her cot. "We heard the nilbogs say that their master wanted it, and that he thought we had it or that we knew where it was."

"Which we don't," Jenna added. She squinted. "Do we?"

"No, you don't," Lou sighed. "Nobody at Maple Cliff knows where it is."

"Klaus thought we knew about it, too," said Hallie. "He wanted us to tell him about the Sterling Cone so he could tell Zyngor. That's all he kept saying to us up in that attic room in his dungeon."

"The room that collapsed on him and killed him," Jenna added.

Hallie glared at her. "Thank you, Jenna."

"Klaus was clearly paranoid. Zyngor filled his head with lies and deceit." Lou massaged her forehead. "The Sterling Cone is one of the more magical elements of

Pawcombe. It's connected to the job of a Sought Six, which means it's useless even to Zyngor unless there's an active Sought Six team. That must be why he's looking for it now—because he knows about you guys."

"But what is it?" Hallie repeated. "What does it look like?"

"Hmm. Well, it looks like a shiny silver pinecone. It's one-of-a-kind, and it's extremely valuable," said Lou. "Whoever has it can use it to grant themselves one wish."

"Klaus mentioned that," said Jenna, tapping Hallie's arm. "A wish... He said the Sterling Cone would grant Zyngor his wish to make Pawcombe a better place."

Lou scoffed, just like Jenna had when she heard Klaus say those words. Her eye and cheek began to throb suddenly, but she tried to ignore it.

"You said the Sterling Cone looks like a silver pinecone," Hallie said hopefully. "Maybe it's here, in Pine, hidden among the other normal pinecones."

Lou shook her head. "We thought so, too, but we've had volunteers searching Pine for the last several hours while we waited for you guys to get here and while you were cleaning up. We just got a report after you all went to sleep. It's not here."

Hallie dropped her head. "I guess that would have been too obvious, anyway."

"So, let me get this straight," said Jenna. "Zyngor wants to find this shiny silver pinecone and use it to control Pawcombe, but he thinks we're trying to stop him from doing that?"

"Well, you are," said Lou, "now that we know that's what he wants. As the Sought Six, it's your job to stop him. Even if those volunteers had found the Sterling Cone, they would have had to hand it over to you guys to dispose of it." Lou smiled suddenly, a smile that couldn't be wiped away. Jenna thought she might be delirious with exhaustion.

"Why are you smiling?"

"I was just thinking about going outside and seeing you guys there with the gryphons."

"Kind of happy to see us alive, eh?" said Hallie.

"Yeah, just a bit," said Lou, winking at her and ruffling her hair. "But when you told us you used the gryphons to escape that cave... I just... I was impressed. That was really clever."

"That was my idea," Jenna said quietly but proudly. Hallie rolled her eyes.

"I'm smiling," said Lou, "because I was so scared when we first got here. I didn't know what any of your instincts would be, or how you would deal with the pressure of being the Sought Six. I do wish you didn't have to face Klaus and then find a way out of Cedar all by yourselves, but you did it. You know what that tells me? You aren't helpless."

"But Mom..." Hallie swallowed and darted her eyes back and forth from Jenna to Lou. "We don't know what we're doing."

Lou just smiled. "I didn't either, when I was your age. But you aren't alone, remember? You have me, Annabel, Levi, and Denny. All of us are here to help you."

"You guys will be there for everything? All of you?"

"Even *after* we destroy the Sterling Cone?"

Lou nodded. "No matter what."

Jenna dropped her eyes to her sword, which was leaning against the wall next to her cot. She wondered why she never used it against Zyngor in her dream. She reached for it and pulled it only slightly out of the sheath.

"Hey, there's something written here," she said, peering in the dark.

"There is?" said Hallie. She picked the candle up off the bedside table and held it over the top of the blade.

"Asiuol," Jenna read slowly, sounding out each letter. "What's Asiuol?"

Lou allowed herself a grin.

"What's Asiuol? It's written on the blade," Jenna repeated. She thought of Lou's sword, which was the same as hers. "Does yours have that?"

"Yes, it does," said Lou. "That's the name of this sword. It was forged by Pawcombe's blacksmiths years ago, and they named after me because I was the only one who could use it. It's different from the others with its weight and its aerodynamics. I was the only one who ever seemed to be able to get the hang of it, so only a few Asiuols were ever made. There are lots of Roses, lots of Wind Riders, but not many Asiuols at all."

"Named after you?" said Jenna, looking at the letters again. "Oh! It's Louisa backwards!"

Lou nodded. "You know, it didn't surprise me one bit when you chose an Asiuol sword for yourself, Jenna. I figured at least one of my girls might. Being able to use it must be a family trait."

Hallie looked at the Asiuol. "I wonder if I'd be able to use it... Jenna, here, let me try it."

"No way, it's mine!"

"It's the middle of the night," said Lou, replacing Jenna's excuse. She leaned forward to give them each a kiss. "Come on, back to bed. It'll be light soon." She walked back across the room to her bed and Hallie climbed into her cot next to Jenna's. Jenna fluffed her pillow, but before lying back down, she looked across the room

"Mom?"

"Hmm?"

"We *will* find the Sterling Cone, right? I mean, if Zyngor thinks we have it, which we don't, then he doesn't know where it is either. We've got a chance. Right?"

Lou said nothing but smiled so reassuringly that all Jenna could do was smile back. Lou blew them both a kiss and then blew out the candle. Jenna expected to have a hard time going back to sleep, but the next thing she knew, it was morning.

CHAPTER 19:
THE SINGING PONY

Jenna

A BRIGHT AND SUNNY morning it was, too. Jenna could smell bacon and eggs as they walked to the mess hall, which was what Pine City Centre called its cafeteria. The people who worked at Pine City Centre gave them each a new set of clothes (hunter green T-shirts and grey sweatpants), which were much softer and drier and less caked in green nilbog blood than their other ones had been. It was amazing, Jenna noted, how much better she felt after a bath and a change of clothes. Even with a bad dream interrupting her sleep last night, she felt as good as new. A hot meal would be the cherry on top.

"Something smells good," said Thomas, rubbing his stomach as they walked. "Please excuse the metaphor, but I'm so hungry I could eat an elephant."

"I hope there's enough for us all, then," said Annabel.

"Huh? Why wouldn't there be?" said Alan as his own stomach growled.

"Pine City Centre started a meal program recently," said Annabel just as they arrived in the mess hall, "for people with no food to eat."

"Isn't this the one you organized yourself, Annabel?" said Levi, but he was met with a piercing stare from Annabel, as if maybe he wasn't supposed to point out her involvement.

"In hard times, we all must help any way we can," she mumbled.

"All these people are here because they have no food? But there's... there's so many of them," said Jenna, scanning the room. There were three long tables filling the room, just like any other cafeteria, and they were all full of people. Some of them were kids around their age.

Annabel sighed, resting her hands on Jenna's shoulders. "That's Zyngor's doing. He's been working even harder than usual lately to recruit his army. Some people who refused to follow him ended up dead. Others," she said, waving her arm over the crowd, "just had their homes and villages destroyed."

Jenna felt a pang of guilt in her gut. They—the Sought Six—were the reason Zyngor was working so hard to build up an army. These poor people wouldn't have lost their homes if it weren't for—

"Stop," said Annabel, staring down at Jenna. "I know what you're thinking. This is *not* your fault. You guys can't help the days you were born. You didn't make Zyngor do this. He made his own choice."

"So, you're saying these people are all here right now because they refused to follow Zyngor? They're on our side?" said Hallie, also gazing out at the dozens of people. By now, some of them were noticing the group standing at the head of the room. One little girl, probably four or five years old, tapped her mom on the arm.

"Mommy!" she squealed excitedly. "Look, Mommy! It's the Sought Six!" She leapt from her chair and rushed to the front of the room, to her mother's apparent horror.

"Honey! Get back here!" she hissed, but the little girl didn't listen. She stopped in front of the group and became shy.

"Hi," said Jules, bending so that she was at eye-level with her. "What's your name?"

"Shauna," said the girl.

"Nice to meet you, Shauna. I'm Jules." She held up her hand. "High five!"

A big smile spread across the little girl's face as she jumped up to smack Jules' palm with her own.

"Whoa, what an arm!" said Jules, pretending to be pushed backward. "You know, we could use someone like you on our team." That seemed to make the girl very happy. Her mother arrived at her side and took her hand.

"I'm so sorry, Miss Jules," she said, chuckling a little.

"That's okay," said Jules. She smiled at the little girl. "See you around, Shauna."

Shauna waved fervently at them all, and then followed her mother back to their seats. Jenna hadn't even noticed how silent the cafeteria had become until everyone resumed their conversations again.

"How many people were watching that?" said Jules, now a tad embarrassed.

"Most of the room," said Denny, beaming. "You handled that with such elegance, my dear. I know that little girl will never forget your kindness."

"You think?" Jules dropped her head a little. "I feel bad for these people, especially the kids. Imagine being hungry and not having any food to eat."

Right on cue, Alan's stomach growled again. "You were saying?" he said.

Denny began ushering them all to an empty spot along one of the tables. "We can talk more about Maple Cliff's efforts to help the people of Pine once we get back to Maple. But if we want to be of use, we must keep ourselves fed and fit. After all, without fuel, a fire goes out. Ma'am?" She raised her hand to get the attention of a woman wearing an apron and a hair net, who promptly rolled over a cart with ten plates of food on it.

"Here we are, Masters and Misses," said the woman. The plates were piled high with steaming scrambled eggs and fat strips of juicy bacon. "I do apologize. I know it's not what you're used to at Maple Cliff. I'm afraid our supplies are quite meager at the moment. There seem to be more and more people here every day, bless them."

"It looks delicious," said Jenna, taking her plate. "Thank you."

"Yes, thanks," Hallie added, taking a bite. She smiled at the woman; proof that the food was indeed tasty.

"Oh, it's my pleasure," said the woman, who seemed to be entirely thrilled that she had their approval. As she walked away with the empty cart, Lindsay leaned forward on the table so she wouldn't have to shout.

"Are people going to treat us like royalty everywhere we go?" she said.

"Pretty much," said Annabel, not looking up from her plate. "You'll get used to it."

"It only gets annoying when the newspaper people want to talk to you," Levi added. He lifted his fork to his mouth and lifted his gaze to a window looking out on the pine trees. He put down his fork and his face became strained. "What the... did I summon them or something?"

Jenna turned around to look out the window. There were three men and two women standing out there, all dressed in brown tweed suits. Some were carrying old-fashioned cameras, and some were carrying notepads and pencils.

"Who are they?" Jenna asked.

"Reporters from *The Singing Pony*," Levi answered, still staring out the window. "Unbelievable. How did they know we were here?"

Hallie nearly choked on her juice. "The singing what?"

"*The Singing Pony*. It's the name of the newspaper in Pawcombe," said Annabel, staring out the window at the reporters. She stood up. "We should go see what they want, Levi."

"Yeah," Levi agreed, standing up with her. He smiled at the group. "We'll be right back."

Alan waited until they were gone before looking excitedly at Lou and Denny. "Are we going to be interviewed?"

"Hopefully not," said Lou, sighing and handing him a napkin because he had a piece of scrambled egg on his cheek. "Those reporters don't often ask easy questions. It's much less stressful to just avoid them."

"Okay, I just have to ask," said Lindsay, "why is it called *The Singing Pony*?"

Denny made a murmuring noise as she sipped her coffee and flapped her hand happily while she swallowed, like she had been waiting for one of them to ask that question. "It's because, long ago, when Pawcombe wasn't quite as populated as it is now, a little pony was the deliverer of newspapers. He would carry a pouch on his back and go door-to-door every morning, letting out a happy whinny to let residents know their paper had arrived. How precious is that?"

Jenna chuckled at the idea of a little Shetland pony trotting along with a pack of newspapers on its back. Just then, Annabel and Levi arrived back in the mess hall with annoyed looks on their faces.

"What?" said Jules, although it sounded like she knew what the answer was. Jenna was pretty sure she knew, too.

"They're not going anywhere until they get their *statement*," said Levi using air quotations on the word 'statement'. He forced a smile at the six of them. "They want to interview you guys. News of Klaus' death has spread and apparently the people of Pawcombe have *questions*." Once again, he used air quotations.

"But... but what do we say?" said Hallie, looking anxiously between them all. "We didn't kill him."

"No, dear, of course you didn't," said Denny, massaging her shoulder, "but you were the last ones to see him alive. All you have to do is tell the truth, even if the truth is saying 'I don't know'. Simple enough, right?"

"And if you don't want to answer a question, just shoot a look at one of us," Annabel added. "We'll be out there with you, making sure the reporters don't get to ambitious with their questions."

Lindsay gulped. "Ambitious?"

"Doesn't seem that long ago we were the ones being interviewed," said Lou, shaking her head. Then, she stood up. "Might as well get this over with. Come on, guys."

As soon as they got outside, the door had barely shut behind them when the reporters swarmed like moths to a flame. Flashes from the cameras all but blinded them. Citizens of Pine (and there had to be at least fifty of them there that morning) had gathered around Pine City Centre, apparently just to get a glimpse of the Sought Six and listen to their interview. As their voices and gasps filled the forest, Thomas stayed close to Denny. Jenna took Lou's hand. Annabel and Levi took a big step forward with their arms out.

"For crying out loud, what did I just tell you guys?" Levi snapped at the reporters. "Give them their space."

"Yes, yes, please keep your distance," Denny added, also acknowledging the crowd. "I assure you; you'll get your answers just fine from where you are. The Sought Six will speak loudly and clearly, won't you, kids?" She smiled and nodded at them, and since they all seemed to understand that speaking loudly meant the reporters wouldn't come any closer, they all nodded in agreement.

"Right, well, let's begin," said a woman with mousey brown hair, the youngest of the group. She opened her notepad. "Miss Jenna and Master Thomas, I understand you two were the ones Mr. Vandnav was chasing when he met his demise. Yes?"

"Yes," Jenna said quietly. She cleared her throat. "Yes, that's right."

The woman began scribbling. "Where were you when all this was happening?"

"In his dungeon," said Thomas. "The dungeon of Vandnav Hall, where he lured us and tried to kill us."

"Must have been awful for you," said the woman, but she didn't look at them. She was still writing furiously.

"Well, it wasn't fun," said Jenna. The crowd chuckled a little at her response, which took her off guard. She hadn't meant to be funny.

"That black eye you have there—for those of you in the crowd who can't see, it's a purplish shiner underneath Miss Jenna's right eye—how did you get that?"

"Klaus—um, I mean, Mr. Vandnav—hit me in the face."

The reporters were all writing and taking photos. The crowd began murmuring amongst themselves and Jenna was grateful to see that most of them appeared to be on her side, disgusted by Klaus' actions.

"Master Alan," said another reporter—a man in a bowler hat. "I understand you've been eager to gain experience with a sword. What was it like to finally get a taste of action?"

Alan looked dumbfounded that they could change the subject so quickly. "Taste of action? Um, I mean, it was alright, I guess... We all worked together as a team. We protected each other from the nilbogs."

"You get a lot of good kills?" the man asked, winking at him. He might as well have been asking Alan if he had scored a lot of goals at a hockey game.

Alan squinted. "I... Sorry, what?"

"Ask another question, Bruce," said Annabel, through what sounded like gritted teeth. Jenna looked over at her. Her jaw was most certainly clenched.

"Did any of you suspect Mr. Vandnav to be a traitor?" said another male reporter. This one had a large belly nearly bursting through his waistcoat.

"Suspect him? No," said Hallie. "We had no reason to suspect anything."

"He used to be just like us," Jules added quietly. "We thought we could trust him."

"Of course, of course," said the man, scribbling away on his notepad. "But surely there were signs... Had Mr. Vandnav been acting distant as of late?"

"They've only known him for a few days, Alastair," Lou spoke up. "There is no 'as of late' about it."

"Sure, sure," he nodded.

"Now let's talk about the big issue at hand," said the young woman reporter, raising her hand so they'd all look at her. "Where are you at with Zyngor? Do you have any idea what his plan of attack might be?"

The six of them looked between each other.

"Is it true that he's hunting the Sterling Cone?" the woman went on. "What are you doing to find it before he does?"

Nobody knew how to answer.

"They're doing their jobs," Levi finally said, "and that's all anyone can ask of them."

"Quite right, and on that note, I think that's enough questions for one day," said Denny, making a move to usher everyone back inside.

"If I may turn my attention briefly to the previous Sought Six team," said the man in the bowler hat just as one of the photographers snapped another photo. "Pawcombe hasn't had to deal with the death of a past or present Sought Six member since Miss Jessica and Master Gabriel. Does it feel the same now as it did then?"

Annabel's entire demeanour changed, so much so that everyone noticed. Her head whipped toward him and her eyes flashed. "I beg your pardon?" she gasped, taking a step toward them.

"It most certainly does not," Levi cut in. "Klaus was a traitor and he got what was coming to him. Jessica and Gabriel were not traitors and their deaths were tragic. They left us in mourning. Klaus' death, however, has not."

Jenna tugged Lou's sleeve. "Who are Jessica and Gabriel?" she whispered. Lou was trying hard not to look at her.

"That's enough," said Annabel, who seemed to have composed herself a little bit. "We're done here. I hope you got all you needed, because if you bother us again while we're still in Pine, you'll be bringing those cameras back to your office skewered on an arrow." And with that, she shoved past everyone and stormed inside.

CHAPTER 20:
MISS JESSICA AND
MASTER GABRIEL

Hallie

"IT'S JUST OVER HERE, I know it," said Thomas, rushing between the bookshelves of the Maple Cliff Library and aiming a flashlight up at all the books.

"Thomas, it's after hours," said Lindsay. She looked over her should for the third time since they arrived. "It's the middle of the night, for pity's sake. We shouldn't be here."

"Mrs. Mugford won't mind," Thomas said confidently, running his index finger along the spines of the books and held the flashlight in the other hand. "When I met her my first time in here, she told me I'm welcome anytime."

"Yeah," said Lindsay, glaring at him, "during regular library hours. We're breaking and entering."

"What are we looking for that couldn't have waited until the morning, anyway?" said Hallie, crossing her arms and yawning. "You still haven't said."

"Just follow me," Thomas insisted, "and keep up."

Ever since hearing the names Jessica and Gabriel in Pine a week ago, Thomas had been obsessed with learning who they were. He had spent every bit of his free time in the library, scanning the shelves from top to bottom. The only problem was there hadn't been much free time over the past week. Denny had increased their combat lessons to practically every day, and their other three mentors had been more than happy to impart more of their wisdom.

All the adults—Lou in particular—had really been spooked by the events at Vandnav Hall in Cedar. Hallie couldn't blame them, really. There were a lot of things that had thrown them through a loop—Lou in particular. First of all, someone she thought was her friend had turned out to be a traitor. Second of all, she was forced to use her skills with a sword that she had buried for twelve years. And thirdly, her children had almost been killed. Actually, that one was 'first of all' to Lou.

"Can't we go slow and enjoy the view?" asked Jules, pointing out the windows between the bookshelves at the silvery moonlight on the maple leaves. "My legs are killing me."

"Man, so are mine," said Alan, shrugging his shoulders. "My arms, too. But I don't think we have much choice in the matter."

"Guys, come on, it could be worse," Lindsay argued. "I mean, we could *not* know how to use swords and bows, and then get killed the next time someone attacks us. Would you rather that?"

Jules huffed. "No."

"Fine, but practising every single day for the last week?" said Alan, rolling his shoulders in their sockets. "My hockey team doesn't even practice that much."

"Hockey isn't a matter of life and death, Alan," said Lindsay. Hallie swallowed. Hearing it put like that, she felt the weight of Pawcombe on her shoulders.

"I can't feel my thumb," said Jules, wiggling her left thumb. "It's numb."

Alan chuckled at the rhyme. "Nice one, Dr. Seuss."

Jules stomped her foot. "It's not funny!"

"Shh!" Hallie hissed. "Quiet, guys, someone's going to catch us!"

"Annabel told you that kind of pain and numbness is normal for first-time archers," said Jenna to Jules. She ran her hand along each book as they walked down the aisles. "You're lucky. You get a one-on-one teacher because Annabel is the only one on her team who uses a bow, and you're the only one on our team who uses a bow."

Jules sighed. "Yeah, I guess you're right, but there's no way I'm ever going to be as good as Annabel is."

"Here it is! I found it! I knew it was here!" Thomas exclaimed, stopping suddenly and pulling a thick leather-bound book off the top shelf. He blew the dust off of it.

"Oh, gross!" said Hallie as she wafted the dusty air away from her face.

"This is the condensed history of Maple Cliff," said Thomas, balancing the book in his arms.

"This is condensed?" said Jenna, lifting the cover and letting it fall back onto the book. More dust flew out of it, and Hallie groaned.

"Careful!" she said, waving the air.

"I know it's a rather large book," said Thomas, "but Maple Cliff is a rather large place, with a lot of people to account for. Now, if you'll all excuse me, I'm going to put it down on the floor. My muscles are rather sore as well."

Everybody stepped back and then knelt down as Thomas opened the book. He skimmed the table of contents for a moment, and then flipped to a page titled: THE SOUGHT SIX.

"Here we go," said Thomas, dragging his finger down the page as he read. "Of course! Just as I suspected."

"What? What's as you suspected?" said Jenna, peering over Thomas' shoulder.

"Gabriel Fuller and Jessica Scott were the kids who completed the first Sought Six team," said Thomas, eyes still glued to the page. "They were the ones Zyngor killed, making the team unable to complete their job."

"Whoa, hold on a second," said Lindsay, and judging by the tone of her voice, Hallie guessed she was probably thinking the same thing she was.

"What?" said Thomas.

"Gabriel Fuller and Jessica... What did you say her last name was?"

Yes. She was thinking what Hallie was thinking.

"Scott," said Thomas, and right when he said it, his face fell. He understood, too. "Oh, that's... she's... oh dear."

"What?" said Alan, leaning in to see the book, which was difficult as he was looking at it upside down. "What's the problem?"

"Jessica Scott," said Hallie. "Annabel's last name is Scott. They must have been sisters."

"Sisters?" said Jenna. "Sought Six teams are all the same age as each other. They were twins, Hal, just like us."

"Well, wait a minute," said Jules, shaking her head. "Are you sure they're not just cousins? I have a cousin back home whose last name is Mansfield."

"Not unless cousins look this similar," said Thomas, turning the book so everybody could see the picture on the page. It was the first Sought Six team, standing at the edge of the forest. They were all much younger, but there was no mistaking Lou, Levi or Annabel. And, for that matter, Jessica as well. She and Annabel might as well have been clones.

"Man, what a coincidence," said Alan. "Two Sought Six teams and two sets of twins."

"I wonder if they had to look for the Sterling Cone, too," said Jules, staring at the photo.

"Well, if they did, nobody ever found it," said Lindsay. "It's still out there right now."

Alan shook his head. "If you ask me, it's just plain weird. How can a pinecone grant wishes?"

"One wish. Singular, not plural," Thomas corrected, "and it's no ordinary pinecone, apparently."

"Oh, right, it's silver and shiny," said Alan, rolling his eyes.

"We've flown on gryphons and fought nilbogs, but you find a magical pinecone hard to believe?" said Jenna.

Thomas snorted a laugh through his nose.

"Well, anyway," Alan continued, "Pinecones are found in forests. And, in case you guys haven't noticed, this entire *world* is a giant forest. It could take us years to find it!"

Hallie pursed her lips as she peered closer over Thomas' shoulder. "I don't suppose that book says anything about the Sterling Cone, does it?"

Just then, the giant grandfather clock in the library common area chimed so loudly that Hallie's heart skipped a beat. It rang once, signalling 1 o'clock in the morning. Thomas checked his watch, as if he didn't trust the grandfather clock to be correct.

"I'm afraid more research will have to wait until tomorrow. We've been out of our beds long enough." He slid the book back onto the shelf.

They all headed for the stairwell to make the five-storey journey from the ninth floor down to the fourth, but Jenna stepped back at the last second. Alan reached his arm out to hold the door.

"What is it?" he said.

"I have to go to the bathroom," said Jenna.

"Can't you wait until we get downstairs?" said Jules.

"No, I really have to go now. There's one up here. I, um, I'll see you guys in a bit." And with that, she took off down the hall.

"She really shouldn't be by herself, even in Maple Cliff," said Thomas, checking his watch again.

Hallie lifted an eyebrow. She knew her sister well enough to know when she was up to something. "You guys go, I'll wait for her," she said. She waited until Alan

225

let go of the door and they were out of sight. Then, she followed Jenna, not to the bathroom, but back to the aisle of shelves they were just in.

"Jenna," she said, and Jenna practically jumped out of her skin.

"I thought you were gone already."

"What are you doing?"

"Nothing," she said, pulling the large leather book back off the shelf. Hallie watched as she flipped back to the page about the Sought Six they had just been reading. She gripped it tight near the spine, and pulled. It ripped out cleanly.

"Jenna, what the—"

"You don't seriously think it's a coincidence, do you? Because I don't."

"What?"

"The twin thing," said Jenna, folding the page and slipping it into her pocket. Hallie groaned as Jenna put the book back onto the shelf.

"What are you going to do with that page?"

"I'm going to bring it to Annabel. I'm going to ask her."

"You can't do that! What if it upsets her? She's never even mentioned her sister before, so she obviously doesn't want to talk about her. This isn't a good idea, Jenna."

Jenna stood up. "Sorry, Hal, but something's fishy here. What are the chances that both Sought Six teams would have a set of twins? I mean, really?"

"Okay, I admit it's weird," said Hallie, crossing her arms. She groaned because she knew there was nothing she could say to convince Jenna not to ask Annabel about the picture. "Just pick your moment, okay? Don't, like, blurt it out over dinner or something. Don't catch Annabel off guard. We like her, right?"

"Of course," said Jenna, as if the question was one of the dumbest she'd ever heard.

"Then don't upset her, please," said Hallie. "She's been so nice to us, and she's helped us so much."

"I know that. I'm not going to upset her."

"By bringing up her dead sister? You just might."

Jenna opened her mouth to retort, but closed it at the last minute. Finally, she said quietly, "I'll pick my moment."

"Thank you." Hallie motioned her head toward the stairs. "Now, can we please go?"

Jenna didn't say anything, but merely yawned in response. Hallie took that as a 'yes', and so off they went, back downstairs to bed.

CHAPTER 21:
THE TRIALS OF THE TWINS

Jenna

ANOTHER WEEK OR TWO of combat training came and went. Honestly, time had gone by so quickly that Jenna didn't know exactly how long it had been. The only good thing about so many days of straight training was that the six of them were becoming quite skilled with their weapons. In fact, Jenna had even been able to disarm Levi a few days ago. She still hadn't figured out how to disarm Lou, and she wasn't sure she'd ever learn. With each day of practice, it became more and more obvious why Lou had the title of 'the best swordswoman in Pawcombe'.

Every bit of their time was taken up with something or other; weapon training, horseback riding lessons, studying maps of the forests—and, albeit rarely, a bit of free time. Thomas' free time continued to be spent in the library doing research, but this time about the Sterling Cone. Unfortunately, he hadn't been able to dig up any information on where it might be hidden.

Jenna still hadn't found the right time to talk to Annabel about the library book page that was burning a hole in her pocket, which made Hallie happy. She simply had to ask her, though, and she knew it would only be harder to do the longer she waited.

"Just leave it alone, Jenna," said Hallie as the two of them walked the halls of Maple Cliff one afternoon. "It's really none of our business, anyway."

"I beg to differ." Jenna lowered her voice as they passed one of the butlers dusting the picture frames. "Why would she keep something like this a secret? What's one of the first things we say when we meet someone new? That we're twins."

"Only if they're daft enough not to see it for themselves. We're identical, Jenna." Hallie exhaled sharply. "Besides, not everyone is the same. Maybe Annabel and her sister didn't get along. Maybe they fought all the time."

"We fight."

"Not all the time."

They left the hallway they were perusing and emerged through a door onto the curved stairway lining the walls of The Tower. They were only two floors up, so it wasn't much of a descent. Still, they had to walk in single file because the stairway wasn't very wide.

Everybody in The Tower was rushing around from one side to the other, going in and out of the many doors that curved around the walls. They acknowledged Jenna and Hallie with kind nods or greetings, but otherwise they were busy with their work. It made Jenna nervous to see how busy they all were. Maybe something new had come up about Zyngor.

"Where is everybody, anyway?" said Hallie, looking around. "I know Jules is still at the archery targets and Thomas is in the library…"

"Denny is giving Alan and Lindsay a riding lesson," said Jenna. "Haven't seen Mom or Levi since this morning. Haven't seen Annabel all day." She put her hand into her pocket and touched the library book page.

The door to Conference Room 1 was open, and Jenna looked inside as they passed it. She stopped walking.

"Speak of the devil," she said. Hallie looked in the room as well. Annabel was in there, sitting by herself at the oval table and looking out the window in a sort of trance.

"Jenna, don't—"

But Jenna wasn't listening. She had already started walking into the room. It wasn't long before she heard Hallie jogging to catch up to her.

"Jenna, leave it alone," Hallie hissed, grabbing her sleeve. Jenna pulled her arm free and cleared her throat.

"Annabel?" she said once they were close enough to her.

Annabel kept her green eyes glued to the green trees outside. "Jenna, Hallie. Come in." How she knew who was there was beyond them; she hadn't even looked at them.

"What are you doing?" said Hallie.

Annabel didn't answer. She barely moved.

Jenna took another step forward. "Where's Mom?"

"Out for a ride with Levi."

"How come you didn't go with them?"

Annabel shifted her eyes to meet theirs. She gave them a sly grin before returning her gaze to the window.

"Oh," said Hallie, understanding. "They wanted to go alone?"

"They didn't say so, but yes."

"Why?"

"Lou and Levi have always been... close. Even when we were kids. But since she's been here, they haven't been able to spend any real time together." Annabel finally turned in her chair to face them rather than the window. "What can I do for you, ladies?"

Jenna waited a moment in which she felt Hallie become tense next to her, and then she sat down in the chair next to Annabel.

"We found this in a book in the library." She reached into her pocket and retrieved the page with the picture of the other Sought Six team. "You were a twin?"

Hallie buried her face in her hands and groaned, but Annabel took the page from Jenna and cracked a smile. She ran her fingers over her—or, more likely, Jessica's—face.

"Am," she said.

"What?" said Jenna.

"I *am* a twin. She's still my sister."

Jenna felt her cheeks become hot. "Oh, right. Sorry. So, um, what was she like?"

Hallie stared at her with daggers. "Jenna!" she hissed.

"She was kind," said Annabel. "Much kinder than I ever was. She saw the good in everybody, and she was sweet to everybody. Even when they didn't deserve it."

Annabel stared at the picture for a few more moments before sniffling and wiping her nose with the back of her hand. "I had a feeling you guys would go hunting for answers. After that interview with *The Singing Pony*, how could you not?"

"Annabel," said Jenna, nervously. She opened her mouth several times to keep talking, but each time the words seemed to get caught in her throat. Finally, she swallowed and said, "It's not a coincidence that both Sought Six teams have a set of twins, is it?"

Annabel's green eyes sparkled in the sunlight that shone in through the great window. For a moment, she said nothing; she barely reacted. Jenna was about to repeat herself when Annabel finally shook her head.

"No," she said rather coldly, "it's not."

Jenna's mind was running a mile a minute. "So, Sought Six teams need all six of the kids to be born on specific days, *and* two of them need to be twins?"

"No wonder they're so rare. Twins are rare enough on their own, let alone adding the Sought Six into the mix," said Hallie.

"Yes, twins are a freak of nature," said Annabel, nodding slowly, "but in Pawcombe, they're also a force of nature."

"Why?" said Jenna, leaning so far forward that she almost fell off her chair. "What is it about twins? Why does a Sought Six team need them?"

"It's complicated," said Annabel, staring at her hands and twisting her pinkie rings.

Jenna exhaled deeply. "Can you explain it?"

Annabel paused. "The thing is, I don't know for sure," she said. "I can try to explain it. But our team never got that far. We didn't get the chance."

Jenna and Hallie exchanged nervous looks but kept quiet.

"Apparently," Annabel began, "many years ago, Zyngor removed his heart from his body and hid it somewhere. What makes it more complicated is that he also split it into two pieces. Basically, that means he won't die if we use our swords or bows on him. He'll be injured and will slow down, that's for sure, but he won't die. He can't be properly killed unless his heart his destroyed by the Sought Six. More specifically..."

Jenna gulped, getting a sinking feeling about where she was going with this.

Annabel sighed. "One twin has to retrieve one half of Zyngor's heart, and the other twin has to retrieve the other half—wherever they may be. The other four must do their part and assist, but the twins are the ones who must perform the final act. It can be done no other way."

"How come nobody told us this before?" said Hallie, after a moment.

"For the same reason you had to find out about the nilbogs on your own," said Annabel, "and the same reason we didn't tell you about things like the Sterling Cone right away. We didn't want to overwhelm you. As it is, I probably shouldn't have told you about the twin-thing without the others. But you two, of all people, should know."

"Well, what... What does... What does it look like?" Hallie gulped. "Zyngor's heart, I mean."

Annabel shrugged and shook her head. "I don't know. We never got that far."

"How much longer until we have to start looking for it?"

Annabel shook her head and sighed. "I don't know. But it's not right now. Right now, we have to focus on finding the Sterling Cone. We absolutely cannot let Zyngor find it first."

Again, Jenna and Hallie exchanged nervous looks.

"It's a silver pinecone that's so shiny it practically glows. Once we know where to look, it won't be too difficult to find," said Annabel, seeing their concern. "It's figuring out where to look—that'll be the hard part."

Jenna's brain felt like a ball of mush. "And... how are we supposed to figure that out?"

"That's what I'm sitting in here thinking about, actually." Annabel stared out the window again. "I'd like to be alone, if you don't mind."

"Oh, sure. Jenna, let's go," said Hallie.

Jenna stood up and slid the page off the table. She was about to pocket it when she felt Annabel's eyes burning a hole through her back.

"Leave that here," she said.

Jenna put the page back without a word, and then she and Hallie walked quickly out of Conference Room 1. Even though the door hadn't been closed when they entered, they closed it on their way out.

CHAPTER 22:
ARMIES ADVANCE

Jenna

D ENNY WALKED ON FOOT alongside six horses, one for each Sought Six member. She was certainly dressed for a day of walking—jeans, field boots, and a denim shirt. She also wore a bright pink scarf that matched the bright pink scrunchie holding her silver hair in a low ponytail.

She turned and looked up at each of them smiling that big, bright smile of hers. "Is everyone having fun?" she asked. "How do you like riding the trail?"

"Love it," Jenna answered for everyone as Belle marched along happily beneath her. "This is so much fun!"

Denny beamed. "I'm so glad."

Jenna was ecstatic at breakfast that morning when Denny told them she wanted to take them for a trail ride today. It may not have been the sunniest of days, but it was a perfect day for riding. At least, that's what Denny said.

"You've all been working so hard lately," she had said, spreading some jam onto a scone. "I think a little fun is well-deserved. Oop, my scone is crumbling! Whoops! So what do you say, kids? Noon?"

She took them through a part of Maple they hadn't seen yet, and it was truly breathtaking. They were riding along the top of a lengthy hill that towered over a lot of open fields. Jenna didn't even know there were so many open fields in Maple, since she had only seen the trees so far.

"Remember, sit up straight and look where you want to go," said Denny, shifting her glance from horse to horse, rider to rider. "Alan, push your heels down, dear. Hallie, very good. Lindsay, very good. Jules, darling, sit up straighter."

Jules leaned forward and held tightly to the thick black mane of Nuit, Levi's horse. "I'm never going to get the hang of this." She seemed to be focusing more on staying on his back rather than steering him. "It's so bumpy and jerky."

"It'll be a lot more comfortable if you just sit back and relax," said Lindsay, who was quite a natural atop a beautiful bay horse named Fleur. "Let your body move with him."

"Easy for you to say," said Jules, gripping more of Nuit's mane. "Your grandparents live on a farm. You're used to this."

Jenna chuckled as she gave Belle's neck a gentle pat. Belle wasn't bumpy or jerky at all, but she supposed if she was sitting as tensely as Jules was, it might feel different. The breeze blew her hair back and probably tangled it a bit, but she didn't care. It was a chilly wind, but Belle's body was so warm that she barely noticed.

"Remember, eyes forward and heels down. Sit up nice and tall," said Denny, watching them all. She clapped her hands delightedly. "You're all doing so wonderfully well! I can't wait to tell the others what a success your first trail ride was."

Then, suddenly, Belle stopped. She stopped hard, as a matter of fact. Jenna was glad she happened to be at the end of the line of riders, otherwise there might have been a horse collision. Belle grunted and her ears pinned back against her head. She adjusted her stance, swinging her body around and facing herself down the hill.

"Whoa, easy," said Jenna. "What is it, Belle?"

Belle pawed at the ground and shook her head. Jenna looked forward in the direction Belle was now standing. There was a mass of people down the hill and over the forest—hundreds, maybe thousands. They were all wearing dark clothing and shiny armour and carrying weapons. They were marching in the direction of Maple Cliff. Jenna felt her stomach drop.

"Oh... what... hey, guys, do you see that?"

"Huh? See what?" said Alan. He brought his horse to a halt and looked behind him.

"Denny!" Jenna called as quietly as she could. She had no idea how well the sounds of their voices might travel over to those people, and she didn't want to find out.

Denny spun around and Jenna pointed down and across the land.

"Oh, merciful heavens," Denny gasped. Her smile faded.

"What?" said Hallie, twisting on the back of her horse. "Who are those people?"

"Zyngor's army," Denny said bluntly.

Now, Jules sat up straight. "What?"

"They're on the move, but they're still far enough away. That forest down there is mostly wetlands, so they're going to have to go around it. At this rate, it looks like..." Denny looked up at the sky, across the field to the army, and then back in the direction of Maple Cliff. "Yes, at this rate, they'll probably reach us by sunrise, the day after tomorrow."

"So soon?" said Jenna, staring down at the army. Belle was still staring as well. She snorted, as if to express her personal disdain.

"We knew they'd be coming. After the attack at your school, then Winston Pearce, and then Klaus' death... It was only a matter of time, really," said Denny. She inhaled deeply and forced a new smile. "Well, we can't stay out here. We must keep walking. Come on, let's go home."

"But... Denny," said Jenna, swallowing hard. "Well, what... what are we going to do?"

"The only thing we can do. We're going to fight."

Everyone looked between each other.

"You're ready, my dears," said Denny, nodding confidently. "You've done so well with your training, not even including what you've done in the dungeons of Vandnav Hall. Maple Cliff is prepared to match that army down there, don't you fret about that. As I said, we knew they were coming. While you kids were training, we've been preparing."

Jenna didn't know it was possible to feel better and to not feel better at the same time.

"What's next, then?" she finally said.

"We go back to Maple Cliff," said Denny, beginning to walk again, "and we inform the others what we've seen."

"And then?" said Hallie, squeezing her horse onward.

Denny kept her eyes forward. "Then, we wait."

When they got back to Maple Cliff and made sure the horses were happy in their stalls, they told the others what they had seen. Word spread very fast after that. Lou, Levi, and Annabel reacted exactly as Jenna had expected: Lou was worried, Levi was fired up, and Annabel was passive. Denny was up very late that night sending out notices to the residents of Maple, warning them of the incoming attack on Maple Cliff. Some very brave people offered to venture out and fight the army before they even got to Maple Cliff, but Denny assured them it was no use. She had seen with her own eyes that Zyngor had acquired far too many fighters.

While Denny stayed up and did her work, Jenna slept uneasily. Hallie probably did as well, judging by how many times she tossed and turned, whacking Jenna in the face with her arm. Eventually, they both found a comfortable spot and drifted into dreamless sleeps.

But then, once again, a hand landed on Jenna's face. She made a half-awake move to push it off, but it wouldn't budge.

Why wouldn't it budge?

She tried to move, but the hand was pressing down hard on her mouth, keeping her still and quiet.

Her eyes snapped open. She tried to yell out, but she couldn't. Whoever was covering her mouth wasn't letting go. She jerked her head to Hallie's side of the bed, where she was also being held by a hand over her mouth.

"Shh!" this person hissed. "Calm down. It's me, Annabel." Then she released her hands and stood back.

Jenna sat up. It was indeed Annabel, but she was wearing a hooded sweatshirt with the hood lifted over her head. She looked rather like a thief in the night, especially since she also had her bow and a quiver full of arrows over her shoulders.

"Annabel? What are you doing?"

Hallie lifted her watch off the bedside table and peered closely at it in the dark. "It's the middle of the night!"

"I need the two of you to come with me now," Annabel whispered. She pressed a finger to her lips.

"What?" Jenna rubbed her eyes. "Why?"

"Change into your jeans," said Annabel, heading toward their bathroom door, "and put your shoes on." She peeked into Lou's adjoining room to make sure she was still asleep, and then gently closed both doors.

Jenna and Hallie were so groggy that they didn't question Annabel's motives, even though their minds were filling up with plenty of questions. They hobbled their way over to Annabel and followed her out into the hall. Jules, Alan, Lindsay, and Thomas were already out there, shoes and jackets on and looking every bit as groggy.

"What's going on?" said Jenna, looking at Annabel. "Why are we all here? Where are we going?"

"Follow me. Quickly and quietly. Keep up." She darted down the hall, her wavy chestnut hair bouncing behind her. Everyone followed, but not nearly as fast. Eventually, she led them outside into the crisp nighttime air.

Across the field and into the forest they went, never letting up on speed until they arrived at a large red maple tree. Annabel turned on her heels and waited for everyone to catch up.

"Why are we here?" said Jenna. She looked at the tree. "Wait a minute, is this tree a Root Path?"

"Yes."

"Where does it lead?"

"You'll find out soon enough."

"This is a Root Path?" Alan stared at it. "How can you tell?"

Annabel shook her head. "There isn't really anything distinctive. The more time you spend in these forests, you just get to know which trees are Root Paths and which ones aren't." She retrieved a matchbox from her pocket. "There is one way to tell, come to think of it." She pulled out a match and scraped it against the box to ignite it. Then she held it right next to the tree bark. Everyone watched as the flame flew the other way on the match, as if being blown away from the tree by wind.

"Whoa, what's it doing?" said Alan, his eyes widening.

"See that? Root Paths don't burn," Annabel explained, shaking the match to put it out. Just then, Jenna noticed a paper bag Annabel was carrying. It appeared to have something lumpy in it.

"What's in the bag?" she asked.

Annabel looked down at it, as if she had forgotten she was holding it. "Nothing," she said simply. She cleared her throat. "Is everybody ready to go?"

Jenna groaned and wondered if there was even a point in asking where Annabel was leading them, since she hadn't gotten a straight answer so far.

"Go where?" she said anyway. "Where are we going?"

Annabel said nothing. Instead, she held out her hand for Jenna to take. Then, Jenna held out her hand for Hallie, Hallie held out hers for Lindsay, and so on. When everyone was connected to each other, Annabel knocked on the tree four times.

A gut-punch. A strong gust of wind. A bout of light-headedness.

When Jenna opened her eyes, there were no more maple trees surrounding them. Now, they were within a type of tree that Jenna recognized, but hadn't seen yet in Pawcombe.

"Welcome to Willow, everyone," said Annabel. She dusted herself off and flipped her hood, which had fallen, back on top of her head. "Stay close to me. We're here for a reason, and that reason isn't to get lost."

Jenna took deep breaths and massaged her stomach, hoping the effects of the Root Path would wear off soon. She looked up and around as she followed Annabel on the path. Even in the dark, she could see the wispy willow branches flowing slowly and rhythmically in the breeze, as if they were moving underwater. There was something about this forest that was more peaceful than Maple, Cedar, or Pine. Maybe it was the fact that there was no sign of people.

Right on cue, something snapped off in the distance, like a twig someone might have stepped on. Hallie reached for Annabel's arm.

"What was that?" she whispered.

"I don't know," said Jenna. She looked as hard as she could up the path, but she couldn't see or hear anything other than the wind moving through the willow branches above them.

"Shh," Annabel hissed. She stood very still, which encouraged everyone else to stand very still as well. Her eyes darted all over the place, but no other part of her body so much as flinched.

"Maybe we should just keep walking," Jenna suggested, but Annabel shook her head.

"We're not alone."

CHAPTER 23:
CITIZENS OF WILLOW

Hallie

HALLIE STOOD UP STRAIGHTER. Annabel's words had sent a chill up her entire spine. They weren't alone? What did that mean?

"Who's here?" Alan whispered. Annabel ignored him. Her back stiffened as her eyes shot sharply to her left, like there might have been someone behind her. Hallie couldn't bring herself to turn around and check, though.

"Notice I don't have my bow aimed, gentlemen," said Annabel, raising her voice slightly. "I think you should return the favour." Then, she slowly turned around. Everybody else copied her actions and then they saw who she was talking to.

It was hard to mistake who—or what—these creatures were. The top halves of them were humans, but the bottom halves were horses. Each of them had a bow aimed at the group, as Annabel had predicted.

"Are those... centaurs?" Jules gulped.

"They certainly appear to be," Thomas whispered in response. "I'm afraid they look rather angry."

"Do you have any idea who you're aiming those arrows at?" Annabel went on, stepping forward. The centaurs didn't budge. One of them—a blonde one with the golden hair on his human head matching the golden hair on his horse body—grunted and tightened his grip.

"Doesn't much matter," he said. "A trespasser is a trespasser."

Annabel sneered. "Not when you're a Sought Six requesting sanctuary."

The centaurs lowered their weapons, but they didn't seem entirely happy about it. They looked briefly at each other, and then back at the group. The other centaur, with reddish-brown hair on his head and body, pointed a finger at them.

"These children are the Sought Six?"

Annabel said nothing, but she finally put her hood down. The centaurs immediately recognized her and became rather pale.

"Miss Annabel," the reddish-brown one gasped. He blinked a few times. "I mean, I suppose you'd be known as Ms. Scott now, having grown up."

"Yes, Bafoe, it's been a while," said Annabel. She looked at the blonde centaur. "Are words failing you, Euwo?"

The blonde centaur, Euwo, gulped. He bowed his head. "They are, ma'am. Forgive me."

Finally, Annabel turned and acknowledged the rest of them. She motioned for them to come forward, so they did.

"These six children are Pawcombe's new Sought Six," she said. "They've already seen and done so much, and all to preserve Pawcombe and its citizens. All of its citizens."

The centaurs exchanged looks once again. Hallie couldn't help but detect a flicker of contempt.

"Yesterday, we learned that Zyngor is marching an army toward Maple Cliff. They'll be there in just over twenty-four hours." Annabel gripped tighter onto the paper bag, the contents of which were still a mystery. "Bafoe, Euwo... you're both smart enough to know why we've come here tonight."

Bafoe nodded. "You want to speak to Ralthoar."

"Yes," said Annabel, "we do."

"Well, I don't know what he'll say, especially at this hour," said Euwo, "but we will bring you to him."

Annabel sighed in relief; a sigh Hallie could hear but the centaurs could not. "Thank you," she said.

"This way," said Bafoe, extending his arm and inviting them to continue walking in the direction they were going.

As they walked, Hallie listened to the silence. Nobody said a word and even the wind had stopped blowing. It was rather a shock when Hallie happened to look behind her and saw three other centaurs following them about twenty yards back.

"Annabel," Hallie hissed, "behind us! There're three more centaurs."

"Four," said Annabel, not looking back. Hallie turned back around. There was a fourth one there now.

"Why are so many centaurs awake?" said Jenna, constantly looking behind them. "It's the middle of the night."

"Centaurs are highly intuitive creatures," said Annabel, eyes forward. "They know when something abnormal is happening in Willow. They'll want to know who we are and what we're doing here."

By the time they arrived at wherever Bafoe and Euwo were leading them, there was a whole crowd of centaurs behind them, all of them being as quiet as mice. Euwo stepped toward a willow tree as big as a small house and knocked on it. At first, Hallie thought he was going to disappear into a Root Path, but then a piece of the bark opened up like a door. It soon became obvious that this gigantic willow tree was as big as a house because it *was* someone's house.

There was a rustling sound from behind them suddenly, and when Hallie turned around, she saw that every centaur was bowing. Even Bafoe and Euwo bowed. Annabel nudged them all to do the same, and they dropped to their knees. Hallie kept one eye on the willow tree door and, soon enough, someone emerged.

It was a big centaur with jet-back hair on his human head and on his horse body. It practically glistened in the moonlight, as did his black hooves as they clip-clopped on the path. His dark skin was toned, and his face was stern but gentle.

"Ralthoar, sir," said Bafoe, "the Sought Six requests an audience with you."

"The Sought Six?" said Ralthoar in a rather booming voice.

"Yes, sir."

"My children," said Ralthoar. Hallie looked up, assuming he was speaking to them. He was. He offered them a kind smile. "You need not bow to anyone."

They stood up, as did Annabel, and that's when Ralthoar noticed her there.

"Ms. Scott," he said, nodding courtly, "it's nice to see you again."

"You as well," said Annabel.

"I assume there's a reason you've made the journey all the way to Willow in the middle of the night?" Ralthoar folded his hands in front of his body. "What can I do for you?"

The rest of the centaurs stood up straight again and listened intently.

"Zyngor is on his way to Maple Cliff," said Annabel. "He'll be there in a day's time."

Ralthoar nodded, unsurprised. "And you're in need of higher numbers for your army."

"We are, yes."

Ralthoar thought for a moment. "Is this true, Masters and Misses of the Sought Six? Is Zyngor posing an immediate threat on your lives?"

"Yes," said Hallie. "I mean, um, yes, sir. He is."

Ralthoar nodded. "Well, we cannot have that, can we?" He turned back to Annabel. "How many fighters do you need?"

"As many as you can spare," she said.

"Done." He lifted his chin and raised his voice so the whole crowd could hear him. "We will do our part in the battle at Maple Cliff—the battle for our Sought Six."

None of the centaurs seemed at all distressed by this notion. Quite the contrary; they all seemed eager and ready.

"I admit, I had a feeling we'd have a representative from Maple visiting us soon, asking for aid," said Ralthoar. "Rest assured, you've no reason to believe we won't help you if we can. The alliance between Willow and Maple has always been good. Together, we are strong." He spoke very calmly; Hallie felt warmed by his mere presence, even though he was so much bigger than she was. His human half looked even larger than an ordinary human, probably because he was also part horse.

"We appreciate it, Ralthoar, truly," said Annabel, turning and eyeing the six of them.

"Oh, yes," Jenna agreed quickly, as if someone had nudged her ribs and forced her to speak.

"Is there anything else you need?" said Ralthoar just as both Lindsay and Jules yawned. "A place to stay the night, perhaps?"

"That would be kind," said Annabel. Hallie tapped her arm.

"Mom's going to freak if she wakes up in the morning and we're gone," she whispered.

"It'll be fine," Annabel whispered back. "We're staying here tonight. Trust me, okay?"

Hallie almost asked her what she meant, but Annabel returned her attention to Ralthoar.

"There is one more thing, if I may ask it of you," she said.

"Of course," said Ralthoar. "I'll do my best to oblige."

Annabel stepped forward so none of the other centaurs would hear her. "Zyngor is hunting the Sterling Cone, Ralthoar."

Ralthoar's face immediately hardened. His lips tightened like he was sucking a lemon.

"That's what he wants," Annabel quietly went on. "We need to find it first."

Ralthoar grunted and crossed his arms. "Sorry, I can't help you."

"But you just said—"

"I can't help you."

"The Sought Six left their homes—their *lives*—to come to Pawcombe and stop Zyngor. They're here for Pawcombe's citizens. *All* of its citizens."

Ralthoar said and did nothing.

"Zyngor will use the Sterling Cone to destroy Pawcombe. The Sought Six can stop him from doing that if you just—"

"That is not—" Ralthoar practically bellowed, but he stopped himself. He lowered his voice almost to a whisper. "That is *not* my concern. They have *their* job and I have *mine*. I agreed to let my centaurs join your army. Don't make me retract my generosity."

Annabel stood back, defeated. She forced herself not to say another word, but Hallie could feel the disappointment radiating from her.

"Euwo, please take our guests to the riverside huts," said Ralthoar, louder now so that the crowd would know the conversation had been put to an end. The rest of the centaurs cleared away and went back to their homes as

Euwo hurried the group down the path toward the river. Ralthoar stayed right where he was, his tail swishing and his eyes watching them until they were out of sight.

CHAPTER 24:
BIRTHDAY DOUGHNUTS

Hallie

THE RIVERSIDE HUTS WERE exactly as they sounded: tent-like shelters by a river. At first, Hallie was a little bit put off by the idea of sleeping in tents. Lou took her and Jenna camping one summer when they were little and, after nearly being attacked in her sleep by a bear (it was actually just the wind, but it could have been a bear), she vowed never to sleep outside again. The tents in Willow were quite large, though, and the one where Euwo brought them had seven hammocks in it.

As comfortable as the hammocks were, which surprised Hallie, she stirred in hers for most of the night. Not because she thought she heard something outside, but because she couldn't stop thinking about the look on Ralthoar's face when Annabel had mentioned the Sterling Cone. It had been cold. Distant. And his entire body language had become aggressive.

A few hours later, when it was morning, everyone left the tent to find Annabel tending a campfire by the riverside. Hallie wondered how long she'd been up; if she ever even went to sleep.

"Good morning, sleepyheads," said Annabel, turning to see them all squinting in the sunlight. "I was beginning to wonder when you'd get up. Come over here, I've got something for you."

Everyone walked over to the campfire and took a seat on a few logs surrounding it. The river was slapping against the rocks as it flowed next to them and the fire cracked and sparked.

"Impressive firepit," said Thomas, holding his hands out to feel the warmth. "Did you build this?"

"I did," Annabel answered simply, as if it was an everyday thing for her. She took the paper bag she had been holding the night before from the grass and handed it to Jules. "Jules, you open this."

Jules did. Her face instantly lit up. "Doughnuts!" she exclaimed.

"What? Really?" said Alan, straining to see through the dancing flames to where Jules was sitting.

"There's one for each of you," said Annabel. "Sorry it's not a cake, but your uncle told me you like doughnuts."

"A cake?" said Jules, taking out a doughnut with pink sprinkles on it.

"Today's the first of July," said Annabel, smiling. "Happy birthday, Jules!"

Hallie stopped and thought. She hadn't even realized how long they'd been in Pawcombe; after all, none of them had seen a calendar in weeks. The school year was over now. Summer had begun. And if today really was the first of July, then it really was Jules' twelfth birthday.

"Wow, thanks, Annabel!" said Jules, beaming. "I can't believe you remembered. I didn't even know what day it was."

"Me neither," said Jenna, nudging Jules with her elbow. "Happy birthday, Jules!" Everyone else joined her in a chorus of "Happy Birthday to You", during which Jules' cheeks became bright red.

"Doughnuts for breakfast—cool!" said Alan. He bit into one and got a ring of chocolate icing around his mouth. "My mom never lets me have sugar for breakfast back home."

Annabel chuckled as she tied her hair back into a ponytail. "Well, now you're hanging out with me, and I say go for it." She sat there quietly for a few more moments as everybody began enjoying their breakfast doughnuts, but then she became agitated. "Listen, I have to tell you all something. There's a reason I brought you here to Willow."

"I thought it was because we needed the centaurs' help for Maple Cliff's army," said Hallie.

Annabel paused. "Okay, there are two reasons I brought you here. The second is because"—she took a breath—"the Sterling Cone was created in Willow. If anyone knows where it might be hidden, it's the centaurs."

Jenna made a face. "A pinecone was created in a forest full of willow trees?"

"Genius, don't you think? Who'd suspect it?"

"That's why you insisted on staying the night," said Hallie, understanding. "You wanted enough time to get information about the Sterling Cone."

Annabel nodded.

"Is that why Ralthoar got defensive last night?" said Thomas, biting into his doughnut and catching a few sprinkles as they fell off. "He doesn't know where the Sterling Cone is?"

"Oh no, he knows where it is. I'm sure of it."

Hallie crinkled her eyebrows. "Then, why didn't he tell us?"

"That's what's confusing me," said Annabel. "The centaurs have no reason to hide something like that from Maple Cliff, and especially from a Sought Six team."

"Are you sure the centaurs know where it is?" said Hallie. "I mean, how do you know?"

"I did my research." Annabel picked up a few small twigs and tossed them into the fire. "Thomas, why do you think you couldn't find any books on the Sterling Cone, even though you searched the library up and down?"

Thomas sat up straighter. "You took them out?"

"The moment we got back from Pine."

"Why?"

"I was afraid you guys might take it upon yourselves to travel to Willow by yourselves if you found out the Sterling Cone originated there."

Hallie and Jenna looked at each other, and at the same time, they said, "Why would you think that?"

Annabel raised an eyebrow. "Gee, let's recap, shall we? So far, in the short amount of time you've been in

Pawcombe, you've been ambushed by one of Zyngor's assassins, you snuck into a dungeon full of nilbogs, you nearly drowned in a sewer stream, you escaped a cave by flying gryphons, and, instead of simply asking me, you broke into the library in the middle of the night just to figure out that I'm a twin."

Hallie felt her cheeks redden.

Annabel chuckled as she shook her head. "Forgive me, but something tells me you guys are the 'figure it out for ourselves' kind of kids."

Alan wiped his hands on his pants after shoving the last of his doughnut into his mouth. He cleared his throat nervously. "You, um, you knew we went to the library in the middle of the night?"

"There's not much you can hide from me," said Annabel. "A big part of my job is to keep an eye on you."

"Who else knows about the centaurs' connection to the Sterling Cone?" Jenna gulped. "Does Zyngor know?"

"I was hoping Ralthoar might be able to answer that."

"How are you going to get Ralthoar to tell you the truth, then?" said Jenna.

"I'm not," said Annabel. Her green eyes flashed in the firelight. "You are."

Hallie coughed on her doughnut. "Excuse me?"

"That's another reason I had to bring you guys with me," Annabel explained. "I knew there was a chance the centaurs might not be very willing to divulge information about the Sterling Cone. But they can't refuse a Sought Six."

"They could say no," said Jenna.

Annabel shook her head. "They won't. Word will get out that they denied a personal request from the Sought Six, and that won't bode well for them. Centaurs are proud creatures. They won't want a bad image."

"You want us to go and talk to Ralthoar today, don't you?" said Thomas. "I mean, we don't have much time before Zyngor and his army arrive at Maple Cliff."

Annabel nodded. "Correct on all accounts, Thomas."

Hallie swallowed and turned to face Annabel. "He won't... you know, hurt us... will he?"

"No," Annabel said quickly. "Centaurs are kind. They won't hurt anyone if they don't have to, especially children. But I'll go with you and wait right outside. Okay?"

Hallie felt incredibly uneasy, but she nodded her head anyway. Thomas was right—they didn't have a lot of time.

CHAPTER 25:
RALTHOAR'S TRUTH

Hallie

LATER THAT MORNING, THEY all made their way back down the path toward Ralthoar's willow tree home. Willow appeared to be deserted. There was no sign of anyone. Hallie's uneasy feeling was still very present in her gut.

They knocked on the door to Ralthoar's home, but there was no answer. They tried again. Still, no answer.

"Maybe he's not home," said Jules, scanning the tree for a window to peek through.

"May I help you?" said a voice behind them. Everyone spun around.

"Good morning, um..." Jenna's eyes widened as she realized she had forgotten this centaur's name.

"Bafoe," Annabel whispered.

"Bafoe. Good morning, Bafoe," said Jenna.

"Good morning, young Masters and Misses," said Bafoe. "Are you looking for Ralthoar?"

"Yes," said Jenna.

"You won't find him here, I'm afraid," said Bafoe. "He's in the town square, as is everyone else. They're preparing themselves for Maple's battle."

"Oh," said Jenna. "Well, could you take us there? It's really important that we talk to him."

"Of course, Miss Jenna," said Bafoe, "right this way."

It didn't take long to follow the tree-lined path to get to the town square, which was actually shaped more like a circle than a square. There were large tents circling around a bare piece of land, and although this entire area was covered over by tall willow trees, no trees were growing inside the circle. Centaurs were swarming this area. There were so many that Hallie could barely count them all.

"Ralthoar is in that tent right there," said Bafoe, pointing to one.

"Thanks," said Hallie, and as they approached it, she was surprised to see just how tall it was. Then again, it was a normal sized tent to the centaurs. She reached her fist out and rapped sharply on the wooden pole that was supporting the tent flaps. Just as she knocked, Annabel ducked sideways and hid herself behind a tree.

"I'll be right here," she mouthed. She obviously didn't want Ralthoar to know she was there. Hallie's uneasy feeling suddenly got worse.

The tent flap lifted and Ralthoar was there, holding it up. He looked surprised to see them.

"Good morning," he said.

"Good morning, Ralthoar." Hallie cleared her throat. "May we come in?"

Ralthoar paused. "Of course," he finally said, stepping aside. "It would be my honour. Please, come in."

Inside the tent was a table covered with a large map of what Hallie could only assume was Pawcombe. The map was coloured with a lot of green, indicating trees, and there was also some blue, indicating lakes. A sword was leaning against the table—a huge sword, at that.

"Is that yours?" Jules asked, also noticing the sword.

"Indeed, it is," said Ralthoar. "It's served me well over the years. You all have swords, too, I'd imagine."

"I have a bow," said Jules.

"Just like your mentor, Ms. Scott," said Ralthoar, nodding. "If you're lucky, one day you'll be as skilled as she is. Well, kids, I do hope you had a good night's sleep. How did you find the riverside huts? Comfortable?"

"Look, we don't want to waste your time," said Hallie, "so, I think we should just get straight to the point."

Ralthoar smiled but said nothing.

"You must know why we're here," Lindsay added, doing her best not to break eye contact with him. "We need to find the Sterling Cone, and we need to find it fast."

Ralthoar's smile faded.

"We know it was created here, and we know you know where it is," said Jenna, trying to sound confident. "We know you lied to Annabel about it last night."

"We don't know why you lied," Thomas added, "and we aren't judging you, but we need this information."

Hallie took a breath. "Tell us what you know about the Sterling Cone. Please."

Ralthoar pawed at the ground nervously. "It's complicated, kids," he said.

"Try," said Hallie. "Please, for us."

Ralthoar's eyes slid shut. He wasn't going to refuse them, but he didn't like it.

"Yes, I know where it is," he said. "I'm the only one in this world who knows precisely where it is. It was entrusted to me when I became leader of the centaurs and the protector of Willow."

"So, Zyngor doesn't know where it is, then?" said Jenna, sounding relieved.

Ralthoar squinted. "Not exactly."

"What does that mean?" said Jenna, now sounding pained.

"I told you. It's complicated." He sighed quite heavily. "Not long ago—just before you kids came back to Pawcombe—Zyngor came here to Willow. He knew the Sterling Cone was in my charge, so he threatened the welfare of Willow if I didn't hide it somewhere of his choosing. I couldn't ever let anyone find out where it was hidden. He knew the new Sought Six team would be arriving here soon, and he didn't want them to be able to find the Sterling Cone once its powers were activated."

"Activated?" said Alan.

"The Sterling Cone is useless to Zyngor unless there's an active Sought Six," Hallie clarified, remembering what Lou had told them at Pine City Centre.

"I know that," said Alan. "I just mean he knows there's an active Sought Six right now. He knows we're here. The Sterling Cone's powers are, you know, activated.

Why hasn't he come back to Willow to ask you where it is?"

Ralthoar smoothed his eyebrows and sighed heavily. "He has."

"Excuse me?"

"He's been to Willow. To me. He came after the news of Mr. Vandnav's death reached him."

Hallie shuddered at the mention of Klaus.

"He seemed quite put out—didn't like how effectively you all had been handling yourselves in Pawcombe." Ralthoar paused. "He did ask me to reveal the location of the Sterling Cone. He said he was ready to make his wish."

"What did you tell him?" said Hallie.

"I told him exactly what he wanted to hear. I told him I couldn't say the exact location out loud, in case anyone was listening, but I did tell him he could find it for himself in the crooked woods of Oak."

"You what?" said Alan, shocked.

"I told him I hid the Sterling Cone in Oak."

"Look, maybe you think you're doing the right thing by listening to him, but we're trying to help everyone," said Alan. Hallie nudged him in the arm, hoping he'd shut up, but he kept going. "*Everyone*—that includes centaurs, you know. You don't need to make our job any harder by siding with Zyngor."

Ralthoar looked shocked and, for a moment, Hallie was sure they were dead meat.

"*Siding* with him? No, you misunderstand me, Master Alan," said Ralthoar. "I told him I hid the Sterling Cone in Oak."

Alan crossed his arms. "No, I don't think I misunderstood you."

"Wait a second," said Lindsay, holding her hand out in front of Alan and staring at Ralthoar. "You *told* him you did?"

Ralthoar nodded, and now Alan understood, too.

"Please don't think ill of me," said Ralthoar, folding his hands and pleading to them. "I had no choice but to obey him—or, rather, make him *think* I was obeying him. He would have unleashed a massacre over Willow if I didn't tell him what he wanted to hear. I never wanted to betray my loyalty to Pawcombe. I never wanted to betray the Sought Six. That's why I lied to him, don't you see?"

"Why Oak?" said Hallie. "Why not Cedar or Birch or something?"

"He resides in Oak," said Ralthoar through a long sigh. "I thought it might keep him there and away from all of you, and it has. You haven't seen much of him in the time you've been in Pawcombe, have you?"

Hallie shrugged. "No, I suppose not."

"I only wanted to do my part in protecting our Sought Six."

"So, if it's not in Oak like he thinks it is, then where is it?" said Alan.

Ralthoar darted his eyes left and right. He was looking for any shadows on the tent wall, listening for anybody's breath. When he was sure they weren't being spied on, he sighed and lowered his voice.

"There's a maple tree on Forest's Edge Way. It's right off the path. You'll know it by its bark. It looks purple compared to the rest of them. If you hit the lake, you've gone too far. The Sterling Cone is buried about a foot beneath its roots."

"Maple?" said Alan, sounding rather exhausted. "Are you kidding me? We've travelled to half the forests in Pawcombe and it's been in our backyard this whole time?"

"I am sorry," said Ralthoar, and he truly did look sorry.

"Wait, is that the reason Zyngor is on his way to Maple right now?" said Hallie. "Does he know it's there?"

"No, he doesn't. He may know by now that it's not in Oak, but he doesn't know where it really is. Up until a few moments ago, I was the only one privy to that information." Ralthoar shook his head pitifully. "But now that he's on the move, there's no doubt in my mind that he knows the Sterling Cone is not where he thinks it is— that I lied to him. He may be wicked, but he isn't stupid."

"But what—what does that mean?" Jules stuttered.

"It means that before long, he's going to come back to Willow." Ralthoar swallowed so hard that his Adam's apple shot up and down his throat. "I just hope I'm the only centaur killed in his rage."

Before anyone had time to react, they heard shouting from outside the tent. There were cries of horror and cries of anger. There were pounding footsteps, like there were suddenly a hundred people stampeding through Willow. Jenna lifted the tent flap ever so slightly, but it was enough for Hallie to see out. The hundreds of footsteps were coming from nilbogs, all with swords. They were attacking Willow and taking the centaurs by surprise.

Ralthoar's face became pale. "Oh no," he said, looking so desperately sorry at them. "He's already here."

Hallie's heart sped up. "Annabel," she muttered. Jenna opened the tent flap even further.

"Miss Jenna, please stay inside!" Ralthoar exclaimed, but it was no use. There weren't only nilbogs on the attack—there were people as well. They were cutting down the tents in the town square and slicing through the hanging willow branches. The centaurs, although caught off-guard, were defending themselves well. Most of them already had swords on their belts or bows over their shoulders, as if it was some sort of fashion accessory.

"Annabel!" Jenna cried. She was nowhere to be seen.

"Jenna, close that!" Hallie shrieked. "Are you trying to get us killed?"

"We can't stay here!" Jenna shrieked back. "Look what they're doing to the other tents. If we stay here, we *will* get killed!"

"But we can't go out there—we don't have our weapons here!" cried Jules.

Ralthoar snatched his sword off the ground and unsheathed it. "Stay hidden, kids," he said urgently as he trotted for the tent flap. "I'll make sure nobody comes near this tent. Leave through the back flap, and hurry. I don't know how long I can hold them off." And with that, he left the tent. Judging by the loud grunts and yells, as well as clanging swords, he was immediately ambushed upon leaving.

"Well, I say we follow his orders," Thomas said nervously, "and leave through the back flap." They all turned and looked behind them, where there was indeed a back exit to the tent. There were screams coming from out the front entrance, followed by clashing swords and pounding feet.

"Yeah, let's get the heck out of here," said Hallie, speeding toward the back flap. Someone else screamed in pain outside and Hallie forced herself not to think about what was happening. The morning sun had completely gone away, and grey storm clouds replaced it. The wind had picked up as well.

"I don't like this," said Jules, standing firm to steady herself in the wind.

Hallie looked around and noticed there was nobody in their immediate vicinity; all the commotion was happening inside the town square, not behind it.

"Do you think they're here to..."—Alan gulped—"to kill Ralthoar, like he thought?"

"I hope not, and not just because Ralthoar doesn't deserve to die," said Jenna, holding her sandy-blonde hair against her head so it wouldn't fly all over her face in the wind. "If they're here to kill Ralthoar, that means Zyngor has figured out the Sterling Cone isn't in Oak, and that means—"

"Nothing's keeping him away from us anymore," Thomas finished for her. He also held his hair against his head. "This isn't good. This isn't good at all."

"I say we just start running," said Hallie, "and maybe we'll find a way out of here without anyone seeing us." She turned around and started to walk, but instantly bumped right into someone. She grunted and stumbled back, but then she lunged forward and hugged this person.

"Oh, Annabel! You're alive!"

She was dirty and sweaty, her chestnut hair had lost most of its bounce, and she had a bloody nose, but she was there. She had already made quite a dent in this fight; there were hardly any arrows left in her quiver. Everyone else rushed to hug her as well, but the hug was interrupted by the clanging of swords and the screeches from people, centaurs, and nilbogs on the other side of the tent. Annabel hurried them further into the forest and behind a group of willow trees.

"Listen to me," she said, breathing heavily. She wiped her forehead. "Before I woke you up to come to Willow, I hid your weapons and some armour in Maple Cliff. 7-1-9-3. Remember that."

Hallie shook her head. "You... wait, what?"

Clang! Clang! Squish!

"I don't care what's happening when you get back to Maple Cliff," Annabel went on, ignoring the commotion behind them. "Our army will hold Zyngor at bay. Your job is to find the Sterling Cone. I heard Ralthoar tell you where it is just now, so arm yourselves and then go find it.

Find it and destroy it. Then, and only then, may you go and help the others. Got it?"

They all nodded vigorously, but nobody looked confident.

"There's a Root Path around here that'll take you right where you need to be," said Annabel, scanning the forest. "You're going to take the Root Path, prepare yourselves, and join the battle at Maple Cliff."

Hallie felt a wave of fright rush through her. "What? No! We're not leaving you here!"

"You've all done everything you can here," said Annabel, reaching to gently stroke their faces or hair. She offered a smile to them, but not without tears in her eyes. This was the first sign of weakness they had ever seen in Annabel, and yet, she had never looked stronger. "You can't stay here. It's not safe. You're needed in Maple. Lou needs you. Levi needs you. Denny needs you. I... I don't need you. You can't help me here anymore. You have to go."

Someone screamed loudly in pain from the town square. Hallie flinched so hard that she threw herself back against a tree. She covered her ears, as the screams and clanging of swords were relentless. Annabel began searching frantically for one specific tree.

"This one!" she finally said, reaching out and touching one. "No... no, not this one." She muttered something under her breath that Hallie couldn't quite make out.

There was an unsettling slicing sound off in the distance, followed by a loud screech that Hallie recognized to be a nilbog's cry. Her heart was beating so fast that she thought it might leap out of her chest.

"This one! This is the one!" Annabel exclaimed, pointing at a tall willow tree and being careful not to knock it herself. "I'll make sure you aren't followed. Hurry!"

Jenna and the others rushed to the tree and held hands so they could all travel the Root Path together. Annabel rushed out of the forest.

"Annabel, no!" Hallie pleaded. "Come with us!"

Annabel looked back at her with a mix of adoration and pity. "Go, Hallie. Please."

"Hal, come on!" Jenna yelled, reaching for her hand.

"Just go! Go while you still can!" said Annabel, pushing Hallie away. Hallie waited a moment more, watching as Annabel rushed off toward the commotion with her bow loaded and aimed.

Hallie turned and took Jenna's hand.

"Alan, now!" Jenna yelled. Alan knocked on the tree four times and, quicker than a snap, they were out of there.

CHAPTER 26:
BURIED SILVER

Jenna

THEY GATHERED THEMSELVES UP next to a tree right outside Maple Cliff. There was a door to inside not ten feet from them. They couldn't hear anything—no battle cries, no clanging of swords, and no horse's hooves pounding against the ground.

"Perhaps we're early," said Thomas. "The battle doesn't seem to have started yet."

"That doesn't mean they aren't here," said Jenna, trying and failing to see around Maple Cliff. They must have been at the very back of the building, out of harm's way. No wonder Annabel insisted they take that particular Root Path.

"Do you think Annabel is going to be alright?" said Hallie, almost reading Jenna's mind.

"Of course she is," said Alan. He shrugged his shoulders coolly, but he didn't look very sure. "I mean, it's Annabel. She has to be."

"Let's just go get our stuff," said Jenna, trying not to think about any gut-wrenching scenarios. She made her way to the door and almost tripped over the long blades of grass. It had to have been a long time since someone trimmed the lawn back there. "Annabel said she got some armour ready for us, right?"

"And she put it with our weapons," Lindsay added, "but then she said 7-1-9-3. What on earth could that mean?"

"Maybe it'll be obvious when we get inside," said Jenna, reaching for the door handle. It did nothing other than wiggle a little in its place. Then, she noticed the padlock beneath the handle.

"Oh, well that's just great," Hallie groaned. "How are we supposed to get inside now? Go around the building?"

"No way, we aren't armed!" said Jules. "And if there's even the slightest chance that Zyngor's army is here already... Nuh uh."

"Guys," said Jenna, staring at the padlock. "Look at this lock. It's a four-digit combination lock."

Hallie shrugged. "So what?"

"What was that number Annabel gave us?"

Lindsay's teal blue eyes widened. "7-1-9-3," she said.

Jenna dialled those numbers.

Clunk.

"Open sesame!" Alan exclaimed, pounding his fist into his palm. "Thank you, Annabel!"

Jenna exhaled. "I hope she's alright," she mumbled, opening the door.

This room, if it could even be called a room, was long and thin. It was more of a twenty-foot hallway made entirely of stone from floor to ceiling.

"Ugh," said Hallie, holding her nose. "I feel like we're back in Klaus' dungeon."

"At least there aren't any nilbogs," said Jules.

"Not here, anyway." Jenna bent and picked up a sword. It was a Rose. "Here, Hal, this one's yours." Their swords, Jules' bow and quiver of arrows, and a bunch of pieces of armour were spread out all over the floor.

"What is this place, a storage room for weapons?" said Lindsay, securing a piece of armour over her shoulders that covered most of her body. "If these are all the same size, they're going to be big on the rest of you. I'm the tallest, and it's long on me."

"As long as it stops me from getting stabbed, I don't care." Jenna tightened her sword around her waist and then scanned the floor for some armour. "Come on, we don't have a lot of time."

When everyone was dressed, they quietly left the room. They shut and re-locked the door so it wouldn't look suspicious to anyone, and they began to make their way around to the front of Maple Cliff.

"Forest's Edge Way is a street that's just down from Maple Cliff's entrance," said Jenna, jogging from tree to tree and hiding behind each one. "I remember it. Mom showed it to us when we first came to Pawcombe, remember, Hal?"

"Yes," said Hallie, huffing as she sprinted to join Jenna behind the tree. Their armour clinked as they moved. Hallie sighed. "Someone's going to hear us if we don't get a move on."

At last, they arrived around the front of Maple Cliff and rushed into the forest toward Forest's Edge Way. On one side of the dirt path there were miles and miles of maple trees. On the other side—well, there was no other side. The forest ended abruptly and dropped. Maple Cliff wasn't the only cliff surrounding the big open field below.

"I guess now we know why they named this street Forest's *Edge* Way," said Jenna. She pulled Thomas' sleeve. "Careful, you're walking too close to the edge."

Hallie looked out over the edge as well. "You know, I don't remember that field being so far below Maple Cliff. That is the field we walked across to get to Maple Cliff on our first day here, isn't it? Surely..." Then her face became pale, and she pointed a shaky finger down to the field. "G-guys... look..."

There were two crowds of people, one on either side of the field. The crowd closest to Maple Cliff was the army fighting for the Sought Six. Jenna recognized a few of the men and women in armour as employees of Maple Cliff, but they were so far away that it was difficult to see everybody clearly.

"Jenna, look! There's Mom," said Hallie, pointing to the head of the crowd. Lou was indeed there, armed and sitting atop Belle. She was next to Levi, riding Nuit. They appeared to be leading the army.

"And there's Uncle Levi, too!" Jules exclaimed rather loudly.

"Jules, shh!" Jenna hissed. Her gaze moved to the other side of the field where Zyngor's army was. At least, she could only assume they were Zyngor's army. This crowd was littered with slimy green nilbogs.

"Where's Denny?" said Hallie, looking everywhere. "Isn't she fighting, too?"

Lindsay pointed. "She's right there. See the pink on her armour?"

Jenna couldn't help but chuckle. Leave it to Denny to wear armour with pink engravings.

The air suddenly filled with the clean swishing sounds of thousands of swords being unsheathed. Everybody in Zyngor's army was preparing for an attack. They held their swords at the ready and they began shouting things Jenna couldn't make out.

She whipped her head back over to Lou, who was calmly taking out her Asiuol sword. She held it high in front of her, which must have been some sort of command because then every archer in Maple Cliff's army loaded their bows with arrows. Lou lowered her sword, and each archer released their arrows. Jenna watched as they flew clear across the field, hitting members of Zyngor's army.

"Do you see Zyngor anywhere?" asked Jenna, scanning the angry army as they looked up for more incoming arrows.

"Negative," said Thomas, adjusting his glasses. "At least, I don't see anyone who could be Zyngor."

"I don't like that," said Jules, fidgeting with a buckle on her armour. "That means he could be anywhere."

Lou brought her sword up and down once more, and more arrows flew across the field toward Zyngor's followers. With that, Zyngor's army charged forward. Lou wasted no time kicking her heels into Belle's sides and charging forward as well, Levi and the rest of Maple Cliff's army right behind her. The area suddenly echoed with battle cries and screams, not to mention the pounding of nilbog feet, human feet, and horse hooves.

"I hope Annabel gets here with the centaurs soon," said Jenna. She refused to take her eyes off Lou galloping across the field. When the two armies met in the middle of the field, there was instant chaos and bloodshed. With everybody mixed up around each other, it was next to impossible to make out any faces. The only way Jenna could keep an eye on Lou was because Belle's snow-white body stood out against the green field.

"Jenna!" said Hallie, snapping her fingers in Jenna's face. She had been trying to get her attention for a while.

"Argh, what?" said Jenna, flinching.

"We have to find the Sterling Cone, remember?" she said. "That's why we're here. Remember what Annabel said."

Jenna nodded. They rushed off down the path, away from the edge of the cliff. It was probably for the best—Jenna knew it would have driven her crazy to stand there and just watch the battle happen. Besides, someone could have easily seen them up there if they happened to look.

"Okay, so we're looking for a purple tree?" said Jenna, trying to remember what Ralthoar told them back in Willow.

"Purple? There's no such thing as purple trees," said Lindsay.

"Isn't that what Ralthoar said?"

"No," said Alan, "he said... um... he said something about a lake, right?"

Jenna rolled her eyes and stopped running. "Thomas, what exactly did Ralthoar say?"

Thomas thought. Then, as if he were reading from a book in his mind, he said, "There's a maple tree on Forest's Edge Way. It's right off the path. You'll know it by its bark. It looks purple compared to the rest of them. If you hit the lake, you've gone too far. The Sterling Cone is buried about a foot beneath its roots."

Alan snapped his fingers. "See? I knew he said something about a lake."

"More importantly," said Jenna, "he said the tree is going to look purple."

"Guys..." Jules had jogged ahead a few feet. "Come over here and look at this." She was kneeling in front of a tree, and its bark definitely had a purplish hue compared to the other greyish-brown trees around it.

"This must be it!" said Alan, dropping to his knees and pushing his hands into the dirt. "Someone help me dig!"

After digging for what felt like an eternity, they all had dirt stains up to their elbows. Jenna sat back and looked at the hole they had made around the tree.

"This must be deeper than a foot," she said. "Maybe this isn't the right tree after all."

"It's got to be," said Alan, still digging. "We have to keep trying. We have to—whoa! What *is* that!" He snatched his hands back and leapt backward, as if something might have bitten him.

"What?" Hallie shrieked, crawling to his side. "What happened?"

"There's something down there," he said, pointing to the hole. "It was... it was... smooth."

"Smooth?" said Hallie. "You yelled blue murder for smooth?"

"You don't know," he sneered. "Smooth could be bad. What if it was a snake?"

Jenna peered down into the hole. "Jules, give me one of your arrows." She took the arrow and began digging around the loose dirt. Nothing came slithering or flying out at her, so she assumed there were no animals down there. Something did, however, make a tapping noise against the arrowhead.

Tap. Tap. Tap.

"Do you guys hear that?" said Jenna.

Tap, tap, tap.

Lindsay leaned in excitedly. "What's this?" she said, reaching down and pulling more dirt away. Then, Jenna saw a shimmer. A silver shimmer. She reached down and gripped her fingers around something smooth. Smooth, but very oddly shaped. She pulled it out of the ground.

There, in her hand, was a shiny silver pinecone. Despite being buried in the dirt, there wasn't a speck of dirt on it. It was so shiny that it was almost glowing— Annabel was right about that.

"That's it?" said Alan, leaning forward to get a better look. "That's the Sterling Cone?"

Lindsay looked at him. "What were you expecting?"

"I don't know, I guess I thought it'd be bigger. It's the same size as any old pinecone."

"Guys, focus," said Jules, waving her hands. "Now that we've found it, how are we going to destroy it?"

"Maybe we can break it," said Jenna, standing up. She wound up her arm.

"Jenna, wait!" Hallie exclaimed, grabbing her arm to stop her. "What are you doing?"

"Throwing it against a tree," said Jenna. "Maybe it'll smash."

"And if you miss?" Hallie demanded. "Then what? We have to go searching through the forest for this thing that we've already spent weeks looking for."

"Yeah, I say we use our swords," said Lindsay. Jenna put the Sterling Cone on the ground and Lindsay wound up with her white-gold sword. She swung it down in a direct hit, but the Sterling Cone only seemed to bounce off the blade. Jenna dodged after it and picked it back up. There wasn't a dent on it.

"Here, let me try," said Jules, loading her bow with an arrow. Again, Jenna put the Sterling Cone back on the ground. Jules aimed and fired. Another direct hit, but this time it was the arrow that bounced off the Sterling Cone.

"Heads up!" Alan exclaimed as he and Thomas ducked to avoid the arrow, and it flew into a bush. Jenna picked up the Sterling Cone. There wasn't a dent on it.

Hallie groaned. "What, is it protected by magic or something?"

"There must be some way we can destroy it," said Alan. He scratched his head. "What is silver's kryptonite?"

Jules made a face. "Krypto-what?"

Alan lifted his eyebrows. "You know, like in Superman? The thing that can beat him...?"

"Unfortunately, there isn't much that can damage silver—at least, not seriously. It's rather a strong metal," said Thomas.

"You don't say," Jenna muttered, staring at the untarnished, undented Sterling Cone in her hands. "There's got to be something we can try."

"Well, silver readily tarnishes in water, but only if the water contains levels of hydrogen sulfide," Thomas went on, "and certain silver compounds are highly explosive. Then again, there's no way of knowing the Sterling Cone's exact makeup."

Jenna sighed. "In a language we can understand?"

"I don't know how we're going to destroy it," said Thomas.

"Great," Hallie muttered. "Well, let's just walk. Maybe we'll find something that—"

They turned and began walking down the path, but they barely got two steps forward before the noticed someone standing in their way.

It was a man. A man with black hair buzzed nearly down to his scalp. He was tall—probably at least seven feet—and he was wearing a long cloak that made him look even bigger than he already was. His neck was so skinny that the bones and veins protruded out. His eyes, dark and menacing, were wide.

Jules screamed. Hallie almost fell backward. Jenna quickly tucked the Sterling Cone into the pocket of her sweatshirt beneath her armour. None of them had ever seen this man's face before, but that didn't matter. They knew exactly who he was.

CHAPTER 27:
THE MAN FROM THE
NIGHTMARE

Jenna

JENNA GULPED. "ZYNGOR?"

"So, this is Pawcombe's Sought Six," said Zyngor, slinking toward them. His voice was raspy, as if he had a sore throat. "At last, I get to meet the children I will have the pleasure of killing."

"Stay away!" Alan yelled, stepping forward with his Wind Rider aimed at Zyngor's face. Zyngor looked amused. He lifted his hand as if he were swatting a fly, and Alan flew backward into a bush off the path.

Jenna was so stunned that she could barely move. Had that just happened? Had Zyngor somehow thrown Alan using... magic?

Zyngor spat a laugh as he watched Alan gather himself back up.

"Bravery is a noble quality, young man." He pulled a sword off his belt that was black from base to tip, just like Jenna had seen it in her dream. He tapped the tip of his sword with his fingertip to test its sharpness, drawing a dot of dark red blood. He licked it away as if it were icing from a cake. All the while, he didn't take his eyes off them.

"What— What do you want?" Hallie stuttered.

"You know what I want," Zyngor wheezed. "You're smarter than that."

"We..." Jules gulped. "We don't know what you want."

"That's a lie," said Zyngor. He lifted his hand and wiggled his fingers, threatening to do to her what he just did to Alan. "I'm feeling generous, though, so I'll let you try that answer one more time, *Miss* Jules."

Jules' cheeks went white as a sheet. "Um... um..."

"Too long," said Zyngor, and he flicked his hand again. Just like Alan before her, Jules flew backward and rolled along the dirt path.

"Jules!" Thomas exclaimed, rushing back to help her up.

Again, Zyngor spat a laugh. "You can't blame me for having my fun while I can." He waved his fingers all around. "This little trick of mine only works on the Sought Six."

"We're not giving you what you want!" Jenna practically shouted. She could hear her heartbeat in her ears.

"With boldness like that, you should be on the battlefield." He looked them all up and down. "Judging by the way you're dressed, I'm actually left to wonder why you're *not* on the battlefield."

"We were sent to look for the Sterling Cone!" Jules shouted quickly, and then immediately covered her own mouth.

"Ha!" Zyngor spat. "The truth comes out at last. See, that wasn't so hard, was it?"

"So— So what? That doesn't mean we found it," said Lindsay.

"Oh, but I'm afraid it does." Zyngor spun his sword around in his wrist and began walking toward them. "You see, I know that Ralthoar deceived me."

"He..." Jenna swallowed. "No, he didn't."

"He did!" Zyngor bellowed. The mere volume of his voice released an involuntary squeal from Jenna's mouth. He pointed his sword violently at them. "He deceived me and betrayed me. I should have killed him when I had the chance."

"What did you do to him?" Jenna demanded. "And Annabel... What did you do to Annabel?"

"I didn't do anything," said Zyngor. He tilted his head, which somehow made him look even taller. "I sent some of my army into Willow to deal with Ralthoar. If Annabel Scott got in the way, that's not my problem. She always was a feisty little brat, anyway."

"If you ordered it," Jenna said through gritted teeth, "you might as well have done it."

"Well, in that case, I did the same thing to them that I'm going to do to you." He tightened his grip on his sword and his eyes sunk deep beneath his eyebrows. "Your time as the great and powerful Sought Six has come to an end."

No one wasted any time. They all ran, and Zyngor bounded after them. Jenna tried to lead them back the way they had come, but suddenly, one of the trees ahead of them exploded. Its trunk burst with such a force that tiny wood chips flew outward in every direction, causing the topmost branches to come crashing down.

"Move!" Jenna yelled, leaping off to the side and hoping the others would as well. The branches made a deafening *thud* when they hit the ground and Jenna wondered if the people on the battlefield had any clue what was going on up there.

"What happened?" Hallie shrieked. "Why did that tree just explode?"

Jenna glanced back at Zyngor who looked sickly proud of himself. He made sure she was watching before he pointed his index finger at another tree and then turned his wrist over. The tree he was pointing at instantly exploded with the same force as the first one.

"He's going to blow up every tree up here if he has to," Alan gasped, also watching from his spot on the ground. "What do we do now?"

Thomas looked over the edge of the cliff, which, now that Jenna was also looking closely at it, really wasn't all that steep. Thomas gulped and shifted closer to the edge.

"Tuck and roll," he said, promptly sliding himself off.

"Thomas, wait!" Hallie exclaimed just as another tree—one much closer to them—burst into a cloud of bark and leaves. This time, one of the chips of wood flew across Jenna's cheek, causing the skin to break and blood to dribble down her face. She winced in pain, and Jules and Lindsay inched their ways over the edge of the cliff.

"Come on," said Jenna, pulling at Hallie's and Alan's arms. "We have no choice!" And with that, all three of them slid over the edge and down the hill. It may not have been very steep, but it was steep enough that they couldn't control themselves on the way down. They tumbled, they bounced, and they slid. It was a good thing they were wearing armour.

At the bottom, they were only a short distance away from the two armies who were viciously attacking each other. Some of the horseback fighters for Maple Cliff were running over nilbogs like they were dandelions. Jenna looked all over but she couldn't see Lou anywhere.

"Is he following us?" she said, now looking back up the cliff. Her heart sank when she saw Zyngor standing there, staring down at them. His face was scrunched and his eyes were practically shooting arrows themselves.

"Let's go! We've got a head start!" said Alan, motioning for them all to follow him into the forest.

As they raced for the trees, something cracked in the air like a bolt of lightning. It was quite like the one that happened at school the day the lights went out, but this time the entire area shook with a force that knocked nearly everyone off their feet. Riders fell off their horses, and nilbogs (who already had trouble balancing on their stumpy legs) toppled over like dominoes.

Jenna looked back onto the field, where the fighters were gasping in horror as they backed away from one spot. When the crowd cleared, there was Zyngor.

"Keep running!" Jenna urged as they all quickened their pace.

Just then, a group of nilbogs noticed them running away. Hard as they tried to keep going, the nilbogs rushed over with their swords raised and their toothless mouths open wide.

The next few minutes were a blur. Jenna blocked an attack with her Asiuol, stabbed one nilbog through its belly, and cut off the sword-arm of another one attacking Hallie. Luckily, some of Maple Cliff's army were also keeping Zyngor busy for the time being. The longer he was kept away from them, however, the angrier he seemed to become. Jenna couldn't help but notice something else as she looked out onto the field, as well.

"Hey, guys, the centaurs are here!" she exclaimed. "Look, they got here!" She didn't recognize most of them, but she did see Euwo's blonde hair and body.

Alan sliced his Wind Rider through the nilbog he was fighting. "That must mean Annabel is here, too! Do you see her?"

"Negative," Thomas answered, scanning the field. "Oh, Jenna, behind you!"

Jenna turned around just as a nilbog was about to slice her in two. She leapt sideways into a tree, narrowly avoiding the strike. The nilbog, however, wasn't giving up. It followed her over to the tree and cornered her. She covered her eyes and waited for the sword to hit her.

But it never did. She opened her eyes.

Levi was there, having jumped in and defended her. Where he came from, she didn't know—but she didn't much care.

When the nilbog finally lost that battle, Levi turned and lifted Jenna off the ground.

"You okay?" he said.

"Yeah, fine," said Jenna, "thanks to you."

"Oh, Uncle Levi!" said Jules, rushing over and hugging him. "Am I glad to see you!"

Jenna looked around. "Where's Nuit?"

"Ran off when a stupid son of a—I mean, when a nilbog shot me off." Levi lifted the shoulder pad of his armour to reveal a fresh, bloody wound from an arrow.

"Uncle Levi!" Jules exclaimed, covering her mouth. "You're hurt!"

"Are you kidding? I could run a marathon," Levi seethed. The air hitting it must have stung. "It's only my right shoulder. No major organs there."

He hurried them all off the field and into the beginning of the forest. The trees were thick enough that anyone on the field might have a hard time seeing in, which Jenna was grateful for in that moment.

"I see the centaurs are here," said Levi. "When did you all get here from Willow?"

"Just a little while ago, but we didn't come with the centaurs," said Jenna. "Annabel sent us ahead on a Root Path."

"Annabel," said Levi, concerned. He looked out onto the field. "I thought she might be with you guys. I didn't see her when the centaurs arrived."

Jenna suddenly felt a little dizzy.

"You knew we went to Willow?" said Jules.

"Annabel left us a note," said Levi, wiping sweat from his forehead. "Although that still didn't put Lou's mind at ease, as you can imagine."

Hallie lifted her eyebrows. "She's upset?"

Levi shrugged. "Well, it's not like you were kidnapped, but yeah."

Jenna tried, once again, to locate Lou on the field, but once again, she couldn't.

"Guys, what about the Sterling Cone?" said Levi, frantically looking between them. "That's why Annabel took you to Willow, right? What did you find out?"

"Where it was hidden," said Lindsay. "We found it."

"Yeah, it was here in Maple the whole time," Alan grumbled.

Levi's entire face lit up with relief. "Where is it? Does one of you have it right now?" He frantically looked between them all.

"Jenna does," said Jules. "Or, Hallie, do you have it? Which one of you has it?"

"Doesn't matter," said Levi, pushing Jenna and Hallie away from the group. "Jenna, Hallie, take the Sterling Cone. Find a Root Path—*any* Root Path. Just take it away from here. Away from him. Destroy it."

"But... what about the others?" said Jenna.

"Someone has to stay here and keep him busy," said Levi. "He wants to kill you all, but he can't chase you all."

"We can't split up," Hallie argued. "If one of us dies, the Sought Six is over." Hearing those words made Jenna's heart skip a beat.

"That's exactly why you have to split up." Levi looked over his shoulder when a nilbog screeched as it was killed. "Six kids can do more than one thing at once. That's your strength. Use it. Zyngor may be powerful, but he can't be in two places at once."

Hallie scoffed. "Are you sure about that?"

Levi held their shoulders in his hands and his chocolate eyes softened. "It'll be alright. You can do this. You have to. The Sterling Cone cannot end up in Zyngor's hands. You two need to destroy it. Think of it as practice."

Hallie looked appalled. "Practice? For what?"

"For later, when you have to destroy Zyngor's heart," said Levi. Jenna's stomach dropped, as did Levi's voice. "I know Annabel told you about Zyngor's missing heart. You two are the twins. It'll be your job to carry it and destroy it, when the time comes. It just so happens that right now, you're the ones holding the Sterling Cone. So, it's your job to destroy it."

"But what if we can't... I mean, we don't know how... How do we..." Jenna was trying to say something along the lines of, "How exactly do we destroy the Sterling Cone, Levi?" but the words failed her.

Just then, the loud and sharp crack of a lightning bolt echoed throughout the field. The wind picked up, even within the shelter of the trees. Jenna half-expected to see Zyngor right there with them any second now.

"Go, now," said Levi, pushing them. "Hurry! You're wasting time."

Jenna lunged forward and threw her arms around her friends. Hallie did the same, and all six of them held the hug for as long as they could. Then, with another crack of a lightning bolt and a few screams from the battlefield, Jenna and Hallie ran off into the trees—no direction or plan. They simply ran.

CHAPTER 28:
THE WISH

Jenna

J ENNA AND HALLIE HELD each other's hands so that if one of them found a Root Path, they'd be able to travel on it together. They knocked on every tree they passed.

"There has to be one around here somewhere!" Hallie shrieked, knocking on another one.

"Keep trying! We have to—"

And just like that, they felt the gut-punch and light-headed feeling of being pulled in by a Root Path. When they landed face-first on the ground, Hallie spat out a few leaves that ended up in her mouth.

"Oh, gross! Blegh!"

"I guess we found a Root Path," said Jenna, brushing herself off. She looked up. A crow cawed loudly from the branches of trees she didn't recognize. At least, they weren't ones she had seen so far in Pawcombe. "Where are we? Look at those branches. They're almost... crooked."

"Crooked," said Hallie, also looking up at them. "Uh oh, I know what trees these are. We're in Oak, Jenna."

"Oak?" Jenna looked around and the crow cawed again. "Well... um... at least it's quiet. It doesn't look like anyone's around."

"Yeah, they're all in Maple fighting for Zyngor," said Hallie.

Jenna pulled the Sterling Cone out of her sweatshirt's pocket. "Let's just get rid of this thing. This forest is giving me the creeps."

"But we don't know how to get rid of it," Hallie whined. "Thomas said water wouldn't do it, and even fire wouldn't do it. What are we supposed to do? Find some way to make it self-destruct?"

Suddenly, the sky filled with dark grey clouds. A crack from a lightning bolt filled the air. The ground began to shake. By now, they knew what was about to happen—who was about to show up.

Jenna pocketed the Sterling Cone again.

"Where is he?" asked Hallie, pulling her Rose sword from its sheath. She and Jenna stood back to back, swords at the ready. The wind was blowing so fiercely that they could hardly hear anything else. There was one final moment of commotion, and then it stopped. The wind went away.

But now, another sound rang in their ears. Footsteps.

At the same time, they turned and looked in the same direction. Emerging from the darkness and shadows of the oak trees, sword out and a menacing expression on his shallow face, was Zyngor.

"How nice of you to visit me in my solitude," he said, forcing a smile that was much too big. He looked like a clown without makeup. "What do you say I make things a little homier for you, eh?" He pointed his index finger at a tree.

"Get down!" Jenna yelled, and just as she and Hallie hit the dirt, Zyngor flipped his wrist. The tree burst apart, causing wood chips to fly everywhere.

"Move! Move!" Hallie urged, and they rolled away just in time to avoid the falling oak branches from above. In the time it took for them to roll away, Zyngor had exploded two more trees. The whole area was now littered with broken bits of wood.

"If you think that's amusing," Zyngor sneered, "wait until you see what I'm going to do next." He shot them a sick grin and raised his hands. He aimed for a tree and flicked all ten of his fingers at it. Jenna and Hallie watched a lightning bolt shoot out from his hands and ignite the tree it hit. One of the branches fell, all ablaze, and ignited the other fallen branches already on the ground. Within only a few moments, most of the area was on fire.

Zyngor spat a laugh, like a snake spitting venom. Jenna looked around at the forest, each tree burning mercilessly.

Except two.

"Hal, look," Jenna muttered as discreetly as possible. "Those two trees over there, on either side of the path. They aren't burning. You think they might be—"

"Root Paths," Hallie finished. "Root Paths don't burn—they *must* be!"

The sky suddenly darkened as Zyngor looked up at it, and the wind got stronger. It was as if he was commanding even the weather.

"Did you really think I was going to let you live?" he growled, turning back to them. He stalked forward, his cloak flowing behind him in the wind like a phantom.

"Stay away from us!" Jenna shouted.

Zyngor allowed himself a deep, throaty chuckle. He kept on walking, but he only got a few more steps before a burning oak branch fell directly between them from the tree above. Its embers splashed onto the forest floor, just barely missing them all. Hallie shrieked as Zyngor bolted back a step.

"The choice is yours," Zyngor said after a moment. "Death by me, or death by fire. Look around. How long do you think you'll last?"

Jenna did look around. Every single tree was on fire except for the two with Root Paths. Branches were breaking and falling quickly. The heat was scorching and she and Hallie were practically drenched in sweat.

"You're fools if you think you can beat me," Zyngor continued. His voice was like a razor blade to their ears, which seemed to be getting sharper by the second. "Don't be fools. Don't make the same mistakes as Ralthoar."

Jenna felt her eyes well up.

"Or the same mistakes as Jessica and Gabriel."

Hallie whimpered.

"Or the same mistakes as Annabel."

They both became stiff as boards. Thoughts of what may have happened to her in Willow overflowed in their minds. Jenna was so angry she felt like she could explode with it, and the quickening of Hallie's breathing meant she felt the same way.

Keep cool, Jenna thought, hoping her thoughts would radiate over to Hallie. *He's just trying to get under our skin.*

They had to get out of there. There was one Root Path to their left, and one Root Path to their right, but getting to either one without Zyngor following them or killing them—*that* was the challenge. There was no way he'd let them go until he had what he wanted, but they couldn't give him what he wanted.

They knew what they had to do.

Jenna took Hallie's hand, and she understood. Then, she drew the Sterling Cone from her pocket and held it so Zyngor could clearly see it. His dark eyes flashed and a growl grew and stretched across his mouth.

"So, you *do* have it," he said, but he didn't sound surprised. "Very well, ladies, I'll make you a deal. Give it to me, and I'll leave you and your friends alone."

"Yeah, right," Hallie sneered. Jenna scoffed her agreement. She remembered hearing similar words from Klaus.

"Why wouldn't I? What have I got to gain by bothering you once I have what I want? It'd be a waste of my time and energy. Is that what Denny told you, that I'd still come after you? Be careful who you listen to around here."

Jenna and Hallie said nothing.

"The Sterling Cone will make Pawcombe a better place for everybody," he went on. "Do you think I want to ruin Pawcombe? Is that what you were told? Why would I want to live in a ruined world? It doesn't make much sense, does it?"

Jenna and Hallie glanced quickly at each other, but then back at Zyngor.

"The Sterling Cone is much more complex than you've been led to believe. Young children are simply not equipped to handle it."

Jenna wished he would stop talking for just a moment so she could hear herself think. She dropped her eyes to the Sterling Cone in her hand. She repositioned it within her fingers. She could clearly see the fire's reflection against the shiny silver pinecone. They were surrounded by fire. She could toss it into the flames and be done with it—but what if that didn't work? She couldn't exactly just fish it out of the fire to try something else. Hallie had a point. It was almost as if the only way to get rid of it was to make it self-destruct.

Self-destruct.

Jenna's eyes widened.

"Yes, that's it, ladies," said Zyngor, misreading Jenna's expression. "You understand. We could all live quite harmoniously in Pawcombe. You stop hunting me and I'll stop hunting you. All it'll cost you is the Sterling Cone, and then we can call it a day." His eyes flashed with an unsettling greed. Even if they had been falling for his words, they wouldn't be anymore.

"No!" Jenna exclaimed, gripping the Sterling Cone in her hand. Then, she looked right at it and took a deep breath. "I wish for the Sterling Cone to be destroyed."

Zyngor's dark eyes grew wide. "What do you think you're doing?" he hissed, looking extremely disturbed. "You can't wish for that!"

At first, nothing happened, but then the Sterling Cone became brighter and shinier by the second. It became so bright that Jenna almost hid her eyes. Then, her heart gave a leap as she watched it start to peel apart. Every bit of the silver pinecone turned into hot ashes and fell out the sides of her hand and to the forest floor.

The Sterling Cone was gone.

Zyngor became mad with rage. He leapt up and flew over the burning branch as if he had wings, his arms outstretched and his teeth bared. In that same moment, Jenna and Hallie pulled out their swords. In the mere action of unsheathing hers, Jenna gave Zyngor a slice across his front. He screeched in pain and fell over. He growled at them, foaming at the mouth. He looked like a rabid animal.

Jenna and Hallie stood back as he hobbled around. There was no blood coming out of his wound. Not a single drop.

He can't be killed, Jenna kept thinking. *We won't be able to kill him, we can only injure him; after all, he doesn't have a heart.*

Zyngor took out his jet-black sword, which looked painful because of his fresh wound, and swung it hard at their heads.

They ducked.

The sword sliced halfway through a tree, and then appeared to be stuck. As he pulled on it, Jenna looked back at the roaring flames, which were spreading fast. They'd all be engulfed in no time if they didn't find some way out of there. Zyngor was also noticing the spreading fire, and when he was unable to pull his sword from the tree, he turned on them angrily.

"Stay back!" Hallie shouted, holding her sword at the ready.

Zyngor hissed at them and flicked each of his wrists. With a force that felt ten times worse than a Root Path, they flew back toward the fire. It was such a strong force that they dropped their swords. They hovered in the air over the hungry flames. Hallie screamed. Jenna looked back at Zyngor, still reaching his hands out in their direction. He was holding them in midair, just a few feet above the fire.

"You're finished, you little fools," Zyngor growled. He watched them hang there, looking terrified at the fire below them. It amused him. "Foolish twins. Take a look at how the last set of twins fared against me. What chance do you think *you* have?"

"Shut up!" Jenna yelled, straining in her invisible hold to look him in the face.

Zyngor just laughed at them. He violently pulled his arms backward and sent them flying back toward him. They landed hard in the dirt, rolling away from the flames. Zyngor kept laughing in a maniacal frenzy. He was a wild predator playing with his food.

Jenna was relieved to feel that she wasn't hurt or in too much pain, thanks to her armour. She turned to hoist herself back up, but then she saw her Asiuol and Hallie's

Rose lying next to her in the dirt. She looked up at Zyngor, who was now stalking Hallie and cornering her against a tree.

She stood up. She sheathed Hallie's sword and rushed toward Zyngor with her sword high above her head. But right when she was about to bring it down on him, he turned around. Using only the invisible force from his hands, he held her off. Hard as she tried to muscle her sword toward him, she couldn't. He towered over her, staring at her with his dark, angry eyes.

"Give it up," he hissed. "What have you possibly got that I haven't?"

Jenna glared at him with every bit of courage she could muster. "Heart," she said.

His dark eyes narrowed for a moment, and then Jenna let go of her sword. She dodged sideways, allowing the force Zyngor was using to drop his body to the ground like a ton of bricks—right on top of the Asiuol. He screeched and yelled out, but there was still no blood coming from him.

"Hallie!" Jenna yelled, taking out the Rose and tossing it over to her when their eyes met. Hallie caught it. She stabbed it straight into the ground, through Zyngor's cloak. When Zyngor realized what was happening, he tried to free himself from Hallie's sword, but he couldn't. He couldn't even get his cloak off because of Jenna's Asiuol through his body.

"No!" he snarled, reaching his arms out for them. They dove sideways in opposite directions, next to the trees with Root Paths.

"Where do these go?" Hallie yelled, pointing at her tree.

"Who cares?" Jenna yelled back, gripping hers. "Just go, we'll have to meet back in Maple!"

"NO!"

Zyngor screamed so loudly in his raspy voice that it sounded like the shriek of a raptor. By now, the fire had spread even further and the flames were beginning to engulf his body. No matter how hard he struggled to free himself, it was no use. The fire was spreading as quickly as if he was covered in gasoline. He screamed in horror and writhed around in pain on the ground.

Jenna could see Hallie hide her eyes through the smoke. "Hal, go!" she yelled. Hallie promptly knocked on her tree four times, and Jenna did the same. The thrust from this Root Path was quick and hard. She didn't even get a chance to see where she landed because she blacked out before she got there.

CHAPTER 29:
THE STORM ISN'T OVER YET

Hallie

SOMETHING SOFT TICKLED HALLIE'S nose. A blanket. Perhaps a dog's fur. She moved her face to look at it, but her eyes were shut. She opened them and sat bolt upright. It was Lou's golden hair grazing her face as she leaned over her.

"Oh, there you are!" Lou exclaimed, pulling her into a hug. "You're awake!"

"Mom?" said Hallie, wrapping her arms around Lou's shoulders. "Where... Where am I?"

"In your bed, in your room, in Maple Cliff," another voice answered, "and it's a bright, sunny day for you to go outside and get some much-needed fresh air."

Hallie suddenly became very aware that she was wearing a set of clean pajamas and sitting on clean sheets. The sunlight was pouring in from the window of her suite. She looked around Lou's body and saw who else was sitting there.

"Annabel!" she exclaimed. "You... You... Where were you out there?"

"Oh," said Annabel, "yes, I'm sorry I couldn't help you guys more. It took a while to get out of Willow. There were a lot of nilbogs to deal with."

"Willow—how is it? Is it destroyed? What about the centaurs? Are they okay? How's Ralthoar?"

"Easy, sweetheart, take a breath," said Lou.

"Willow will recover just fine. It's a bit of a mess, but nothing that can't be fixed," Annabel said calmly. "Ralthoar is fine. He suffered a shoulder injury, the extent of which I do not know, but he's alive. The rest of the centaurs are okay as well. Plenty were injured, but none died. Not when they were in Willow, anyway."

Hallie gulped.

"Every one of Pawcombe's forests involved in the battle lost people, Hallie," said Annabel, her eyes softening. "Nobody was left unaffected, I'm sorry to say. Battles are deadly affairs."

"We thought we lost *you*," said Hallie, swallowing a lump in her throat. "When we couldn't find you, we were afraid you... you..."

Annabel shook her head. "Me? Nah. Come on. I'm tougher than that." She winked. "I'm sorry I worried you. By the time I got back to Maple and went to look for you guys on the field, you and Jenna had already gone."

"Jenna," said Hallie, suddenly remembering. "Mom, Jenna! She had to take another Root Path from Oak... Where did she end up?"

"Shh, relax, sweetheart, it's okay." Lou softly stroked her hair with both hands. "Jenna's fine. She ended up in Cedar, and the locals brought her back here right after we found you."

"She's quite eager to see you, though," Annabel added. "They all are."

"All? You mean… everyone's okay?"

"Everyone's okay," said Lou. "A few cuts and bruises here and there, but they're all just fine."

"Can I see them?"

"Well, I don't think they'd have it any other way," said Annabel, getting up and walking to the door. "They've been waiting out here for the last two hours."

As soon as she opened the door, five bodies came rushing in like running water. Lou was right; everyone had cuts and bruises, but they were all alive.

"Hal! You're awake!" Jenna exclaimed, leaping onto the bed.

"Careful, baby, careful!" said Lou, holding her arms out.

Jenna huffed. "Hey, it's my bed, too."

"How are you, Hallie? Are you okay?" said Jules, taking Hallie's hand. "We—that is, everyone in the whole building!—have been so worried."

"Yes, everyone's waiting for an update," said Thomas. "Now, we can put their minds at ease."

"Jenna told us everything," Alan went on. "Going to Oak, Zyngor following you there and setting the place on fire, using the one wish to destroy the Sterling Cone, and then impaling him with the swords!" Alan stabbed his arm up into the air.

Lindsay rolled her eyes at his energy. "What was it like? Was it scary?"

"Nah, I'd do it again tomorrow… Yes, of course it was scary!" Hallie sighed. "I'm just glad it's over."

All six of them were silent for a few moments, as if they were all thinking the same thing.

"It is over, right?" Jenna said for all of them. "I mean, Zyngor was burned alive."

Lou and Annabel exchanged nervous looks.

"There will be a time when he'll come back, I'm afraid," said Annabel. "He isn't dead yet."

"Because of the whole 'missing his heart' thing, right?" said Alan. Hallie looked at him, surprised. He nodded his head at Jenna. "Jenna told us all about that, too."

"Yes," Annabel answered. "But the good news is he won't be back for quite some time. Burns like that are a severe injury. It'll take him a long time to recover from that."

"What about his army?" said Hallie.

"Those who are still alive have retreated back to Oak," said Annabel. "Without their master, they're rather helpless."

"So, Pawcombe has some peace," said Jules. She allowed herself a smile. "We... We actually did it?"

Lou smiled. "Yeah, honey, you did."

Just then, the door burst open and Denny flew in like a gust of wind. Her cheeks were flushed—or perhaps that was the blush she was wearing. Either way, her cheeks matched the pink of her blouse.

"Oh, sweet child of mine! Hallie, darling, you're awake!" she squealed, rushing to the bed and wrapping her in a hug. "Oh, I am so happy to see you up and at 'em!"

"Thanks, Denny," Hallie murmured into her shoulder.

Denny stood back and clapped her hands together.

"Well, now that everyone is here—oh, good gracious, where is Levi?" She trotted to the door and cupped her hand to her mouth. "Levi? Levi!" She sounded like a squawking bird. Everybody giggled at her, including Lou and Annabel.

Eventually, Levi came down the hall with shaving cream all over his face. He entered the room and smiled a very sarcastic smile. "Yes?" he said, forcing a sweet tone.

"That's a good look for you, Uncle Levi," Jules laughed.

"Yeah, but you're a bit early. Christmas isn't until December," Jenna added.

Levi pretended to be shocked, playing along. "My secret is out," he whispered.

Denny clapped her hands again. "Alright, settle down. I've got a very important announcement to make." She cleared her throat. "This Saturday evening, Maple Cliff will host a grand dinner party in honour of our dear Sought Six. It'll be a celebration of life, happiness, and success. I expect everyone to be prompt at 5 o'clock sharp."

"A party?" said Thomas, adjusting his glasses. "Splendid!"

"That'll be nice, Denny," said Lou. "Won't it, guys?"

"Yes, I think we all agree it sounds like fun and we'll be there," said Levi. He pointed to his face. "Can I finish shaving now?"

"Yes, yes, dear, as you were," said Denny, waving a flimsy hand at the door.

By the time Saturday came around, a lot had happened. The battlefield had been completely cleaned up, trees had been planted to replace the ones that exploded, everybody's wounds were healing well, and since July 6th came and went in that time, Lou turned another year older.

The fire in Oak had been extinguished, luckily before it spread too far. Apparently, Zyngor's army had put it out after they fled the battlefield in Maple. That meant they would have also found what was left of Zyngor's body. Hallie tried not to think too hard about that.

When everyone was dressed for the party, they made their way downstairs to Maple Cliff's banquet hall. They had never seen this room before. It was truly magnificent. The ceiling was high and there was a piece of wooden floor in the centre of the room, probably for dancing. There was a great balcony looking out over the forest, and there were tables full of food. There was even a band of string instruments (three fiddles and a cello). At 5 o'clock, the room filled with people from all over Pawcombe, and it didn't take long for people to start eating, drinking, and dancing.

Alan and Thomas were spending most of their time at the food tables, filling and refilling their plates.

"Have either of you tried the mini quiches?" said Hallie, examining the trays.

"Yup," said Alan, mouth full. "The green ones are really good, surprisingly."

"Why is that surprising?"

Alan swallowed. "Duh, because they're green." He nudged Thomas. "Hey, what do you think is in them that makes them green?"

"Spinach, of course," Thomas answered.

Alan turned pale. "Spinach?"

Hallie chuckled. "You fought the wickedest man in Pawcombe, Alan. A bit of spinach isn't going to kill you."

"Well, we'll see about that." Alan flapped his lips. "I need something to drink. Where did I put my punch?"

While he and Thomas looked around for his cup, Hallie made her way to the dance floor where Jenna was talking to Jules and Lindsay.

"You guys going to go out there?" said Hallie, nodding her head to some of the people who were already dancing the night away.

Jules scoffed. "Nope. No way, no how."

Lindsay leaned closer to Hallie so she could whisper. "Jules doesn't dance," she said.

"Unlike her uncle," said Jenna, pointing to Levi. He was one of the ones on the dance floor having a very good time, and he didn't appear to care one bit who might be watching him.

"Is it just me or is my *cool* Uncle Levi suddenly kind of *embarrassing*?" said Jules, watching Levi's crazy dance moves.

Hallie chuckled. "I wonder where my mom is. She loves dancing." She scanned the dance floor, but no Lou. She looked back at the food tables, but, again, no Lou.

Alan and Thomas left the food tables to join the girls, cups of fruit punch in their hands. "So, are we all going out there or what?" said Alan, pointing to the dance floor.

"No way, no how," Jules repeated, crossing her arms.

Jenna laughed. "It *is* kind of funny to just watch the adults."

"Hey, guys, look!" said Hallie, pointing to the door. She happened to glance over there just as someone else entered the banquet hall, flowers in hand.

"Hey, it's Ralthoar," said Jenna. "Come on, let' s go say hello."

Everyone made their way across the room and caught Ralthoar's eye. His left shoulder was in a sling and he held the flowers in his right hand. He regally bent one of his front legs and bowed to them.

"My children," he said. He handed them each a wildflower. "I picked these on my way over here. Maple has some lovely gardens along the forest pathways. I've made lots of mental notes for Willow."

"Wow, thanks!" said Lindsay, sniffing her flower. "They're beautiful, Ralthoar."

"We're happy you could make it," said Alan. "We weren't sure if you would after what happened in Willow. We're—all of us—really sorry about that."

Ralthoar tilted his head. "You're sorry?"

"If it wasn't for us, Willow wouldn't have been invaded," said Alan.

"Yeah, and you wouldn't have..." Jenna clumsily pointed to Ralthoar's shoulder.

Ralthoar smiled kindly. "I'm the one who held the information about the Sterling Cone. Zyngor would have come to me eventually. What happened in Willow was nothing more than an accident waiting to happen. You did nothing wrong."

"We destroyed it," Jules said proudly. "The Sterling Cone—it was right where you said it'd be."

Ralthoar smiled again. "I'm glad, truly. I admit, it's a shame to see one of Willow's prized creations discontinued, but it's for the best. When something is as powerful as it was, there's always a risk that no good will come from it."

"And you don't have to keep it a secret anymore," Hallie added.

"Indeed, that is also a positive," Ralthoar agreed.

"Ralthoar!" Denny exclaimed suddenly as she appeared behind them all. She was a little bit out of breath from all the dancing she'd been doing. "It's such a pleasure to have you join us this evening! We're all so glad you could make it, aren't we, kids?"

"Thank you for inviting us, Denny," said Ralthoar, bending his leg in another courtly bow. "May I go and inform the rest of the centaurs that it's alright for them to come in?"

"Of course, of course!" said Denny, smiling her bright smile as she flung her hands to shoo him away. "Tell them to come right on in and make themselves comfortable! There's plenty of food, and that dance floor is plenty big enough for everyone!"

Just then, one of the fiddlers waved his arm to get everyone's attention.

"Alright, listen up, everyone! Listen up!" When the dancers slowed their feet and everyone else quieted their voices, the fiddler flashed a smile. "Thank you very much for welcoming us into Maple Cliff. I'd just like to take a minute to acknowledge our brilliant and capable Sought Six, without whom we would have much less to celebrate tonight."

The crowd erupted in cheers and applause as everyone turned to face the group. Hallie could feel her cheeks redden as she smiled and gave the crowd a tiny wave.

"Who's having a good time, eh?" the fiddler exclaimed, and the crowd cheered again. "Then, it's time for the Mull River Shuffle!" He held onto the last syllable so the crowd could cheer along with him, and then he and the other musicians started playing a fun, upbeat song that brought a lot more people onto the dance floor. Levi continued dancing, and so did Denny. Eventually, they began dancing together.

But Lou was still nowhere to be seen.

Hallie scanned the room one more time, and while she didn't find Lou, she did see Annabel standing by the table full of drinks. She watched everyone dancing for a minute, but then she turned her head to the balcony. She stared out for a moment. Then she picked up two glasses of champagne from the table and walked outside.

Hallie stared at the balcony.

"What are you looking at?" said Jenna, tapping her arm.

"Come with me for a minute." Hallie took her sister's hand and walked her over to the balcony's entrance. Instead of going outside, they each took a side and hid as Annabel approached Lou, who was leaning on the stone railing and watching the sunset.

"Hey," she said.

Lou spun around. "Hey."

"What are you doing out here? Levi started a conga line."

Lou smiled. "I just needed some air."

Annabel walked to join her at the railing. Hallie saw her hand one of the champagne glasses to Lou.

"How's Belle?"

Lou took a sip and nodded her head. "She's good. Hasn't missed a beat since her last battle, bless her heart. She's earned her vacation."

"Here, here." Annabel lifted her glass and Lou clinked it with her own.

"Are the kids okay?" said Lou, looking back at the door. Hallie slipped further behind the wall.

"Oh, yeah, they're fine. Alan's freaking out because he accidentally ate spinach, but all in a day's work, right?" Hallie peeked back around just in time to see Annabel wink. "Stop worrying so much."

"That's like asking the mother bear not to watch her cubs."

"Come on," Annabel teased. "Where's the old Lou Dalmore I once knew?"

Lou shrugged. "She had kids."

Annabel scoffed. "Parenting brings out the worst in people."

"I know, right?"

They laughed with each other and sipped their drinks. They were silent for a moment, and Hallie almost signalled Jenna to go back to the party with her.

"He isn't dead, An," Lou said, as if that sentence had been sitting on her mind for some time.

Annabel sighed. "I know that."

"He's going to recover."

"From burns like that? Not anytime soon."

"But he *will* recover. Maybe not anytime soon, but one day." Lou exhaled. "And when he does, you and I both know who we're going to need to call in."

"We don't need to worry about that just yet. She'll help us. She always has."

Hallie shot her eyes to Jenna. "Who?" she mouthed.

Annabel put her arm around Lou's shoulder. "Right now, all we need to do is celebrate those six kids in there. They did good, Lou. They did everything right. Don't tell them I said this, but I'm so proud of them."

Hallie felt as light as a feather. She smiled and looked over at Jenna, who was also smiling.

Lou chuckled lightly. "Why can't I tell them that?"

"Keeps them on their toes if they don't know what I'm thinking," said Annabel. She stood back and looked out over the field. "You guys could go home if you wanted to. We don't know how long Zyngor's going to take to recover from those burns. It could be years."

"The kids will have schoolwork to catch up on before September," said Lou, nodding. "I think we do have to go back."

Annabel looked disappointed, but she understood. "I can't say I won't miss you guys. All of you."

"Well, now that the kids have seen Pawcombe, I don't think there's much chance of keeping them away for good."

"They do seem to like it here, despite its more... challenging... elements."

"We'll visit," said Lou, pulling Annabel into a hug, "a lot."

"You'd better. There's a Root Path in your backyard, for crying out loud. No excuses."

Lou laughed and held her tighter. "I promise."

"You want to go rejoin the party?"

Lou nodded and released Annabel. "Yeah, if you will."

The two of them started back inside, and Hallie and Jenna rushed away from the door as quickly and unassumingly as they could. They joined the others at the edge of the dance floor, where Lindsay was still trying to coax Jules into dancing.

"Let it go, Alan," Thomas sighed.

"I didn't see you eat eight of those spinach egg pies!"

"It's called quiche. *Quiche*. It's French."

"Yeah, well what's the French word for 'disgusting'?"

By now, Lou and Annabel had arrived next to them. Lou wrapped her arms around Hallie and Jenna and gave them each a kiss.

"Are you spies having a good time?" she whispered.

Hallie looked up at Lou, over at the balcony, and then back at Lou. "How did you—"

"I'm your mother, that's how."

Levi waltzed his way over to the edge of the dance floor. Without saying a word, and without stopping his jig, he took one of Lou's hands and one of Annabel's hands, and he guided them onto the floor with him and Denny.

Hallie watched their four mentors dancing like fools, and she chuckled to herself.

"Makes you wonder who the adults are and who the kids are," she said.

"They're the wise ones," said Thomas. "They know the importance of frolicking after a storm."

"Except that the storm isn't over yet," said Jenna, and Hallie felt the weight of her words like a thousand pounds on her shoulders. "Zyngor's still out there."

"But he won't bother us again for a long time," said Lindsay. "He won't bother anyone again for a long time. Annabel said so, and she's never lied to us."

Jenna nodded. "Yeah, I know."

"Come on, you guys, we can do anything," said Alan, puffing out his chest. "We fought Zyngor. We saved Pawcombe and its citizens. Whatever comes our way in the future, we'll handle it. We're the Sought Six, and we can do anything."

Thomas chuckled. "Anything except eat some spinach, apparently."

Before long, they made their way onto the dance floor and joined the adults, who welcomed them with open arms and embarrassing dance moves. Even Jules decided to join the jig. After all, there were much more daunting things in Pawcombe than a bit of dancing.

THE END

CPSIA information can be obtained
at www.ICGtesting.com
Printed in the USA
BVHW071206190819
556214BV00005B/589/P